Hope yo...

THE @Rachel Selwan — Author
VOICE

The Voice Trilogy

BOOK THREE

By
Rachel Selwan

Content Warning: Discussion of suicide,
sex, and major character death.

THE VOICE
Written by Rachel Selwan
First Edition
Copyright © 2023 Rachel Nicole Selwan
Edited by: Sarah McCarthy
ASIN: 9798374264791

"We'll survive, you and I."
— F. Scott Fitzgerald, *More Than Just a House*

TABLE OF CONTENTS

CLAIR

Clair woke to the soft hum of the heater turning on across the room.

She shifted her feet, sliding the cool silk between her legs. She was encased in voluminous pillows, unbelievably soft sheets, and what felt like the world's plushest duvet on the larger than king-sized bed of the colossal suite. The Covenant's suite reserved for the Seraph on Earth. Her suite.

At the Covenant, the governing body of the angels on earth, she was the only angel of her kind. The only angel with the birthright to rule them all.

Yet…

Clair opened her eyes and saw that Chris was already gone, as usual. He was always up before the sun. On the rare mornings that she woke first, Clair loved watching the rays of light dance through his dark hair and admiring the way he looked so innocent and peaceful when he was sleeping. Chris had told Clair that his establishment as the Leader of the Minor Angels was one of the greatest honors of his angelic life. He honored his commitment to the role by uplifting the minor angels, training them to live up to their full potential.

She glanced at the clock. He would be teaching his open session morning yoga class right now. Most mornings, Clair met him after his class for breakfast before she began training herself. She was under the impression that a team was being assembled and they had been on track to leave on their mission in a few days. That was until their departure had allegedly been delayed by a freak storm over the Mediterranean.

It baffled Clair that they could not just fly around the storm. The Covenant was the wealthiest organization in the world with limitless resources at its disposal. Surely they could make it work if they really wanted. Augustus, the highest ranking angel beneath her and the current leader of the Covenant, had assured them that it would be worth waiting, that the extra time for the team to come together and train together outside of a mission would prove invaluable.

It would be *interesting* working with a team. Clair had primarily trained her angelic powers under the tutelage of Sam, the octocentenarian minor angel who had discovered her and Chris back home in Healdsburg, California. She had major discoveries while working with Chris and her best friend Emily, but it was Sam who held her accountable and kept her on a regimented schedule. Sam who pushed her to always work harder, be faster, grow stronger, and make better choices.

It was also Sam who had pitched a fit when Clair decided to go on the Covenant-sanctioned mission. It was Sam who had immediately phoned her grandmother Dotty to tattle on Clair in an effort to change her mind. Dotty had merely asked Clair if she felt in her gut that it was the right decision before giving her blessing. Sam had been extra moody after that.

Clair leaned over onto the side of the bed that had become Chris's, burying her face into his pillow and inhaling deeply. He had taken to showering with a cedar and pine soap, and while it was not the natural scent of the forest that had clung to him what felt like lifetimes ago, it was close and she loved it.

They had been sleeping together for the past week, both figuratively and literally. What Chris lacked in experience he made up for in his desire to learn and please. Clair loved that about him. He constantly checked in with her during their lovemaking, which was new for her. He was quick to ask if something was working or not and encouraged her to teach him what *did* work.

The sculpted muscles Chris had developed over the past six months training at the Covenant's headquarters allowed them explore exciting new moves Clair had not tried with anyone else. Though a small piece of her wondered if Chris would be missing out on something by only sleeping with her in his new angelic life, she also could not bring herself to ask him about it. She knew she was quite the catch, even aside from the whole "reigning seraph" thing. Chris loved her. He wanted to be with her.

Clair could not hold back her smile. All felt like it was right in the world. She was sure the endorphins leftover from the previous night encouraged the feeling, but regardless, they were finally together and she would never let him go again.

Clair sat up, stretching her arms above her head, and slid off the bed onto the cold marble floor. She took a moment to look through the high windows and enjoy her view of the palace's expansive, lush gardens. It was exquisite, but this was not where the action happened.

Feeling spontaneous, Clair dressed quickly in a workout shirt with a built-in bra and a pair of tight, black leggings. If she ran, she would make it in time for his class.

Speeding through the halls of the main castle in the morning sent off shockwaves among the ever-present minor angel staff that were constantly milling about. As she ran past them, they grew wide-eyed and attempted to bow their heads at Clair – a servile gesture that she had adamantly tried to stop. They leapt out of her way and one woman even yelped in surprise.

Clair dashed into the service elevator and joined an alarmed looking woman clinging tightly to a pile of bedsheets. As the doors closed, Clair pressed the button for the level with the lake, before turning to the minor angel and saying a rushed greeting.

"Good morning, ma'am," the woman sputtered, attempting to bow even with her arms full.

"Please," Clair said, leaning to help her with the bundle that was tipping out of her arms. "Let me help you." Clair grabbed the top three sheets before the woman could protest. Clair could tell by the flashing of the elevator buttons that the woman's floor was next. It would only take Clair a moment to help the woman get where she needed.

As soon as the doors opened, another minor angel leapt forward to take the sheets from Clair. The original angel muttered a quiet thanks, averting her eyes as she stepped quickly out of the elevator.

Clair was not sure if the minor angels feared her after her display of power a week ago in the ballroom or if they were just wary of her in general. And how had they known to have someone grab the sheets from her? Clair wondered if she was being watched somehow.

The elevator doors closed and continued to her floor. Clair looked around without spotting any video cameras. There were staff all over the castle and she was probably the most notable angel around right now. She told herself it must have been a coincidence.

The bell dinged and Clair sprinted out into the indoor park, complete with trees, grass, and a large lake to the left of the room. The fake sky projected on the domed ceiling emulated a beautiful sunrise. Clair thought she could feel warmth emanating from the fake sun. It was an amazing simulacrum, all things considered, though she did not understand why the Covenant did not simply allow its soldiers to train outdoors. She would blame the unpredictability of the autumn weather but the Covenant did not permit angels to go outside without special clearance at any time of year.

Clair headed toward the large group of minor angels gathering near the pond. Most were chatting as they spread out their mats, so Clair figured class had not started yet. It was not until she got to the back of the group that she realized she had not thought to bring her own mat. She started to look around for an extra when she felt a tap on her shoulder.

"Here. I always bring two in case I need to use one for my back," said a petite woman with fiery red hair and striking blue eyes as she handed Clair a black mat.

"Thanks," Clair said as she took the mat and laid it out next to the woman's.

The woman took her extended hand. "I'm Jessica," she said. "Are you new here? This is the first time I've seen you at yoga."

Clair was grateful she had spent so much time with Sam practicing to maintain a neutral expression. She was surprised this woman did not recognize her but grateful, especially after the elevator fiasco. Clair hated how the angels working in her wing seemed hyper aware of her presence and practically feared her. No one would expect the seraph to make an appearance in a class for minor angels. Maybe if she kept a low profile, she would have a chance to get to know people. She would have to be careful not to share her name too quickly. "Yes, actually. I just got here a few days ago. This is my first yoga class."

"Oh! Well, welcome. I promise the training gets easier. This class is at least bearable. I couldn't stand the running group class. Wasn't for me."

Clair laughed. "I completely understand. The first time I had to go running I thought I was going to die." Jessica laughed, and they fell into an easy discussion about training. Clair took a moment while they were talking to look around for Chris, who was at least fifty feet ahead of her at the front of the class, instructing his co-teachers on the schedule for the class.

"That's Chris, our instructor," Jessica said, noticing Clair's glances. She smiled coyly at Clair and wiggled her eyebrows. "Who knew they made them like that? Plus, I heard he can make a fireball. Can you believe it? One of us making a fireball. It's amazing. But see that girl on his right," Jessica pointed to the brunette who was laughing at something Chris said. "That's Terri, she's one of his best friends, and the other girl, the one with the severe face and the short black hair is Kioko. She's one of the toughest angels in the Covenant. Usually an elite would never hang around us minor angels, but she and Chris met during his Claiming, and they've been friends ever since."

They both watched Kioko finish talking to Chris and move back toward the elevator. She did not even sense Clair, and Clair smugly wondered how great she actually was at her job.

"Good to know," Clair said, winking conspiratorially with Jessica.

"But Chris is firmly off-limits. I heard he was claimed by the seraph," Jessica leaned in and whispered, widening her eyes at Clair.

"Oh," Clair said, drawing back a bit.

Jessica laughed. "Yeah, don't go messing with him. I can't believe there's an honest-to-goodness seraph here at the Covenant. I don't even know the last time one of them came to Earth. She's supposed to be some super-powerful, gorgeous, indomitable enigma. I know a couple servers who were at the ball a week ago when she was brought in, and you should have heard the way they tell the story of her power. It's scary intense."

"Oh," Clair said awkwardly, trying to think of how to respond to this. She needed to tell this woman who she was – she wasn't some terrifying enigma. She was just Clair. And what did Jessica mean when she said that Clair had claimed Chris?

Before she had the chance to ask, Chris called the class to order. He was so focused on his work that he barely scanned the crowd before instructing them how to stand for the opening breathing lessons.

Clair soon found herself drifting in the silence, focusing on the gentle breathing exercises directing the air in and out of her lungs. She usually hated yoga, but the past few weeks had been a whirlwind and she welcomed the opportunity to ground herself. After so many frenzied days preparing to come here, the immense display of power she had crafted that Jessica had just described as "scary intense," followed by all her nights and days with Chris, Clair had not had much time to really process things. Here among the soft sounds of the pond water lapping against the shore and the synchronized breathing of the group, Clair felt herself begin to relax and just *be*. She sank into the poses and found a little peace.

They were halfway through the class when she felt the ground tremble beneath her feet.

Clair looked up to see all of the water rising from the pond into a vortex which quickly shifted into a giant wave that was about to crash down on the class. She saw the terror in the minor angels' eyes. She turned and planted her feet as the wave began to barrel toward them.

Clair raised her arms, pulling the energy from the air around her, willing the water to stop, turn, and circle. She took the pond that meant to crush them and commanded it into a building-sized sphere of water suspended above their heads.

She glanced around and saw the fear in Jessica's eyes, the shock of the rest of the class, and heard the collective gasps. Clair looked across to the other side of the pond and saw four middle order angels, doubtless gifted with water skills, staring back at her. Their mouths were agape and horror flooded their eyes. In that moment she knew they had tried to hurt these minor angels. They had tried to hurt Chris.

She did not stop to think.

Clair raised her hand and the water angels went flying into the air, suspending them above the swirling ball of water.

"So, you thought you'd do what, exactly?" she shouted up at them, all the anger coursing through her blood and the power she was pulling from the earth fueling her need for vengeance. "Hurt a bunch of innocent angels because you see them as *lesser* than you? Maybe even kill a few for fun? Not today."

Clair made a fist with her hand and the angels dropped into the vortex of water where they swirled, drowning.

"Clair!" Chris shouted, running toward her. She looked at him, the worry in his eyes reining in her fury. She dropped the water, water angels and all, back into the lake. She watched as they came sputtering up and struggled to shore, running away as if the devil was on their tail.

"I wasn't going to kill them," Clair said, shrugging.

Chris sighed, rubbing a hand across his face before pulling Clair into a fierce hug his pine scent surrounding her. She breathed him in, feeling the heat from his body. "Maybe I should save you more often," she laughed into his shirt.

"Maybe," he said, his eyes growing serious as he looked around at the shell-shocked class. "Today's lesson is cut short. We will resume tomorrow at the normal time."

No one paid attention to Chris's announcement. They all stared, slack-jawed at Clair, who was not used to all the attention and simply gave a small smile and a wave.

"Hi, I'm Clair. Sorry I ruined your class. Leave it to me to pick the one day someone tries to dump a pond on you." She forced a chuckle, attempting to diffuse the tension in the air. "Does anyone want to go get breakfast?"

KIOKO

Kioko never thought she would miss the old days. The days before Chris.

She used to come back to the fortress, have a few meals and a lot more baths, and then be on her way again. She had never spent this much time waiting around wondering what was going to happen next.

Kioko did not wonder. She was one to spring into action, not wait for it.

But that was before she had been tasked with finding the minor angel Chris. Before she was tasked with retrieving a seraph from the human world. Before she saw that seraph and Chris together, forced to witness their irrefutable chemistry.

But that was then, and this was now.

Now, she needed to go drag that seraph out of bed at the embarrassingly late hour of nine a.m. for training. It was shameless that the seraph stayed in bed so late while the angels of every other rank trained.

Before the sun rose each day, Kioko devoted an hour to aerobic exercise followed by an hour of strength training. She never skipped a day. Men feared her, angels respected her. Now, she was tasked as if she were the seraph's nanny.

Joy.

She had thought sleeping with fat foreign dignitaries was difficult. This was excruciating.

Kioko sighed, standing in front of the door, before solemnly knocking.

And waiting.

And knocking again.

Where the fuck was she?

"Ma'am?" a demure voice called to her.

A servant was approaching from down the hall. Kioko inclined her head toward the minor angel. "If you are looking for the seraph, she has gone down to breakfast with the rest of the minor angels."

Interesting.

Kioko nodded again and walked away.

Clair had not taken meals with anyone else in her time at The Covenant.

Kioko wondered sourly what had changed.

The dining hall, normally quiet and somewhat reserved, was alive with chatter from the minor angel section. Kioko could see that Clair was among them, next to Chris, laughing at something someone had said.

Kioko strode up to the group and silence fell across the table.

"Seraph," she said, inclining her head toward Clair. "You are to report to training level five, door thirty-five in half an hour."

Clair cocked an eyebrow at Kioko. "Training?"

Kioko narrowed her eyes. "Yes," she said. "Augustus will not allow you on a team-based mission without properly ensuring you are not a liability."

"A liability?" Clair asked haughtily. Kioko inwardly sneered in response to Clair's attitude but maintained a neutral expression.

"Yes," Kioko said. "Being powerful is one thing. Being in control is another."

"I completely agree, Kioko."

She turned to see a minor angel approaching. She did not know him but she recognized him as Sam, the oldest living minor angel. He had arrived at the Covenant with the seraph. She did not know how he knew her name or why he was siding with her, but Kioko masked her surprise and decided to accept any help she could get wrangling the seraph.

"Thank you, Sam," Kioko said, turning back to Clair. "Don't be late."

"Kioko," Chris said, turning toward her. "Would you like to have breakfast with us? We can make room."

Clair glanced at Chris before turning her scrutinizing gaze back to Kioko.

"No, thank you," Kioko said. "I must prepare the room for the seraph." Her formality brought a frown to Chris's face and she chose to ignore it.

Clair nodded and Kioko took her leave.

Kioko had no doubt they would have an audience in the training room today. She began the preparations.

As she made her way through the room, Kioko reflected on how to move forward in this new normal. The training room was massive, a large round space with quadrants for different training exercises – sparring, archery, and plenty of test dummies to practice magic. She had always considered herself bloodthirsty but she could not blatantly attack the seraph on earth.

Kioko walked through the weapons racks, trying to decide how best to test Clair today.

Kioko was accustomed to being the highest ranking angel in the room, other than Augustus, of course. It pissed her off to bow and scrape to Clair who she was certain had not put in half the work Kioko had in all her years with the Covenant.

The Covenant comprised three classes of angels: the thrones angels, the middle order angels, and the minor angels.

In the early days, each class had been subdivided into three ranks, but by the time Kioko arrived, the ranks had largely fallen into disuse.

The thrones angels were the most powerful angels within the Covenant and Augustus was their highest in command. Most middle order angels had special powers connected with the elements. Under the guidance of the thrones angels, they were the angels most often deployed missions to maintain and safeguard the Covenant's position in the world. The lowest class of angels were the minor angels. These were the angels born from humans who had taken their own lives, brought into existence to fulfill a purpose and then move onto the next life.

Before Chris had arrived with his fireballs, it had been assumed that this class lacked any useful magical powers. Minor angels were also known to dust out of nowhere when their purposes were achieved. They were not regarded as the most reliable sort. The Covenant largely utilized them for service-based roles.

As Kioko and a dozen or so other members of her class began to outperform their peers on missions, a specific rank had been reinstated for them: elite.

Kioko was one of the few elite angels hand selected by Augustus to lead her fellow middle order angels, distinguished by her abilities and brilliance. Even among the elites at the Covenant, Kioko stood apart and was Augustus's favorite mission leader. While she was not free to come and go as she pleased, she had more freedom than most.

As an elite, Kioko had always been granted a certain degree of respect whether or not she was a bitch and Kioko used being a bitch to her fullest advantage.

Kioko finished preparing the sparring station and heard the door open. She watched as Clair strode arrogantly into the room with Chris, Erik, and Terri following close on their heels. Minor angels were not typically permitted in the combat rooms. It bothered her that the seraph could so brazenly break protocol, but she enjoyed watching Clair narrow her eyes when she realized Kioko would be training her.

Kioko relished the irritation in Clair's eyes when she instructed her to run the perimeter of the room ten times and then another ten laps counterclockwise. A measly six mile warm up could not possibly be too much to ask of the seraph on earth.

She held back a smile as she brought out the swords.

"Alright, seraph," Kioko said, flipping a blade in her hand. "I am assuming your *trainer* gave you a brief overview of hand-to-hand combat?" Kioko looked over to Sam, who had casually entered the room during Clair's run, clutching an old tome under his arm which he appeared to be reading intermittently. At her practically spitting the word trainer, he had forgone his book and leaned against the wall, crossing his arms. She expected him to be defensive but he maintained his temperate dispassion.

"That was not part of our training regimen, Kioko," Sam said evenly, gesturing to Clair. "We primarily trained Clair's elemental skills."

Kioko scoffed. "Elements mean nothing when the enemy gets too close. You were remiss, Sam." Sam cocked his head but did not protest. Kioko turned to Clair. "Alright, seraph. It looks like it falls to me to teach you the *basics*." That last word came out dripping with acid and Kioko smiled inwardly at Clair's clear vexation. Though Clair did not say a word, Kioko could see her jaw clench and the hands at her side slowly retract into angry fists.

They spent the better part of the next hour focused on hand placement on various weaponry and key attack positions. Clair was a quick study, but it did not come naturally to her. Kioko assumed she must have been getting by on brute strength and magic alone. She would need to work for a long time on foot placement and body fluidity to be any good at combat.

"Good," Kioko said, moving on from the session. Even Clair could tell she was lying. She was definitely not good, but Kioko was done playing around. "Now, we can incorporate the elements."

Kioko instructed Clair to stand across from her and pulled a bubble wand from the box at her feet.

Clair glared at Kioko. "Bubbles. Really?"

"Wind elements are actually some of the toughest to control. True control means being able to manipulate objects with wind without destroying them." Kioko blew the bubbles, dozens of glistening orbs flying into the air between them. She stretched out her hand and the bubbles began to float in a circular motion. "Just like the glass vortex you created in the ballroom, you need to control these bubbles. When you're ready, make them spin in the other direction."

This test was stupid, yes, but Kioko needed to see how Clair could perform without preparation. She believed Clair had practiced for her grand display in the ballroom. Wind was the most notoriously difficult element – this test would be hard for the best air angels. Even Sam appeared to be leaning in to watch what Clair would do.

Clair stretched out her hand, barely tilting her head. The bubbles followed her chin and began to float in the opposite direction. Kioko frowned. "Good," she said, this time meaning it. Maybe Clair was better than she anticipated. This irritated Kioko. She needed to craft a much bigger challenge.

Without warning, Kioko quickly drew the knife from her belt and flung it with full force at Clair's heart. The knife rapidly spun end over end. Clair's fingertips immediately pinched the air and the knife stopped mere inches away from plunging into her chest.

Clair examined the knife floating before her then looked to Kioko with an expression that could only be asking why she had just attempted murder in a training room.

Kioko shrugged. "You might be better than I thought."

Chris was fuming on the sidelines, but Clair merely cocked her head to the side. There was a glint of something primal in her eyes. The knife flipped and went careening back toward Kioko.

Kioko had just enough time to pull the bubbles toward her and freeze them. The knife embedded in the ice before crashing to the ground in an icy heap.

Clair had a feral smile playing on her lips "So there is power under all that brute strength."

Kioko smiled viciously in return.

"Clair," Augustus said, striding casually toward them from the entryway. "I would like a word with you about your upcoming mission." He did not acknowledge the mess with the knife which he had clearly observed from somewhere behind the scenes.

Kioko seethed again. Clair should not be briefed until she was cleared for the team, regardless of her status. Kioko was not going to let some newbie get anyone on her team dusted. She watched with disgust as Clair and Augustus left the room.

Chris walked up beside Kioko.

"Well," he said, propping his arm on her shoulder. He was much too familiar now. She needed to put her shields back up around him. He was just too easy to let in. "That was interesting. What were you trying to prove?"

"Nothing," she said, pulling her gloves from her fingers and tossing them into the nearest laundry bin.

"Didn't look like nothing to me," Chris said, following her to the other side of the room closer to the archery targets.

"Well, we both know that you choose to see what you want to see."

"Ouch," Chris said with a laugh, clutching his hands to his heart as if she had wounded him. She watched his face shift from smiling to serious as he took in her contemplative expression. "What are you worried about?"

"I'm not worried about anything." He was too perceptive for his own good. He could make a good spy if he was not so damn transparent with his emotions. Handsome enough to seduce even the most unlikely woman to bed, maybe even Kioko herself, if not for the fact that he was already obsessed with another angel. Kioko froze. She could not believe she was infatuated with a minor angel. But Chris was different, he was not like the other minor angels. He had powers. He had confidence. A seraph had claimed him, for crying out loud, even if that seraph was just Clair.

He stared at her, and she stared back. Finally, she caved. "I don't think your seraph should go on the mission."

Chris looked perplexed. "Why not?"

"She's untrained," Kioko said. Chris laughed in protest but she continued. "I know Sam 'trained' her in the forest in Hicksville or wherever you landed when you arrived earthside," she said, even though she knew exactly where Chris had landed because she had been a bit obsessed with him ever since she saw him catch that fireball. "But this is different. This is real combat. Real danger. Real magic." She needed Chris to understand. Maybe if she could convince him that Clair would be in some type of danger – even if Kioko did not give a shit about Clair getting hurt, only her team – maybe then he could convince her not to go.

Chris raised his hand and stroked his thumb and forefinger along his chin. The position bent his arm in such a way that the muscles in his bicep scrunched the shirt he was wearing. Kioko had to force her eyes away when he started talking again. "Yes, but Clair is a seraph. The only seraph on earth. She isn't like any of us. She went into Eden. She faced Eve. She's—"

"Special, yes. I know. She's special, Chris, and we're not." Kioko fought the urge to roll her eyes, she had to make him understand. "She's untrained and if she screws up, she could get someone else killed. I'm not worried about her getting killed. I *am* worried about y– everyone else."

Chris smiled slowly. "I appreciate that, but I trust Clair. I'm certain she's my purpose. If I am meant to get dusted protecting her, then that's what will be. But I do agree with you," he started as she had opened her mouth to argue some more. "I agree that she isn't as trained as the tactical team. I know I'm not. I know technically I'm not even supposed to be on this mission." Kioko narrowed her eyes at him. They both knew nothing would stop Clair from bringing Chris. He continued, "we will make sure to stay out of everyone's way. Plus, Augustus is the one sending Clair out with *you* – he must have a reason."

That was what compelled half of Kioko's fear. Why had Augustus insisted on sending untrained angels on a mission she could handle herself in just a few days? Kioko sighed, running her hand through her short hair. She needed to get it cut before they left. She had been really distracted lately and fallen behind on even the simple routine of scheduling her monthly hair trimming. If Clair really was coming on this mission and bringing Chris, Kioko needed to re-evaluate the team. She would not let Chris become a martyr for that girl. He was the special one. The Covenant had not seen a minor angel like him since Samuel – who was definitely not going on the mission.

Kioko looked back at Chris and noticed Augustus had reappeared by the training room door. Speak of the devil. He gave her the slightest nod as she threw up her hands. Augustus's ongoing interest in Chris both made sense strategically and made her uneasy. She continued without giving any indication to Chris that she had noticed the signal given to her by the thrones angel that it was time to wrap up their conversation. "Fine. *Fine.* I will stop fighting it, but you're both going to be doing a lot more sprints," she said more viciously than she felt.

"Yes, ma'am!" Chris jumped to attention, raising his hand to his head in a mock salute. He would pay for that cheek.

EMILY

What was she doing with her life?

Emily had just finished her last client of the day. She enjoyed the challenge of doing hair, of helping people achieve the looks they wanted in a way that flattered each individual client. She appreciated the clients who would ask her whether or not a specific style would work for their face structure or not. Many did not care. They picked what they wanted and they went with it.

Emily envied their decisiveness.

She stared down at the ring on her finger.

She loved Mike. She knew she loved Mike. This was just all feeling so fast… She was not stupid. It *was* fast. It was stupidly fast, she thought as she brushing up her client's hair trimmings and swept them into the vacuum on the ground. It also felt right.

She did wonder, briefly, if the magic of it all at the time – the romantic nature of the gesture, a proposal after all the hell they went through, and the timing of it coinciding with the magic she experienced with Clair and Sam – if it maybe, even just subconsciously, was a choice she made to give herself a dash of magic. If maybe, just for a moment, she wanted to be the center of the story she knew did not revolve around her in the slightest.

Damn her intelligence and self-awareness. Damn her genes.

Emily wished, for the thousandth time, that she had angelic blood, that she could be a bigger part in this new world she had only just discovered. She wanted to fight beside her best friend.

Clair had disappeared again, though it was intentional this time. It had been over a week since her last text. In theory, Emily knew where she had gone but she was not privy to the precise location.

Clair was at the Covenant. Emily had wanted to go with them, but Sam had insisted she stay in town and remain away from them at all costs. Humans were not supposed to know about the presence of angels on earth. It was dangerous for her to even spend time with them at all, according to Sam.

Emily could not bear to stay away. Clair was Emily's best friend and Emily had proven many times over that she was a valuable asset. She had helped give Clair the clarity to learn how to fly for crying out loud. Emily was an integral part of the team. Clair needed her and she needed Clair.

Those months when Clair was gone after Eve it was like a piece of her own destiny had disappeared alongside her.

After Clair's disappearance, the group had splintered. Emily had returned to work, Sam to Chris's cabin, and Dotty… Emily had only seen Dotty in passing. She had seemed barely alive, a silent wraith passing through town, barely functional enough to work her shop. She had disappeared into herself when Clair was in college but this had been much worse. At least when Clair was at school Doty would try. She would nod at passerby or wave on occasion. But when Clair was gone?

Nothing.

Sam was only around when he needed his weekly haircut. He mostly sat silently and stoic, but every week like clockwork he would come into her shop, sit in her waiting room, and get his hair shaped. She supposed it was his way of checking in on her without being too personable.

Emily laughed a little to herself at the memory.

On the days that Sam would come in, the salon would have more business than she knew what to do with – all the women, and some men, wanted to be around him. One woman even lied through her teeth when it was finally her turn in the chair, saying she wanted a short trim for her minor split ends that needed tending.

There were no split ends.

Emily did not blame them. Sam was hot.

Too bad he was an asshole.

She stared back down at her ring.

Time slowed around her as if it was waiting for *her*. Time waited for her to make the decision to either begin her plans to marry the boy she loved… or not.

She tilted her hand in the overhead lights of the salon, watching the perfectly round diamond radiate sparkles in every direction.

When would she want to start planning?

Everyone had always talked about that feeling you got when you were engaged, like you were in a trance thinking nonstop about the venue and dress and colors. Emily was not feeling any of that. She was not thinking about any of that.

She had told her parents, of course. They were happy for her, in that calm, quiet way of theirs. Her mother was mildly concerned about Mike after how badly he had spiraled and then broken Emily's heart with his bad choices, but he had won them over with his new outlook on life and his career. He had insisted that he was going to provide for her and their life together. He had even apologized to her father for not asking for her hand in marriage first, explaining that he had a plan to ask but the proposal had been truly spontaneous. He had explained his rehabilitation, the program he was currently in to maintain his sobriety, and his new appreciation for religion.

If he only knew.

Emily put the broom away and locked up the store before walking to her car in the small parking lot.

When she got behind the wheel, the setting sun danced through the crystal hanging from her rearview mirror, scattering rainbows around her, and she paused.

She did not want to go home. She did not want to see Mike. She watched the light refract, bursting forth a little of its own magic and science, and knew she needed to see Dotty. She needed to feel a little closer to this grand destiny to which she was sure she belonged, even if only as a tiny piece.

Emily started the car.

CLAIR

"Clair, I would like a word with you about your upcoming mission," Augustus said, gliding weightlessly toward her. She envied the effortless way he moved without seeming to exert any effort.

He had the stealth of a deadly predator.

"Of course," Clair said, following him from the room. She could hear the soft thud of Chris's footsteps as he joined Kioko behind her.

Clair knew the two had become close while she was gone. Kioko had been the angel tasked with finding Chris and bringing him to the Covenant; that was bound to bond them together. Chris appreciated Kioko's friendship but Clair saw the way Kioko looked at Chris.

She understood that look.

She had fought for that look.

She would do anything for that look from him.

It was not that she felt threatened by the elite angel – Clair was high off her own power these days. Learning to harness her power, having the opportunity to showcase her strengths in what been an epic display, and even just being among all of the angels at the Covenant was actually feeding her own power. She felt it thrum through her body, begging for release at all hours.

So no, she was not threatened by Kioko. Clair knew she was both more powerful than the elite angel and that Chris would not leave her, just like she knew the sun would rise in the morning and set at night. They were a part of each other now and always would be.

But she was still a woman and she did not have to like Kioko looking at Chris that way.

Augustus and Clair exited the training facility, turning left toward the private elevator at the end of the hall. It was so like Augustus to have segregated elevators, one for higher ranking angels and one for "the help" as he called the minor angels. She normally used the servants' elevator. It was faster and she did not care for the plush interior of the other elevator, outfitted almost like a carriage with its tufted red and gold walls, fake windows, and a potted plant in one corner.

It was an elevator not a car ride. Wasteful extravagance seemed to be all too common here.

Dotty had always taught Clair to value the things that mattered – good food, a roof over your head, clothes for all seasons. They rarely spent any money on frivolous purchases. So though her suite in this castle was grandiose, it did not make her want to stay.

The only thing keeping her here was Chris, though she did not mind having the opportunity to see how the Covenant operated on missions.

Soon she would be back in Healdsburg, Chris in tow, to start building their lives together.

She wanted to be like Emily, who she missed more than she could say. Emily loved with her whole heart. She gave up everything to care for her family. She was fearless and determined yet levelheaded. Emily had a sharp mind and had solved more than her fair share of Clair's problems. She had even handled the magical revelations better than Clair who was the one with angelic blood. She was also engaged to the love of her life, the man she had fought for against all odds.

Whenever Clair thought about Emily's ring, she wondered if she and Chris would ever have something like that, or if she would constantly be looking over her shoulder for his inevitable, purposeful, angelic end. Once a minor angel had fulfilled their purpose, they simply ceased to exist. Punishment, she assumed, for their previous life and the choice they made to end it all. While the detached part of her thought it was a fair deal, to be given a second chance at redemption and then be done, the selfish part of her wanted to shelter Chris for the rest of their existence.

Clair thought that if she stayed and learned enough from the Covenant, she might find a way to save him from that purpose. Sam might be ready to complete his and die, but Clair would be damned if she lost Chris again.

Augustus pushed the button for one of the upper-level floors. "I trust your rooms are still to your liking?"

"Yes, thank you," Clair said, pulling her arms behind her back. Being in close quarters with Augustus was electrifying, but not in the sexual way. His power called to hers, but instead of wanting to sleep with him, she wanted to consume it.

Sometimes, if she gave herself a moment to think about it, Clair scared herself.

The elevator dinged and they exited onto the opulent carpet of the castle. "We are sending you to Argentina," Augustus said, gliding ahead of her.

"Oh," Clair said, cocking her head. "I've never been. What will we be doing in the birthplace of tango?"

"It's a beautiful country, Clair," Augustus said, turning toward her, a small smile playing at his lips. "The ocean, the forests, the towns. All so alive."

They passed a set of double doors on their left and Clair cocked her head, stopping to listen. She thought she heard voices coming from within, but they were very faint. Augustus stopped with her, observing her. "What's in there?" she asked, gesturing to the doors.

"Nothing, actually," Augustus said coolly, continuing on down the hall. Clair strained her ears, but whatever she had heard had stopped. Maybe she was hearing things. She continued following Augustus down the hall.

"So how did a storm in the Mediterranean end up indefinitely delaying our trip to South America?" Clair asked. Augustus stretched his lips into a serpentine smile.

"What is your rush, Clair?" he asked with a little too much glee. "You are welcome to come and go as you please. I hope it is not too much trouble to wait and train in our humble headquarters."

"We had an agreement, *thrones angel*. I will join this one mission and then be on my way. I am ready to be informed about the mission." He prickled and nearly sneered at her reference to his rank before recomposing himself. Clair imagined it had been centuries since Augustus had been outranked and he did not care for the reminder. She would keep that in mind.

"Come now, Clair. All things in good time. Delays happen in big stakes operations like ours. Surely you can understand that we at the Covenant prefer everything to be just right before we risk any of our members' lives."

She could tell he was trying to reverse the power dynamic. She merely stared him down until he spoke again.

"Well, the primary goal of your mission will be retrieving *something* for me in Argentina, but first, you will be making a pitstop in Greece."

She supposed that explained the importance of the storm.

"I will be sending you and your team to meet up with one of my dignitary allies in Santorini. You will need to play the ambassador, have an expensive dinner, dazzle him and his associates with your charms, and under the cover of diplomacy, gather intelligence to figure out where you need to go in Argentina."

"So, you want me to schmooze?"

"Precisely." Augustus's smile turned mischievous. "It's a win-win Clair. You get to see two beautiful countries, experience how we operate, and meet some of the most influential political players alive right now."

"What is the thing I'm supposed to find? And what's in it for you?" Clair asked.

"I get to share you with the world." The way his eyes glinted at her as he said it gave her pause. She did not like his assumption that she was something he could parade about to his friends, but she intended to learn as much from the Covenant as she could and that necessitated taking part on a mission. Clair weighed her options and decided it was not worth fighting Augustus on it *yet*.

They arrived at his office and he gestured for her to sit in the leather chair in front of his desk. Augustus pulled a small folder from the cabinet and handed it to Clair.

"This is a file with information on all of the players you may encounter on your mission. Be sure to memorize their names before you leave. See if you can find any common ground for communication. Kioko is typically my ambassador of choice on these types of missions, so she will be your greatest resource in this endeavor. Mr. Georgiou is quite fond of her."

Clair opened the folder. The man staring back at her from the first page, Bellen Georgiou, was greying with silver specks in his otherwise dark beard. He was portly and marked with wrinkles in the wrong places for laugh lines. If she could only pick one word, Clair would describe him as severe. The woman standing beside him had voluminous fake breasts and over-the-top work done on her face. It was hard to tell if she was barely out of her teens or in her middle age.

Clair noted Bellen's extensive art collection and a passion for watercolors listed in a column labeled "Interests." Apparently he had taken some art classes in college but he had ultimately graduated with multiple degrees in political science. Clair glanced to the woman's short bio which only stated two facts: she was Bellen's wife and her age, which Clair quickly deduced was less than half of Bellen's. The woman's namelessness rankled Clair. She sighed.

"Well, it looks like we can discuss painting. I have limited experience, but I did major in art."

"Good," Augustus said. "He'll be easily impressed with you, anyway, simply because of what you are. Try not to forget that he is only a means to an end."

"While we are on the subject, why are we telling this man of my existence? I don't remember agreeing to being outed as the seraph on earth to humans. Besides, I thought humans weren't supposed to know about us."

"Because power is a vacuum."

Clair raised her chin to stare directly into Augustus's eyes.

"I have powerful allies across the world who have waited for you to come along, Clair. The kind for whom power begets more power. They can never get enough. The more my allies know of your existence the more capital they will share. That means more funding we can provide to the new minor angels who surface. The more funding we get to support the organization in general."

Clair thought about this. It made sense that he would have backers. Even if the Covenant traded well across the global stock markets, they would still need to have connections to keep this place hidden, to keep all the new minor angels out of the public eye. Even with the best hackers and planes and money, they needed support across the globe to keep the existence of angels a secret. But what did he mean when he said that people had been waiting for her to come along? Clair suspected that Augustus viewed her as just another object to be paraded around to further his goals for the Covenant. She was not going to be that for him, but she could play along. For now.

"Alright," Clair said, closing the file and placing it in her lap. "I can play my part."

"Good," he said. "Now, about Chris—"

"What about Chris?" Clair interjected, feeling immediately defensive.

"Oh, nothing untoward, I assure you," Augustus said, amusedly noticing the power shift around them. "I merely wanted to let you know that because of his great success, we are going to re-evaluate all of the minor angels at the Covenant."

"Oh?" Clair said, relaxing back into her seat. "In what way?"

"They will be tested on their potential effectiveness in the field. Not only will they be trained in methods similar to their higher ranking counterparts, they will have the opportunity to serve on missions."

"The opportunity?"

"Yes," he said, pulling the stopper off the scotch on his desk and pouring them both a finger of the amber liquid. He handed a glass to Clair before continuing. "It wasn't something I had considered before." He glanced at her and she understood she was the catalyst for the after. "But they are members of this community, and those who pass the evaluations will be more than welcome to serve a more active role in the organization."

Not only would it give Chris a chance to delve more deeply into developing his powers, but it would also give the minor angels in general more responsibility and respect among the higher-ranked angels. They needed to stop seeing the minor angels as dispensable and start seeing them as equals.

Clair took a sip of the scotch, enjoying the burn.

"I think that's a great idea."

Augustus clinked his glass with hers.

"Excellent."

They rested in silence for a few moments.

"I don't suppose," Augustus started. "That you could convince Sam to join you on your mission?"

Clair snorted. "I think it's astonishing that Sam is still here. And no, I cannot convince Samuel of anything."

"Hmm," Augustus murmured as he ran his finger around the lip of his glass. "Oh, well. Just a thought."

"I can try," Clair said, placing her empty glass on the table. "But I wouldn't get your hopes up. He barely leaves your library."

Augustus sighed. "You would have liked him in the old days, Clair. He was much more fun than he is now."

"How long have you known him?"

"A few centuries," he said evasively. "The Covenant's headquarters were still in the United Kingdom when we met. It was an odd time in our history. Sam was around for a long time before we discovered him, or rather he discovered us. Sniffed us out like a bloodhound. That was back before all this technology helped us locate new minor angels."

"Did you two go on missions together back then?"

"Oh, yes," Augustus sighed. "Only a couple. I think it spooked him." His viperous grin returned at the shift in her expression.

Clair was reeling. A mission had spooked Sam? Nothing spooked that man. He was unflappable. In Clair's mind, Sam was so much more than a minor angel. He had been alive longer than anyone else here, aside from maybe Augustus, she assumed, so the concept of a mission scaring him unnerved her. She had to know.

"What happened?"

Augustus poured himself another two more fingers and took a long swallow. When he looked back at Clair his eyes were the darkest she had ever seen them.

"He met someone. Another angel."

"Who?"

"Your grandfather."

AUGUSTUS

Clair had left quickly after he let it slip that Sam had known her grandfather, as expected.

It still brought him joy to casually throw a wrench into Sam's tightly regimented life.

Augustus left the office and headed back toward the training room. He normally avoided this route as it took him past the doors. Doors that he would apparently need to inspect with Clair at a later date. She had definitely heard something.

He paused in front them and stared at the ornate carvings for a moment before throwing them open and striding into the room before him.

He scanned the room. The table, the scattered chairs, and the small settee planted in front of the fireplace remained positioned as he remembered. The room was cold and empty except for the small relic in the corner. Augustus had been moving with it for what had felt like eternities. It vibrated with ancient magic powerful enough to call upon spirits – though they had yet to answer him.

He trained his gaze on the chairs and then turned toward the couch.

"She heard you, you know," he announced loudly to the room at large. "She is finally here. The time is upon us. All your years of silence haven't stopped the inevitable."

One of the chairs across the table tipped over and crashed to the ground. He cocked an eye at it and a wicked smile slowly spread across his face. He thought he heard a faint whisper on the wind, but could not make out what was being said.

He sighed.

"I will make sure to bring her to you when she is mine."

With that, he turned and sailed through the doors shutting them firmly behind him.

Augustus continued on his way down to the training rooms. Chris was still chatting with Kioko, who had noticed his entrance. Augustus gave her a nearly imperceptible nod and she in turn dismissed Chris.

Chris turned toward Augustus, an easy smile on his face. The boy was practically sunshine and rainbows compared to everyone else in this organization. He would learn soon enough that this life was everything but pleasant.

"Hello, sir," Chris said, striding up to him much too confidently for a minor angel.

"Chris," he said. "Were you on your way out?"

"I was going to find Sam," Chris said.

"Ah, yes," Augustus said. "He's been spending much of his time in the library. How has your training been going since Clair's arrival? I admit I haven't spent as much time checking in with everyone as I'd like."

"Going well, sir," Chris said, looking to Kioko. "The botanical gardens are producing well. Erik is teaching me about the different serums and antibodies we are able to produce for our blood."

Augustus nodded along, glancing between Chris and Kioko, who appeared to be monitoring the conversation even as she tried to feign disinterest. Interesting.

"Is Clair looking forward to the mission?"

"Yes," Chris said, only a slight tick of his jaw giving away his opinion. "As soon as Kioko selects who she wants on the mission, Clair is going to start training with the team."

Augustus knew that Clair would insist Chris go with them. It would not shock him if Clair had not even considered asking Augustus for his permission. Chris had pledged his loyalty to the Covenant and was Augustus's soldier, after all. He knew the quarter-seraph would not take kindly to that reminder. She was very secure in her standing here, even when it came to him.

Kioko, too, had sensed that Chris would be included. Augustus could feel the tension amping up around her when he had mentioned the mission to Chris.

Augustus tilted his head, studying the boy before him. He was glad he had decided it might be time to re-evaluate some of the minor angels and re-rank them into more active roles in the Covenant. The ones he could find, at least. Some were still out there, acting as if they were autonomous.

"Wonderful," Augustus said. "Well, I will walk with you part of the way to the library."

Chris nodded before turning to Kioko and waving goodbye.

They were out of the elevator and down the hall before Augustus spoke again.

"I never did thank you," he said, feeling Chris turn his gaze on him. He kept his eyes forward. "For completing the mission to bring Clair my invitation."

"Oh," Chris said, turning to look in front of them again. They were passing back by the doors to the silent room.

Augustus noticed Chris subtly cock his head toward the door, as if he heard something, before he continued. Interesting.

"It was no problem at all. I wasn't sure what to expect. I thought I had lost her," Chris shared freely.

"But you didn't," Augustus said, making sure to intone a sense of reassurance. "And now, we start something new." They reached the end of the hall where they would go their separate ways.

Chris furrowed his brow, but nodded. "Yes. I won't ever lose her again," he said with such conviction Augustus felt the statement clang against him like magic.

"No," he said thoughtfully as he turned away. "I suppose you won't."

SAM

Sam pulled the dusty tome from the library shelf.

He could not believe they did not store at least some of these books behind glass. He was old enough to have watched too many books be ruined by the passage of time – and some of these were already falling into disrepair.

Shameful.

He brought the book over to a velvet red armchair near the fake fire. It emitted some heat as the flames swirled synthetically, a poor man's attempt at replicating something so unpredictably wild.

He sighed, looking over to the holographic windows. They projected a beautiful, sunny day, resplendent with green trees and birds flying around the recently bloomed flowers.

Sam thought the window's designer, Erik, had a great sense of humor considering he knew it was bleak outside. The cold Russian tundra surrounding the Covenant sucked the life out of everything it touched at this time of year. Fitting for such a miserable organization.

Sam looked back at the book in his hands. He supposed that at least if the books were being stored in the deeper levels underground that if anything were to happen above, they would be spared.

"Except time corrupts," Sam said quietly to himself, gingerly opening the book.

"I guess it does," Clair nearly shouted, slamming the library door and tramping over to him. "You knew him? You knew my grandfather? How could you not tell me?"

Sam sighed. So much for a quiet afternoon. "What are you talking about, seraph?"

"Don't you 'seraph' me, Sam," she shouted. He felt the shelves shake and heard a few books fall to the ground. "You knew my grandfather! You pretended like you had no idea he existed but you met him!"

"Clair," Sam said, gently closing the book and placing it on the coffee table beside his chair. "I did not know your grandfather. Why in the world would I pretend to have not known your grandfather?"

Clair narrowed her eyes, her temper still flared. "Augustus said that you knew him – that you swore off missions with the Covenant after you met him. How could you not tell me?"

"That damned Augustus. Clair, can you not see that he is manipulating you?" Sam asked calmly.

"Manipulating me?" she spat. "This isn't about Augustus. I'm asking you about my grandfather. How come you never said anything?"

"I did not know your grandfather, Clair. I would remember meeting a seraph. I am *not* keeping secrets. Augustus is lying."

"No, he told me that you met James in England during one of the bubonic plague outbreaks and you shared a meal."

Sam stopped breathing. "What?"

Clair cocked her head. "Augustus said he was on the mission with you when you met James. Said you two shared a meal and you told Augustus all about him. Augustus knew what he was. Do you seriously expect me to believe you just magically forgot?"

Sam leaned forward in his chair, searching his memories. He remembered the numerous recurrent outbreaks of the Black Death, remembered going on missions with the Covenant to help the sick and the poor affected by the devastation. He remembered all the death. He remembered all the minor angels they lost back then and all the humans he had consoled in the wake of the most fatal pandemic in human history.

He remembered the night at the pub where he decided he was not going to be a part of the Covenant anymore. Augustus *had* gone on the mission with them. It was a rare night Sam was not with the group. He hazily recalled ending the night knowing he was not meant continue with them and that he could do more good on his own.

How had he arrived at that decision? Sam had a brief, fuzzy memory of another man, of a comforting feeling…

"I hardly remember any of this," Sam breathed, flopping back into the armchair and linking his hands behind his head. "I think I may remember meeting him, but I do not remember any other details. Why would I *not* remember him? Unless…" Sam trailed off uncharacteristically.

Clair deflated. Sam had met Clair's grandfather, a full-blooded seraph, and could only maybe, vaguely remember him. None of this made sense.

The pair sat in silence for a few moments until Sam leaned forward again.

"Clair," he said in an unusually hushed voice that caught her attention. "I suspect I may have had my memories wiped."

"What? That's a thing?"

"Yes, Clair. In fact, I once suggested to Chris that we wipe some of Emily's memories, but that is neither here nor there."

"You suggested what?" Clair exclaimed, fury rising in her blood.

"Oh, Clair, honestly. You should know me better than this by now. I was trying to keep her *safe*. Do not fret, Chris stopped the idea in its tracks." He waved her off

She sighed in frustration and sat back, breathing deeply until she seemed calm.

"So if your memory was wiped, who did the wiping and why?"

"Well, I imagine your grandfather played a major role. As to why, I can only guess it was to protect his identity. He did convince me to leave The Covenant, after all."

"If James wiped your memory, then how would Augustus have known about you two meeting?" Clair asked, staring intently at Sam's increasingly befuddled face. "He said meeting James 'spooked' you. What happened, I wonder?"

"I do not know," Sam said, sliding his hands down his face. He stood and walked over to the small rolling cart bar, another unnecessary item Augustus had included that did not belong in a library. Along with the bar cart, there were sofas, a coffee table, potted plants, and fake windows. He poured himself two fingers of whatever amber liquid was in the decanter. He looked back at Clair. "Would you care for any?" he asked, gesturing to the other cup.

"No, thanks," she said, sitting back in the armchair. "Already had some of the stuff in Augustus office."

Sam scoffed. "Probably better than this stuff."

"Probably," Clair chuckled. Sam sat back down, taking a large sip.

"This has me questioning everything," he said, leaning forward and resting his arms on his knees.

"How so?" Clair asked, pulling one of her legs under the other on the chair.

"If my memory has been wiped, has it happened before? Could it happen again? How much of my long life am I missing?"

Clair cocked an eyebrow at him. "Well," she said. "That's terrifying."

Sam took another long pull of scotch.

"Honestly, Sam," Clair said, looking at him. "I don't think you have. How many higher-ranking angels have the ability to wipe memories? Probably not many. You're the longest living minor angel on record. How many angels have you known who could wipe memories?"

Sam reflected for a moment. "Very few. It took me several centuries to master the skill and even then, I rarely have the stamina for it without at least a week's preparation and I can only blur recent memories. Aside from me, I have only heard of thrones angels with prophetic tendencies mastering the skill... and seraphs."

Clair absorbed the information.

"It does seem like it was James, then. But then the real question is — why? Why not just let you keep your memory of him?" Clair asked.

"It is perplexing," Sam said. "Perhaps he thought I would become a zealot. Maybe I was drawn to him like Chris is drawn to you. Whatever he said to me changed the trajectory of my life."

They sat in silence, each grappling with the implications this could have.

Sam had to know. He had to find out what he was missing. There had to be a reason for his uncommonly long life and now he suspected it was all connected: him leaving the Covenant, finding Clair, them being here, Augustus choosing now to mention this chance meeting...

But how?

Sam squeezed the glass and looked up at Clair. "If James had the power to take memories, maybe he also had the power to give them back."

"Maybe," Clair said. "But he's gone. It's not like we can ask him."

"No," Sam said, sitting up excitedly, staring pointedly into Clair's eyes. "I cannot ask *him*."

She stared back and suddenly her eyes widened. "Me!" she exclaimed incredulously.

"Yes!" Sam said, setting his glass down next to the book, mentally chastising himself for it but unable to stop himself in the buzz of his excitement. "Yes, Clair, you could do it! If James had the power to take memories, maybe you also have that power. And if you have that power maybe you can retrieve memories."

Clair gaped at him. "Sam, you barely trusted me with heavy weights in a gym and now you want me poking around in your brain? No way!"

"Clair!" Sam practically shouted. "This could be the key to everything. This could be the reason I have not found my purpose. Something *your grandfather* said to me changed my entire life. I need to know what that was."

Clair was shaking her head. "I don't know Sam, this is a crazy idea."

"Please, Clair," Sam said, looking down at her. "Please. You have to try."

Clair shifted in her seat then grabbed Sam's glass and took a long pull of the amber liquid. Sam took that as a good sign. She was steeling herself.

Clair sat back, glass still in hand, and evaluated him. It had been a long time since they had sat like this, just the two of them.

Now that she had settled a bit, Sam noticed how much better Clair looked than she had just weeks ago in Healdsburg. Her skin appeared flushed and healthy, her eyes bright. He knew much of it had to do with her reunification with Chris, but he also recognized quite a bit of it came from being within the Covenant itself – the collective energy of all the angels congregated in one area was immense.

It was why humanity had flourished in communities. Why the traditional churches of today harbored so many members. There was an energy, a collective vitality in a group of people who shared similar goals and agreed upon conventions. It was why so many religious and community leaders dedicated so much time to interacting with their flocks. They needed the group, focusing on them and feeding them energy in order to receive energy and power in return.

Sam had studied this energy for a time. He knew it existed like he knew his every breath was somehow numbered.

Yet when Clair looked at him now, all Sam could do was wait. He felt, for one of the few times in his life, fear – fear that she would say no. Fear that she would say yes. Fear that he had missed something, that her grandfather had taken something vital from him. For him. For his life's purpose.

Sam sat, waiting, and counted his breaths as he stared unwaveringly into Clair's eyes.

"I'll try," she finally agreed.

Sam felt himself deflate, sagging into the relief that poured through his veins. Then he did something neither of them expected – he pulled Clair into a bone-crushing hug.

"Thank you," he breathed, before releasing her. She looked a little shocked but nodded, understanding alighting in her eyes. "Clair, thank you."

"I can't promise anything Sam," she said, gesturing back to the sofas around the coffee table. They both sat.

"I know that," he said, rubbing his temples before leaning back. "But you are my best shot."

Clair nodded, both of them lost in their own thoughts for a moment, before Clair looked up and studied Sam.

"What?" he asked, leaning forward.

"I just wonder why James would blur your memories of him. What could he have said that spurred you to leave the Covenant? This must have happened centuries before he even met Dotty."

"I suppose that is what you are going to help me find out, Clair."

"True," Clair said, leaning back in the armchair. "Is it possible that James knew about all of this?" she asked, gesturing between them and then more broadly around them. "Is it possible he knew what would happen in the future and set you up to help guide me or something? If he had the gift of prophecy like you mentioned, I just don't understand how someone could live with all that. Visions of the future, knowing what was to come. I wouldn't be able to handle it. The knowledge would weaken me."

This was the first time in a long time that Sam had heard Clair be vulnerable about the powers that she had inherited, about the magnitude of it all. While he felt she was entitled and much too young to have such power, he was concerned for her. Concerned that the power would prove too much, that it could consume her, that everything she was fighting to protect – that all of them were fighting to protect – could be lost if she was not disciplined enough. He carefully tucked away his emotions about it, like always, and focused on the science of it.

"If your grandfather was prophetic, he may have only seen glimpses of the future," Sam said. "Maybe he could turn his power on and off. We may not ever know, but I doubt anyone could live with the visions of all inevitable futures and remain sane. Even an angel."

Clair smiled. "Even an angel."

They were greeted by a friendly knock.

Sam turned toward the opening library door. Chris strode through the opening and smiled broadly at the sight of them. He shut the door behind him and offered his greetings as he headed in their direction. When he reached them, Chris deftly lifted Clair from her armchair and sat them both on a loveseat across from Sam. It spoke volumes to how far they had come in the short time they had been back together. Chris was good for Clair, Sam could tell. Whether Clair was good for Chris was another matter entirely.

"What're we talking about looking so serious?" Chris asked as he twined his fingers with Clair's, relaxing into the couch.

"Apparently, Sam has met my grandfather," Clair announced.

Chris gawked at Sam and asked accusingly, "Why didn't you tell us?"

"He didn't know," Clair said, defending Sam. "Augustus let it slip during our little chat earlier."

"Her grandfather wiped my memories of our meeting," Sam said. "Clair is going to help me get them back." He said it with conviction, inflicting the energy into his words. He needed Clair to believe it – he needed both of them to have hope.

"That's incredible," Chris said, turning to look at her. He brought his free hand up to her cheek, thumb delicately stroking her skin while he stared into her eyes. Chris looked at Clair as if she was the sun in his universe. "If anyone can undo ancient magic, it's you."

That was it.

Sam knew in his heart, in his soul, that all Clair needed to believe she could restore his memory was the absolute certainty of Chris.

Clair nodded seriously, staring deeply into Chris's eyes. If the pair were not doing him such a huge favor, Sam might find the intensity off-putting.

"I am assuming you aren't starting today so I need a drink," Chris said, breaking the tension. He gingerly placed Clair on the couch and stood, grabbing the bottle and pouring each of them a couple of fingers. "Augustus walked with me down here, and he *inquired* about us."

Clair scoffed. "Pressed, you mean? That man has his fingers in everyone's business."

"Yes," Chris said, sighing. "He actually thanked me for completing my *mission* to bring you his invitation."

It was Sam's turn to scoff, taking a deep swig. "I am sure he stressed the word mission as much as possible."

"Oh, yes," Chris said, looking at Clair. "He knows you won't leave without me. I made sure he knows I won't *let you* leave without me."

Clair smiled, some of the weight she usually carried in her eyes lessening. "Good, because I won't. I'm not losing you again."

"I know that," Chris smiled, taking a sip of his drink.

They all sat comfortably in silence together, ruminating on everything that had brought them to this moment. It was Clair who broke the silence.

"I wonder where the Gate is now."

"Could be anywhere. I doubt it'll come back to Healdsburg anytime soon," Chris said.

Clair nodded. "I wonder if he's still there."

"Who?" Chris asked.

"Adam," Clair said, pausing to taking a long sip. "He was so pained and trapped. His body was a prison. And right before he was taken over…" Clair shuddered at the memory, no doubt remembering the sight of the Ultimate Evil taking over Adam's body. They had heard this before, or at least Sam assumed Clair had told Chris, but it was still surreal to hear about her experience in Eden after crossing through the Gate. "Adam told me to tell someone that when in doubt to come back to the beginning." Clair shook her head. "What beginning? His beginning? Who needed to go back there?"

"What did he say precisely?" Sam asked.

"Well," Clair began, "What he said was '*Clair, you must tell… When doubts… come back… to the beginning…*'"

Clair looked up at Sam, who was shaking his head. He could not make sense of it.

"Clair," Chris said, "I don't care if Adam needs you to go back for him. I never want you going back into the Gate again."

"Of course not, Chris," she said reassuringly, bringing his hand to her mouth for a quick kiss. "I wouldn't."

"Good," Chris said before downing the rest of his drink.

The trio spent the rest of the day talking through various theories about how Clair could restore Sam's memories. It felt like old times, when only Sam and Chris knew of the seraph on earth. Even in the belly of the beast, Sam could not help marveling at the joy his new life had brought him. He knew he could never leave these two to fend for themselves in the Covenant, whatever it may cost him.

CLAIR

Wait a minute, you're going to start poking into Sam's mind, tomorrow?" Chris asked, sitting on the bed next to her. He had just showered and changed into the yuppie pajamas provided by the Covenant, an expensive silk set to match the sheets. Clair missed her band t-shirts and faded plaid flannel bottoms.

Clair sighed, falling back onto the mountain of pillows. After her meeting with Sam, she and Chris had decided to sequester in her room with a good movie.

It was nice, actually, taking time for herself and getting lost in someone else's story. Someone who would face their own struggles, fight their own demons, but who was so far removed from Clair that it did not matter to her whether or not the main character succeeded or failed. It was all about the journey, not the destination, like Ralph Waldo Emerson had said.

In her own life, Clair was stuck. She was the main character and she needed to succeed. She had to craft her own destiny and she could not simply turn off the movie to stop the inevitable chaos barreling toward her.

"Yes," she said finally, throwing her arms over her eyes. "I said I would try. You didn't see him when we first figured it out, Chris." Chris gently pulled her arms away from her face, gazing down at her in that way that made her feel like she was everything, could do anything, could be anything. "He was practically unhinged. I've never seen Sam like that. He *hugged* me."

"He *hugged* you? That is wild," Chris exclaimed with a laugh, dropping her arms and lying down next to her. "He's always been the immovable rock of this group."

"Exactly," Clair said, turning toward him and cuddling up next to his heat. "What if I can't unlock his memories? What if I can? What if I hurt him?"

Chris stared at the ceiling, processing for a moment. "Well," he said, looking down at her, running his hand through her hair. "It's his choice. He wants to know and he believes you can do this. If you can find those memories – whatever they are – he was the one who asked for them, good or bad. If you can't get them, at least you tried."

Clair sighed, closing her eyes. "This is Sam we're talking about, Chris," she said, nuzzling her face into his side. "He doesn't give up. If I fail, he will throw himself into finding another way to try for all eternity."

Clair felt Chris chuckle, even though he made no sound. The vibrations of his body, his warmth, and his nearness were beginning to lull her to sleep.

"Well," he said softly, his hand still stroking her hair. "At least he'll have a project."

He pulled her face toward him and kissed her. She moaned and he ground his hips against her.

"You are my purpose," he told her.

She loved him for that but she also knew it was not true.

If she was his purpose, he would be gone.

Chris was something more than just her partner.

Clair fell asleep to the gentle strokes of his hand gliding through her hair.

The first three days spent trying to access Sam's mind were a series of failures. Sam suggested they research the brain, then when that failed, he guided her through the basics of elemental magic and its uses in the body.

Clair would have cut her pinky off to have Emily here to guide her to enlightenment. Her genius mind would have this all figured out already.

Sam insisted they conduct all of their work in the library despite him wanting to keep it secret. He flat out refused to meet in Clair's suite as that would be considered improper.

His words, not hers.

"You need to focus, Clair," he said, positioning her fingers more accurately on his temples. "Remember, you are using your magic to pull memories from a brain. You need to focus on the organ itself." He released her fingers. "Maybe we should read more studies on the brain."

"Maybe we should," Clair said, not knowing where to look. Should she look at his forehead? Into his eyes? Where did a person look to pull hidden memories from ages ago?

Sam sighed.

"No, I know," Clair said before he could speak again. "Let me try again. I know what I need to do, it's just that you've guided me the past few times and now I need to try on my own. I figured out the glass manipulation on my own. This is just more, well, mental." Clair chuckled at her own pun, causing her fingertips to slide a bit down his temples. "Everything else is manipulation of the physical world. This is theoretical." She repositioned her hands.

"Yes," Sam said without even the slightest hint of annoyance. Clair had to give him credit. He was not as overbearing as she assumed he would be. He was intense, sure, but he was not pushing her or getting angry. Maybe he really did trust her, or more likely he did not want to upset her. Clair was starting to suspect that they needed to ask for outside help to figure out how to retrieve the memories.

Clair tried again.

And again.

She had a brief moment where she could feel his emotions — frustration, hope, sadness — before that, too, slipped through her fingers. She sighed.

Sam was elated, however. He said that was progress, and he would take it. That they would get this. That she could do it. Definitely a far cry from his tyrannical training days in the forest.

Each night as she drifted to sleep with Chris next to her, Clair hoped she actually would live up to those expectations.

CHRIS

When Chris woke up the next morning, he walked down to the bunks to find Terri. They were supposed to visit the hydroponics lab today to look into increasing the output of plant growth underground. Terri enjoyed the science and Chris enjoyed the earth. They worked well together.

When he arrived at the bunks, Chris could tell it was not business as usual at the Covenant.

All the minor angels who typically rushed off bright and early to start working wherever they were assigned were all sitting on their bunk beds waiting for instruction from one of the elite angels who would be in charge of their re-evaluations.

When Augustus had said he wanted to re-evaluate everyone, Chris did not realize it would move this quickly.

Some looked frightened, others confused, but most seemed genuinely excited. The upcoming mission with Clair would need a larger unit, and now that minor angels could rank a little higher in the hierarchy, they all had a chance to get a spot on the team.

Chris wondered how long some of them had been with the Covenant, and why they had only previously been assigned as task workers and not valued members of the organization's functions. Chris knew keeping an organization like the Covenant running must require an enormous amount of coordination and that positions like cooks and cleaners were essential and valuable, but some of the minor angels he knew had backgrounds in other vocations. It did not make sense to him that they would not at least first be considered for wherever their skills could be most useful. He supposed this re-evaluation would make up for that lapse. Even the recently dubbed leader of the minor angels was required to participate. Plus, Chris thought, how could he lead them without participating fully in everything they went through?

He laced up his athletic shoes and went to talk to Terri. She was in the middle of plating her hair down her back. When he approached, she glanced from the mirror hanging off her bunk up at him. "I am blaming you for this."

"What?" he asked, sitting on the bed beneath hers. Her bunkmate, an elderly woman with spiked white hair, was already across the hall talking with someone else. He knew she would not mind.

Terri finished the braid and coiled it into a tight bun at the nape of her neck. "Evaluations? Really? I've been here five years Chris. We don't *get* evaluated for missions. Then you come along and *poof*," she said, miming a small explosion with her fingers.

Chris was trying but failing not to laugh. "Poof?"

"Oh, don't you laugh at me!" She playfully punched him in the shoulder, and he lost it, letting out a large belly laugh.

It felt good to laugh. He had been laughing a lot more lately.

"Hey," Terri said, crouching to his eye level on the bed, "Toss me my deodorant."

He reached into her bag and did as she said. She sighed and stood back up, quickly rubbing the stick against her armpits, then grabbed her water bottle from her bunk. "It's okay that you don't understand, you're still technically *new*, but one day you'll realize that everything that's happened recently is a *big* deal. Minor angels don't last long in the field. When we achieve our purpose – and believe me, I have watched it happen right before my eyes – we just..." she mimed the explosion again.

"Fall in!" boomed a loud voice.

They both looked toward the door where a middle-aged man with graying hair and a severe expression had just entered.

Chris hopped up from the bed and turned in the direction of the newcomer, who was looking around the room with a sour expression on his face. He and Terri ran to circle with the others.

"Greetings, minor angels. I am Wuldrid. It is my misfortune and responsibility to identify which among you have enough skill to be included on the upcoming mission with the elites. You will participate in a series of tests today, starting with mine." He looked around the room at all of them, his stern face somehow managing to harden even more.

"Being part of a ground operations team is physically demanding. Many of you may already know that your skills do not *lend* you the ability to move within a coordinated team effort. However, we have no choice but to test you anyway. Grab a water bottle and make sure you are wearing the appropriate apparel for a physical assessment. You have five minutes to be outside on the front lawn. Anyone latecomers will run additional laps."

With that, he turned and left, and the room exploded in a flurry of movement and excitement. They were almost never allowed outside and for many of the minor angels, it had been years since they had breathed fresh air. Even those who knew they would fail the fitness test were eager to get outside. Chris nudged Terri and they began walking toward the staircases that would lead them to the front lawns.

It had snowed unseasonably early overnight; the once brown exterior of the castle was blanketed in a layer of fresh white powder. Chris was grateful for the clothing the Covenant had supplied. His jacket was lightweight enough to move his body freely, but warm enough that he could not feel the touch of the cold. He believed it had to be some new scientific-magic hybrid invention they had developed here, but he would need to figure out the details later.

Wuldrid ordered the minor angels into three lines. "As I am sure all of you were made aware, the castle is warded. Nothing can get in or out without us knowing. No satellite software or military tech can breach these wards, so do not concern yourselves that we are outside and not in the underground training facility some of you are already familiar with – we will get there later.

"Your first challenge is to run around the perimeter of the castle grounds ten times. Anyone caught cheating will be immediately failed and not allowed to test in any of our other mission qualifiers. If you feel you cannot go on, or have reached your limit, stop where you are, hold your hand to the sky, and one of the patrols will be along to collect you. Everyone understand?"

He looked around at all the nodding.

"Begin."

"I. Hate. You." Terri inhaled between each word.

Chris was lying on the floor next to his old bunk, for once extremely happy that the floors in the housing units were metal and cool. "It's not like… I told them…I wanted this," he said, attempting to slow his heart rate. Terri was on the ground next to him, rolling her water bottle across her forehead and breathing heavily.

After the miles of running, Wuldrid – may he be cursed, as far as Chris was concerned – took them through a series of pushups, sit ups, and weight training exercises, recording how much they could lift and carry before collapsing.

None of the physical training Chris had done with his fellow minor angels for the past several months compared to this. He realized a bit late into one of the dozens of reps of sit ups that the field mission angels must have a much more intense exercise regimen outlined for them. Even Chris, who had tested well the first time the Covenant decided to explore the prowess of minor angels after witnessing him craft a fireball, had struggled to complete each task. After all, Chris had used his bolstered status as the leader of theminor angels to work in the greenhouse, teach beginner yoga classes, and train with fire. He had not thought to increase his physical endurance for a mission.

Surprisingly, most of the minor angels had successfully made it through the physical part of the evaluation. A few, especially those who had older angelic bodies, had conceded during the run and were taken back to the barracks. But no one cheated, which meant they were all allowed to go through the next stage of evaluation.

"What do you think part two entails?" Terri asked, rolling to her side and using her elbow to push into a seated position. Chris remained on the ground.

"No idea, but at least we have an hour before we jump back into it."

Terri groaned. "Do you think it's something physical? Because I'm not saying they're trying to kill us, but they might be trying to kill us."

Chris chuckled. "I don't think they are trying to kill us."

"I suppose," Terri said, breathing evening out. "There are definitely easier ways."

Chris elbowed her in the side, causing her to fall back on the floor. "Don't be so morbid. We can do this, I know we can."

"You're always so damn optimistic!"

"One of us has to be," he sighed, smiling at her. She just rolled her eyes.

"Well, I'm going to go decompress with a good book for an hour before the torture begins again."

"Sounds good," he said, watching her feet walk away as he remained sprawled on the ground.

He wondered how Clair's training was going. He was already looking forward to a shower in her suite, *their* suite he supposed, since he was basically living there with her. Maybe he could convince her to shower with him…

He was pulled from his daydream by his friend and colleague Erik sauntering over to him. "Hey, Chris," Erik said casually. "How much time do you have before the next session?"

"A little less than an hour," Chris responded, sitting up, wrapping his arms around his legs, and staring up at Erik. "Why?"

"New plant species was just created downstairs. It's a cross between a tomato and a strawberry. Thought you'd want to check out the flower which just started to blossom."

"Yes!" Chris said, standing too fast and gripping his old bunk-bed post to steady himself. Erik laughed.

"I thought you might need this," he held out a small vial filled with purple liquid. "Rejuvenation brew. Trust me, it's worth it. No side effects, helps you regain your energy. Drink that and meet me in the garden."

"You got it!" Chris said, watching Erik walk away.

Chris downed half the vial, surprised that it tasted almost like those sour candies Clair loved, Sour Patch Kids, before dashing over to Terri's bunk. He tapped the book obscuring her face.

"Hey," he said, swinging the half-full vial above her.

"Oh. Em. Gee!" she squealed, snapping the vial out of his hands and downing it. "I take back all the negative things I've ever said about you."

"Sure," he chuckled. "Until the next time I bug you."

"True," she said, sighing as the potion's effects hit her. "Thanks, Chris, I mean it."

"No problem," he said. "I'll be back before the next phase."

"You better be," she said. "You started all this. You and your fireballs and your seraph girlfriend."

Chris chuckled and walked toward the door that would lead him to the hallway with the correct elevator.

As he walked, he considered what Terri had said.

First, if he had never met Clair, would the minor angels ever have had this opportunity to be truly considered respected members of the Covenant or would they just still be the labor force?

Chris thought about the fireball. He had learned how to make them on his own before Clair came into his life. It was likely that other minor angels could do the same. But, Chris had also been in close proximity to the Gate for most of his angelic existence. Was he truly exceptional or had he simply absorbed the powerful magic around him?

Did it matter?

Chris decided that it did not matter. Everything had happened because fate had intervened in all of their lives and changed them.

Chris could not help but think that fate looked a lot like Clair.

Second, girlfriend? Clair was not his girlfriend. The word was too pedestrian for what they were.

Lover was too limiting. It was not just about sex with them, although that was great.

They shared a love that was deeper than the sea. He would drown the stars to save her.

He loved her. She loved him. They were *magic* together.

No, he thought. Clair was not just his girlfriend. If she was the sun, he was a planet caught in her orbit. As terrifying as it was for Chris to admit, she was his purpose. Everything about his second life revolved around Clair.

As he stepped into the garden, he decided that he was more than okay with that, no matter what it meant for his short life.

SAM

If Sam could peek into Clair's brain, he was certain he would hear her cursing him out and considering the different places she could hide from him in this forsaken castle. He knew she would rather be doing anything else right now, but she was here, with him, trying for what felt like the millionth time to restore his memories.

Sam peered into Clair's concentrated eyes yet again and he could tell that she was reaching her limit. He knew that all it would take to break her was a single snide remark, one throwaway comment about her not trying hard enough.

Sam felt nearly as exhausted as she looked and he could practically taste his negativity manifesting in the sassy quip on the tip of his tongue.

His brusque personality would not be particularly effective here. They were in an unfamiliar environment and Clair was feeling defeated. His punishing words usually triggered a fire in Clair that pushed her forward but that was not going to work for Clair – not now. Not here, in this castle where they were all fighting to maintain their bonds within the pull of the Covenant. As much as it fed them energy, the Covenant equally feasted on their energy. No, this would never be the same as their training sessions spent in the quiet forest back in her hometown. He had to maintain a gentler approach if he ever hoped to see those wiped memories again.

"Clair," he said, and she blinked. "I want to try something else."

She sighed, shaking her head. "I am trying my best. I'm thinking about your brain, your memories, and my grandfather. I've tried moving the little angels around your head and even into your brain but nothing is changing."

Sam was momentarily horrified that she had pushed what she and Chris called little angels into his brain without his knowledge, but he did not show it. He knew the little angels as influences, the small, invisible dots of energy that reacted to the choices people made around them, amplifying and energizing the choice. Talented angels could harness their power to create magic and Clair's mastery of them was unparalleled.

"I believe you," he said, and Clair looked almost surprised. "I keep ruminating about what you are even supposed to think about and we have both reached the same conclusions."

She nodded, bringing her hand up to her cheek, cracking her neck. She sighed again.

"What?" Sam asked.

She stared at Sam as if he should be able to read her mind.

"I don't know how James did it," she exclaimed in frustration, her eyes narrowing at him. "I'm upset he didn't leave a handbook." Clair scoffed at her own suggestion.

"Yes, that would have been helpful," Sam chuckled.

She sighed, shaking her head.

"A piece of me knows this is just another test from Augustus," Clair said, touching the golden bracelet on her wrist. Sam paused. He had not actually considered that this was all, in fact, some sort of test or power play from Augustus, for Clair. Sam had been so concerned about finding his lost memories that he had lost sight of why he remained here. In losing focus, Sam had left his friends vulnerable.

A power play to what end? To get Clair to ask him for his assistance? To see if she could do it? To get Sam to kowtow to him? Who was Augustus manipulating and for what purpose?

"But another piece of me doesn't care. Screw him. He doesn't get to control everything," Clair said defiantly. She dragged her hands through her hair. "Like everything else I have figured out, the answer must be simple and it's probably right in front of me."

Sam thought Clair mastering her powers was anything but simple, but he was not about to stop her if she was in the midst of a breakthrough.

She examined his head, his ears, his hair, his nose… She was studying him as if the answer was written into his skin.

He knew the moment the answer came to her.

"Oh," she said, blinking. "Could it be…"

"What?" he asked, releasing a breath he did not know he had been holding. "What is it?"

She cocked her head.

"It's not about you," she said.

"What do you mean, it's not about me?" he said, thoroughly confused.

"I mean," she said, studying him, her eyes slightly clouded over. "The answer to getting your memories back. It's not about you or your brain. It's about me."

Sam knew the skepticism was showing on his face. Not everything was about her.

"I swear I'm not being narcissistic right now," she said, chuckling. "I mean it's about me being what I am. It's about the seraph bloodline. It's a seraph power, dealing with memories."

Sam felt his eyebrows hit his hairline. "Okay. So we just have to figure out what James did?"

"I think I know what he did," she said, grabbing the decanter of bourbon off the table to quickly pour herself a glass. She took a deep pull from her glass in one hand as she handing the decanter to him with the other. She hoped the alcohol would relax her enough for what she needed to do. "Drink up, we're about to get personal."

He took the decanter from her and took a swig of the alcohol straight from the source. He did not want to slow her roll by bothering with a cup. "Now what?"

"Now," she said, shaking out her hands and stepping back out of his personal space, "I find your soul."

CHRIS

The second part of the evaluation was led by a wiry, short, boy-faced angel with black rimmed glasses. Erik, the very angel who had just shown Chris how to artificially pollinate a cross-bred fruit in the garden.

"Hello, everyone. My name is Erik. I run the technology department here. Many of you may recognize me as your fellow minor angel, a class which I will maintain, though I was recently re-ranked as an archangel. The Covenant has decided to bring back this obsolete term as the official ranking for minor angels in positions of leadership or those with notable special talents. You are all here to be evaluated for the rank. This ranking does allow its members to be considered for support roles on missions. Thankfully, the Covenant has wisely decided to utilize my skills as a non-combative asset."

Chris heard Terri sigh in relief next to him. Erik must have heard it, too, because he looked over at her and smiled before glancing down at the mound of papers on the cart he had rolled before them.

"This next test is, in fact, a test in the scholastic sense," Erik announced. He gestured to the angel closest to him and handed him a large box filled with pens. "We know you all wake with different information preprogramed in your minds. This test will determine what that information is and the ways in which it could be useful for the Covenant. Each of you will take a packet and complete it at your own bunk.

"Do not," Erik said with surprising sternness, "I repeat, do *not* cheat on this test. The Covenant is trusting you as it would any elite angel and assuming you are answering these questions to the best of your own personal ability. The Covenant is known for conducting random tests. Should you, for example, demonstrate on this test that you know the difference between a plant that could save a life and a plant that could kill you, you might find those very same plants in your breakfast tomorrow morning."

Erik paused for effect and silence fell over the room. Many of the minor angels exchanged furtive glances. Erik smiled, a little sinisterly.

"Now that I have made my expectations perfectly clear, you will have four hours to complete the questionnaires." He held up one of the packets, which Chris deduced were the actual tests. They had to be at least an inch thick and knowing Erik, the pages were probably double-sided. "Please feel free to cross out any questions you may not know. Once you are done, place your test back in the crate. Any questions?"

A kind minor angel Chris recognized named Dylon raised his hand. Erik looked over at him and nodded. "After we're done with this test, what's next?"

"Nothing yet," Erik said, adjusting his glasses on his nose. "You will resume your normal schedule in the morning, while we evaluate."

Erik looked around at the group. Seeing no more questions, he continued.

"This is an unprecedented opportunity for you, minor angels. Pace yourselves and do your best. Physical ability is one thing, but knowledge is the true differentiator. The Covenant looks forward to learning about your talents."

Chris saw the determined faces around him. The Covenant was giving them a chance at more, not just in combat, but in its intelligence operations.

"Grab a test and begin."

CLAIR

t was genius in its simplicity.

In theory.

"Now, I find your soul," she had confidently announced.

Clair watched Sam's eyes widen. They did not talk about spiritual things and really, what could be more spiritual than the soul? Her gut was telling her this had to be it, the only thing that a seraph could do that none of the others could. She hoped she was right.

Sam looked at Clair, and she sensed his internal struggle. Not only would he be doubting her theory, he was debating willingly allowing her to search for a soul within him. Ultimately, his curiosity won out, as she knew it would. Sam wordlessly took another long pull of the bourbon before setting the decanter down and facing her, his arms loose at his sides.

Clair raised her hands, but just before she began, he spoke.

"Please be careful," he said. This was the first and only sign of fear she had ever seen in him. Clair was so thrown that all she could do was nod in affirmation.

Clair raised her hands and closed her eyes. She felt for the little angels, enveloping them around her and Sam. She felt for the energy of the earth and the blood flowing through her veins. She heard Sam's heartbeat pumping a little faster than it should be, the only sign of his anxiety.

Clair observed the *thump thump thump* of his heart alongside the little angels whose essence she sensed twisting and glowing around him. It was like stepping into an alternate universe. Sam was no longer a physical being in front of her. He was an amalgamation of light, sound, and energy – unconstrained colors and wisps radiating with his essence.

Clair brought her hands together and pushed them against Sam. She continued to push through his skin into his body and then deeper, past anything that could be seen. Past the tangible perfection of the human circulatory system, nerves, receptors. Clair pushed the little angels past the realm of the phenomenal.

Clair felt tears spring into her eyes.

She could see his soul. It was beautiful. Golden, soft, filled with light. She could feel its slight density flow through her fingers as if she was running her hands through the clouds.

She slid her hands across his soul, searching for a clue. As she reached what could only be described as the center of Sam's soul, she brushed against a very slightly elevated thick spot, like something fine had dried on the surface of a table, giving it a rougher texture than the rest.

Clair rubbed the spot with her mind, feeling it scrape.

She stopped. She did not want to remove it, she wanted to restore it.

Clair thought about water, calling to mind the sensation of a damp cloth in her hand pressing upon the spot. The bump slowly relaxed and accepted her touch. She gently smoothed it until it became flush with the rest of its existence before letting it all go, dropping her hands and collapsing to the ground, breathing hard.

When Clair looked up, she could see Sam staring down at her.

He was crying.

CHRIS

t had been a week since Terri, Dylon, Chris, and about ten other minor angels passed the first two stages of the re-evaluation and made it through to combat testing which started today.

Chris had never been more tired.

Back in Healdsburg, whenever Clair was enduring physical training with Sam, Chris would be collecting plants for recipes or tonics. Sometimes he got to hike with Clair but he had largely escaped the physical fitness side of training.

Now he understood why Clair was always so prickly toward Sam.

This was hard. *Hard* hard. Even painful at times.

There had been moments during the testing where Chris realized that despite all of his efforts, minor angels would never be able to perform at the same level as the elites. It did not matter what Sam had accomplished in his unusually long life. It did not matter what feats Chris could manage with his self-taught fireballs. The elite angels had a natural edge against the originally-human minor angels. They would always be classified as a minor, nothing more. That did not sit right with Chris. A person's value should not be based on the gifts they are physically capable of giving to the world.

Chris did not care for the Covenant's tonics that were designed to enhance and speed up recovery from physical exertion. He opted to fast to optimize his strength like Sam had taught him. It felt more natural, more grounded and in sync with his body. The tonics they prepared made him feel off. Fasting was harder but ultimately, he did not want to be reliant on what the Covenant provided him. He could train his own way and be able to move on if he had to, without needing a supply with him like some of the other minor angels.

Even after following Sam's angelic fasting routine, Chris's body was screaming at him. The last week had been filled with nothing but training. It had been a nonstop cycle of running, lifting, training the powers that made them exceptional, and pushing all of them to their limits, crashing, and getting up to do it all over again the next day.

At least he had Clair. She was always there to help soothe him at the end of the day and during his rare breaks.

The Covenant had archangel track minor angels on a stricter diet now, pushing protein and vegetables at them as well as low glycemic carbs. Chris had never wanted a cupcake so badly in his life.

Terri, for all her grumbling, was outperforming him. She could run faster, jump higher, lift more. She was a champ but she made sure to let him know she blamed him for this new routine. Despite her complaints, he had noticed her mentioning more than once that she was hoping to see Erik from the technology department again.

It seemed like the minor angels who had passed the tests were receiving less hostile attention from the ranked angels. Chris wondered if, after all was said and done, there would be a culture shift among the different ranks.

This was the first day in a week that started differently. Wuldrid himself had made an appearance in the bunks to direct them to a different level in the Covenant where the middle order angels trained. They entered a combat arena, a room like the one where Kioko had challenged Clair.

It was a wide open space, with numerous sets of circles taped on the floor, staggered at different intervals where competitors could face off against each other. There were some higher-ranked angels already training in the room. Chris saw fire sparring against fire, water against water, and earth against earth. The volume of noise and activity had him and the other minor angels turning this way and that to get a better look at everything.

"This way," Wuldrid shouted over the chaos, leading them into a far corner of the room where a lone practice dummy sat in the center of a large circle. It was humanoid in shape, sculpted from heavy plastic and set on a firm platform.

Wuldrid walked over to a wall filled with some type of bladed weapon and plucked one from the holder. It was only then that Chris noticed Kioko leaning against a wall near them, her arms crossed as she scrutinized the group. He waved openly with a warm smile. Kioko did not react.

Wuldrid glanced from Chris to Kioko and back again, before shaking his head and instructing the group to line up along the circle where they could still see him.

"This," he said as he held up the blade, "is a modified version of the Ancient Egyptian khopesh." Wuldrid walked along the line, giving each of them an up-close view of the sickle-shaped sword. "It was mostly used in Egypt, but it found its way across Middle East and central Africa. It largely fell out of use a few thousand years ago, but we have adapted the weapon to suit our combat needs. It is one of our preferred weapons at the Covenant and you will all need to learn to wield it properly. Kioko will demonstrate proper use of the weapon and explain why we chose this particular blade to replicate."

Kioko sauntered over, grabbing the khopesh and walking over to the dummy in the center of the ring.

"As stated," she said, tossing the blade from hand to hand without looking at it, "our weapon is merely stylized in the same vein of the original." She pulled her hand back and sliced at the dummies stomach, ripping it open and spilling stuffing onto the floor. Chris felt his stomach tighten at the sight.

"Our blade is sharpened along the interior and exterior curves. The curved area was originally designed to allow its user to get around a shield. We use it for clean, close-range slicing." She used the back end of the blade to slice the dummy's head from its shoulders in one of the cleanest cuts Chris had ever witnessed. To slide so smoothly through the fiber and stuffing, the force behind her attack must have been intense but somehow she made it look easy. "And the pointed tip makes it useful for stabbing as well," she said, thrusting the blade into what would have been the dummy's heart, leaving it there, and walking away.

"Thank you, Kioko." Wuldrid drawled, extracting the sword from the dummy with some difficulty.

"Khopeshes were also used as axes for cutting wood, and as a tool for the soldiers at camp," interjected a minor angel Chris had not spoken with before. "The blade could be held almost like a knife and used to cut a variety of vegetables and meats."

"Very correct. You are, Mr....?" asked Wuldrid.

"Rajesh," the minor angel said with a slight blush.

"Correct, Rajesh," Wuldrid said with an approving nod. "This blade served many purposes for its original creators. You are one of the ones drafted into the tech division, correct? But you're interested in swordsmanship?"

Rajesh looked surprised he was even being addressed. He was alternating his weight from foot to foot.

"Yes," he said. "I like to read historical fiction in my respite time, when I'm not cooking or cleaning."

"Good," Wuldrid said. "Well, I am sure the tech department wanted you to get some hands-on experience. I will report that we should get you involved with our weapons development team."

"That would be – I mean, yes! Thank you," Rajesh sputtered.

Chris smiled. This was great. Maybe some of the minor angels he was concerned for would be allowed to flourish in professions other than service or even fighting. Maybe they would not have to use a weapon on another person after all.

"Now," Wuldrid said, walking over to another box on the ground. "These are the practice swords you will be using for training. All angels start with them because they are specially modified."

Wuldrid pulled a handle of a khopesh from a box. It did not have a blade attached.

"Here is the switch." He pointed to a small button on the underside of the handle. "When pressed, the practice blade will activate." He pushed the button, and a glowing blade appeared from the handle, emitting a slight buzzing sound.

"These blades are projected like holographs, but they still have a corporeal form," he said seriously as he looked around the room. "That means you will feel it when struck, but it won't kill you or draw blood."

Chris heard Terri sigh next to him, and smiled to himself.

"Everyone, come and grab a training sword," Wuldrid said. "Get the feel for the blade in your hand."

Chris waited his turn before grabbing one of the handles.

It was lighter than he had imagined. The handle was wrapped in a worn brown leather and topped with a metal pommel. He could tell these swords had been in use for ages by the number of scratches etched into the leather.

Chris felt around the handle for the switch, locating the small button just below where the blade should be. He pressed it and the holographic blade popped out. Chris heard a very faint buzzing coming from the handle. He gave it a couple casual swings to get a feel for it.

He peered in closely to examine it. The blade was completely see-through. He enjoyed the off-white tint to the design, and gingerly ran his hand along the flat edge. This was not like the electronic sabers he had seen in movies.

"Playing with it?" Kioko asked as she grabbed a practice sword and walked up beside him. "You're with me today."

"Really?" Chris asked, following her over to one of the sparring circles. He felt the eyes of some of the other minor angels on his back, but focused his attention on her. "I thought you weren't speaking to me anymore."

"I never said that," Kioko said, turning on her practice khopesh.

"You've basically been avoiding me since Clair arrived."

"I haven't been avoiding you," Kioko said flatly. "I just haven't been seeking you out."

"You never sought me out before," Chris said, testing the blade in his hands and decided to start with his right hand. He was not sure how he was supposed to stand or best hold the blade. The most he had worked with knives was in the kitchen or out in the garden.

Kioko sighed heavily, her arm falling slack at her side and her eyes rolling back into her head. "Didn't that Sam character teach you two *anything?*" she asked angrily. She strode over to Chris, correcting his posture and hold on the handle. Her touches were efficient and smooth, and never inappropriate. She had never been inappropriate with him, even before Clair...

"No," he said, memorizing the stance. "Sam was always more focused on Clair. We both were. She was the one who needed to be prepared."

"You *all* needed to be prepared," she said severely. "From what I've seen, none of you even knows the basics of how to handle a sword." Kioko walked back to her position across from him. "Do you want me to come at you first, or do you want to come at me?"

Chris stared at her. It was not until that moment that he realized he really did not want to have to fight anyone. He knew he needed to learn to defend himself, Clair, and their friends. He wanted to be someone who could stand next to her, not behind her, but the thought of fighting to kill…

"You come at me," he said finally.

She nodded and they began.

SAM

xperiencing Clair work her magic within him was a religious experience. He could see the little angels floating around them, and his own body was giving off a glow.

Sam was so entranced by the beauty of it all that her initial scrape had deeply shocked him. It did not hurt, but it felt… off. He remained motionless as she paused and pursed her lips. He sensed the influences shifting around him and suddenly he began remembering.

Sam slumped into an empty chair.

They had been in this part of the city for too long. He did not know what Augustus hoped to accomplish here, or what he was looking for, but Sam felt it was time to move on.

He just needed to convince Augustus.

"Ale," Sam said, gesturing to the filthy barkeep.

"The ale here is shit."

Sam turned to the man sitting down next to him. He was averagely built, with hazel eyes and brown hair. He was staring at Sam.

"Well, that is all they have," Sam said, dropping a coin in the barkeep's grimy hand in exchange for an equally grimy cup of ale. He leaned his elbows against the table in front him and took a sip.

It was shit.

The man laughed.

"Told you," he said, angling his body toward Sam. "New here?"

"You could say that," Sam said, glancing at him out of the corner of his eye while scanning the rest of the tavern.

"We do not see many minor angels here," the man said a little too casually.

Sam chocked on the beer, a little foam spewing from his nose as he sputtered. The man thumped him on his back. "Good thing I know this is not the way you end," he said with a chuckle.

Sam turned toward him, setting his beer on the table. "How do you—who are you?"

"James," the man said as he held his hand out. The moment Sam touched him, he knew. He drew his hand back as if he had been burned. "You're…"

"Yes, I'm a Seraph." James said, taking a draw from the draught. "And you are a minor angel?"

"Yes," Sam said, in awe. "I never knew it was possible. I did not think you existed here. I have never met a seraph and I have been alive—"

"A long time already," James finished. "But you have much more of this life ahead of you."

"Much more…" Sam said as he fell back hard into his chair. "You know what my fate will be?"

James turned toward him, cocking his head. "Yes."

"Tell me."

"No," he laughed. "That I cannot do. But I know you will be important somehow. I can feel it. That you are important already. But this angel you are traveling with…"

"Augustus," Sam said, nodding his head.

"Yes," James said. "I know him. He is not good for you. He is not a part of your path. You need to move on. Get away from the Covenant. Look for purpose elsewhere."

"But why?" Sam asked, confused. "I have learned so much with them—I could learn more. They are the only angelic community I have ever encountered. The things we could do there—you should join us."

"No, I will not," James said firmly. "You need to get out while you can. Trust me. I can sense it. If you stay, you will meet your end, but it will not be your purpose."

"How is that possible? How could I meet an end that was not destined?"

"Destiny can be manipulated, cut short, deceived. Not all minor angels turn to dust after finding their purpose, Sam. Some are killed."

Sam was stunned. All this time, Augustus had led him to believe that he would be safe until he found his purpose. Until it was his time to die. He was held hostage by the anxiety of the unknown.

"Listen, Samuel," James sighed. "Your purpose is elsewhere. You need to leave. I have already said too much and been around you too long." He glanced around the room and a contemplative look flickered across his face. "I promise you will remember enough," he said as he touched Sam's forehead.

Everything went white.

Sam came back to himself slowly.

He remembered being at the tavern that night. He remembered knowing he was done with the Covenant, being sure Augustus was not part of his path. He remembered the hungry look in Augustus' eyes when Sam told him he was leaving. He remembered Augustus demanding to know who he had met and where they went. Sam insisted had not met anyone – he was sure of it. This certainly changed things.

"Your grandfather," Sam said, looking at Clair. "He pushed me away from the Covenant. He was the one who got me away from Augustus the first time."

"He was?" Clair asked in almost a whisper, leaning toward him.

Sam recounted the memory, realizing that Augustus must have sensed the seraph energy around him after his meeting James.

"James knew," Sam said. "Even then, that my life would be long. That I would be here with you. He knew."

Clair blinked, inhaling deeply. She was drained. The energy that constantly hummed through her had dulled to a low hum, as if her blood had gone slightly numb from the effort. "But he didn't know about me. He didn't even know about his own child. He left before my father was born – before Dotty even knew she was pregnant!"

"But he sensed it. He must have been prophetic, Clair. Many seraphs are," Sam said, dragging his hands through his hair. "What else would have drawn him to me? What have I done in my life that compares to this?"

Clair shook her head.

Sam had done amazing things in his long life. Beautiful things. Terrible things. He had wasted as much time as he had used.

This must be his destiny, just as he had assumed from the first day they met. They had always been destined to complete this journey together. Clair was supposed to be right here, right now, unlocking this memory for Sam. Unlocking the limitlessness of her own potential.

Sam was fulfilling his purpose.

He wondered how close he was to the end.

CHRIS

"Alright, angels. Front and center."

Chris thought Kioko was in rare form today as he ended his workout and ran over to join the others. There were five other elite angels with Kioko. He did not know their names, but he knew one as an earth affinity, two fires, and two water. Erik was also with them, laptop perched on his palm, glasses smudged on his face.

Chris knew Clair was with Sam. She typically called Dotty around this time. Chris hoped the lovely older woman was well. Thinking of home also reminded him of Emily. Chris had not seen Emily during his brief mission to Healdsburg, but Clair had filled him in that she was engaged. To Mike.

To Chris, it seemed like a really fast turnaround for Mike to transition from a burnout who had hurt Emily to an upstanding business man worthy of marrying her, but when he thought of Clair he understood. Love was fast sometimes. He and Clair had shared a whirlwind romance.

While he was thinking about Clair and weddings, he wondered, again, how much time they had. If he achieved his purpose he could disappear before they could build a life together. They had only been back together a short while after Clair's time in Eden and his in the Covenant. He wanted more time. He would always want more time.

"Fall in," Kioko shouted. "The Covenant has decided to allow promote all the minor angels standing before me to the rank of archangel. Congratulations." She paused to give the group time to absorb this information.

"As archangels, you are now eligible to assist on missions. Our next mission will be with the seraph. It will require a full team – tech, offense, defense, scouts. If I call your name, step forward."

The room held its breath. Not only had they been promoted, they were being considered for roles on a full-fledged mission. It felt like all of their grueling work had led to this moment. Not just for him, but for all of them. Chris assumed he would be going on the mission, if only because Clair would not leave without him. They could barely stand to be separated for long anymore, and he knew she would threaten whoever she had to in order to include him.

As for his peers, this was a huge step toward equality for the minor angels.

"Terri," Kioko called, and Chris turned to search for Terri in the crowd. She was near the back and her eyes had grown wide, but she made her way confidently toward the front.

"Richard." A minor angel Chris had only recently spoken to stepped forward. He looked like he was in his mid-sixties, with a long beard and thick biceps.

"Chris," Kioko said. He walked over to stand next to Terri, Kioko's eyes never leaving his. When he fell into formation, she turned back to the room.

"Flora, Gabrielle, and Hatashi, you will be on recon, scout, and meal duties for this mission, as well. Lower odds you'll encounter hand-to-hand combat, but you will need to be able to keep up." The three minor angels who stepped forward nodded enthusiastically. "Alright," Kioko continued, looking at the remaining archangels. "The rest of you will continue your training and be tested in other areas. As your skills sharpen, you will have the opportunity to be re-evaluated for missions on a quarterly basis. You are all dismissed. I have been both impressed and heartened by your effort."

Kioko waited for them to file out before turning to the select group beside her. "As for those of you chosen to join me, this mission promises to be an adventure, but not without assumed danger. We cannot guarantee your safety or that you will return from this mission. However, mission completion comes with benefits." Kioko continued to review some of the perks of performance, evaluations afterwards, and better living conditions. Many of the recently promoted archangels seemed thrilled. Others still looked apprehensive. "However, just because you tested into the mission does not mean you have to go." She took a beat to look each of them in the eyes. "You are allowed to forgo this mission. This will not eliminate you from consideration for future missions. There is no shame in knowing your limits. Any who wish to be exempt, speak now."

Kioko stared around at the group, but no one spoke up. "Good," she said, turning toward the middle order angels she had brought with her. "You will have until midnight tonight to back out, in private, if you wish. Simply come find me. Everyone, this is the rest of the team. Offense and defense – fire, water, air, and earth. We also have a tracker."

Erik waved his hand in the air. "I'm tech support," he said, chuckling.

Chris raised his eyebrows at Erik. He had never seen the man out of his office for more than an hour before. Erik noticed Chris staring. "Of course, I want to go and watch the seraph on a mission. I'm practically recording history. Like Bilbo Baggins, it is time to step out the front door and into the unknown. Plus," he said, typing away on the keyboard one handed. "It's been a while since I have gotten out, and I heard the first stop is Greece."

At the mention of the location, everyone, including Chris, perked up.

"Correct," Kioko said. "We will be beginning in Greece, staying with a local contact. From there, we will continue onto the next point."

"Where will we go after Greece?" Terri asked.

Kioko turned to look at her. "We don't know precisely, and I do not have clearance to reveal where we suspect we are heading."

"We don't know?" Terri asked with confusion.

"There is a clue in Greece," Kioko sighed. "We will need to find the next location based on that clue. Sometimes things are not always as straightforward as I would like them to be."

"You and me both," Terri grumbled, stuffing her hands in her pockets. Kioko smirked.

"Now, let's go over supplies and squad roles."

"Shouldn't we wait for the seraph?" Erik asked, looking around as if expecting Clair to materialize out of nowhere.

Kioko pinched the bridge of her nose. "No," she said. "The seraph will fall in with the rest of us, but her role is less…defined."

What did that even mean? Chris decided he would need to discuss it with Clair later.

"Now, let's move on. We are each going to need to bring three tactical outfits, tents, and supplies. Come with me and we will get you all outfitted with backpacks."

CLAIR

She was running.

Her breath came hard and fast through her nose. In and out. In and out. The hallway was dark and both sides blocked her from going in any direction but forward. The grey cement walls shrank around her, caging her in with every step she took.

But she had to find it. It was here, somewhere. Whatever it was, she knew she had to have it – it belonged to her, it was everything. She knew it. It had to be here. It had to be. It would change everything, this thing.

Clair turned a corner and found herself in a wide, round room, as grey as the walls in the hallway behind her and just as cold.

It was somewhere in the center of the room. She knew she had to find it. It called to her.

Clair ran toward it, but the floor beneath her feet began expanding as the walls shrunk inward, threatening to destroy her. The ground beneath her feet turned to fire and flame…

She woke up.

"What happened?" Chris was leaning over her in bed, his hair tousled from his abrupt wake up. The full moon bled through one of the high windows, bathing him in a muted light.

"Just a bad dream," she said, pulling him down toward her. He flipped her onto her side, pulling her into his warmth. "Just a bad dream."

"Do you want to talk about it?" he asked, the rumble of his voice ever-deeper from sleep. She could tell he was only half-awake, half-listening to her. Training had been hard for him today. The remaining minor angels had been promoted and a small handful were approved for mission work.

Of course, Chris had been one of the top performers, one of the ones instantly selected. She knew it was not because of her. The rank of archangel had been brought back for him because he was that impressive. He had achieved this all on his own. Chris had his own life and accomplishments, and she loved him for it.

"No," Clair said, slowly running her fingers along his. "Sleep."

Within moments his breathing turned soft, slow, and quiet. The rhythm of his chest moving lulled her back to her own slumber.

Just before she fell asleep, Clair wondered when she would stop wanting more than this.

Clair debated asking Chris not to go.

She almost tried convincing him. She almost suggested taking Sam instead, before she had her coffee and came to her senses. That bastard would rather stab himself in the eye than join a Covenant-sanctioned mission, and she would rather not spend the entire mission assaulted by his snark.

Plus, she knew deep down that he would say no. Just like she knew Chris would be deeply hurt if she asked him not to go.

It was not that she did not want him with her. She always wanted him with her. She was overjoyed to have him, especially after everything they had gone through. She refused to let him go. But Clair was also terrified that at any moment he would complete his purpose and leave.

Be reduced to dust. Just… disappear into nothing.

The scariest part of loving a minor angel was that he could simply cease existing at any time. Though she had not seen it happen, a minor angel had recently left the Covenant.

Chris had been stunned. He knew the angel and they had been training together in a big group.

Chris told Clair that the man had handed Terri a weapon from the rack, showed her how to properly hold it, and suggested she try a few practice swings. When she turned back around after a few successful strokes, he was gone.

They had looked everywhere for him, thinking maybe he had left the facility.

It was only after someone thought to search Erik's camera recordings that all they watched him disappear in somber silence.

So, Clair supposed, Chris also technically had not seen it happen yet. But he was affected and so was she. Just not in the same way.

Clair knew she would die if she lost Chris. She knew it with the same certainty that he had that his purpose was to protect her, to be with her.

She did not want to risk Chris's life, but Clair needed to know what she was up against. She needed to go on a mission with the Covenant and the only way she could know Chris was truly safe was if he was by her side. She knew his ultimate loyalty was to her, not the Covenant. They had to do this together.

She had spent a long time wondering whether this supernatural organization may be her destined nemesis. It did not appear so, at least not yet, but she was not ruling out the possibility. She needed to learn how they operated. Because if she had to, Clair knew the best way to destroy an organization was from the inside.

DOTTY

lasted coffee pot.

Dotty slammed her mug onto the counter, a satisfying *crack* of ceramic meeting her ears as the bottom broke.

That wretched caffeine machine was staring at her again. Day in and day out that damn machine sat on her counter and taunted her. Every morning it rested, existing, serving no purpose, not being used. In the evening, she would stare at the glowing light of its little clock until the numbers would begin to blur before her tired eyes.

She could not unplug it.

She would not unplug it.

The minute she unplugged it, she knew in her tired, wise, old bones that something bad would happen to Clair.

Dotty had been staring at that coffee maker when Clair materialized back into this world. When everyone thought Clair was lost forever, it was Dotty alone who still believed, who knew she would return. As certainly as Dotty had known when her husband had left this earth, Dotty knew Clair was alive.

The dreaded coffee pot had become part of an essential superstition that ruled her life. Dotty had no choice but to leave it plugged in and sucking up all her electricity. Never being used but mocking her. It knew, that damn machine knew it had a hold over her heart and mind, and there was nothing she could do about it.

She glared at it as she picked up the kettle from the stove. She growled at it as she filled the kettle with water. She watched the numbers on the minute side tick up as she set the kettle to boil. For *tea*. The correct caffeine source, always.

The kettle began to whistle, a beautifully natural sound. Not the incessant *beep beep beep* and *pffft pfft pffft* of the coffee machine spewing sludge into its pot. The kettle was refined, dignified even. But Clair loved her coffee, and Dotty loved Clair.

And, she realized, as she poured her hot water into her mug before adding a teabag, she needed to stop talking to herself.

A knock came from the front door. Dotty sighed.

"Dotty?" a familiar voice called from the front of the house.

"Coming, dear," she said, setting the teacup on the counter and walking toward the door. She opened it, revealing Emily standing before her, still clad in her apron from work. "Has something happened? Have you heard from Clair?"

"Oh," Emily said, looking at her and then back to her car as if she was debating leaving. "No, I'm sorry I didn't call first. I just wanted to talk to you."

Dotty stared at her. "You wanted to talk to me?"

"Yes," Emily said, reaching to put her hands in her pockets and realizing she was still wearing her apron. She hastily took it off and slinging it over her arm. "I haven't heard from Clair in a while, and was wondering if you had?"

"Ah," Dotty said, stepping to the side to allow Emily inside. "Yes, I have heard from Clair. Come sit, I just made a kettle of hot water. Would you care for a cup of tea?"

"Yes, please," Emily said. "That would be great."

Dotty walked through the living room into the kitchen with Emily on her heels. When they arrived, Dotty went to grab another mug — emblazoned with Clair's college mascot — while Emily sat at the little table in the center. "I have many options, do you know what you want?" She asked, looking at the girl.

"No, I don't. Anything without caffeine."

Dotty poured the water and picked out a nice herbal honey blend. "Sugar? Honey?"

"Honey would be great, thank you," Emily said.

Dotty grabbed the little pot of honey and a spoon and walked over to the table, setting both in front of Emily. They were silent as Emily made the tea to her liking.

"So," Emily said, "You heard from Clair?"

"Yes," Dotty said. "She called me about a week ago. They should finally be leaving on their mission in the next day or two. Apparently, there was some training involved, or some test, or something new that the blasted Covenant made up before they could leave."

Emily laughed. "Yes, she called me about that one. Something about the minor angels getting to test into the mission program or something. Why wouldn't they be allowed in the program from the start?"

"Big dick syndrome."

Emily choked on her tea and Dotty had to slap her back a few times before she recovered.

"Excuse me?"

"The Covenant is all about power, and that power determines your level in the organization, at least according to what Sam and James have told me over the years. Minor angels have no power or powers, so they are relegated to the bottom-most tier. Allegedly, before Chris showcased his fire skills to the Covenant in the wake of Clair's disappearance, no one knew that minor angels could wield elemental powers. I assume that sketchy Augustus character is doing everything he can to maintain his power over the Covenant. He must know that Clair wouldn't go on the mission without Chris. Augustus is old, even older than Sam. He's smart and conniving. In allowing the minor angels a 'fair shot' to join missions now, he not only wins Clair's favor, but it appears as though Chris's participation on the mission was not only sanctioned by him but also his idea. It makes him look fair and benevolent among the minor angels, who largely outnumber the more middling angels and have suddenly discovered they could have powers and deserve rights."

"Wow," Emily said and looked down into her mug. "I had not thought of it that way. Do you think Clair can see through what Augustus is doing?"

Dotty cracked her first smile since Clair had left for the Covenant. "I think Clair doesn't give a rat's ass about what Augustus does or thinks, as long as he doesn't get in her way."

Emily laughed. "Too true. That's our Clair."

"Yes," Dotty said, pausing to take a sip of her tea. "Our Clair."

They lapsed into comfortable silence for a moment, enjoying the easy companionship.

"And you," Dotty said, staring into Emily's eyes. "You are our Emily." She glanced at the ring on her finger. "What are you going to choose?"

Emily looked down at the ring as well. "Doesn't this mean I've already chosen?" There was no laughter in her voice, only a question.

"If it's what you want," Dotty said. "If not, it's just a piece of jewelry."

Emily sighed. "It's funny," she said, pulling the ring from her finger, resting her elbows on the table and twisting it between two fingers. "Clair and I sat right here the night Mike gave me this ring. She sat where you are now and basically said the exact same thing – that it was my life. My choice. My story."

"It *is* your story," Dotty said. "It *is* your life. Your life can be with someone else and that's *your* choice to make. It's your choice to decide what you want."

"Is it?" Emily said, setting the ring on the table. "Nothing in my life has been my choice. I didn't choose to be here. I didn't choose to leave college and sacrifice my dreams. I had to stay. I had to help my family. I had to make a living."

"What you are failing to see," Emily looked up at Dotty. "Is that it *was* your choice to help your family. You chose to put your dreams on hold. You chose to help your family, make a living, and survive. You chose to forgive an old friend. You chose to become involved with magic, and angels, and fate. You chose, and the sum of your decisions so far has been pretty remarkable."

Dotty saw tears form in Emily's eyes as her hand stilled, leaving her pinching the ring in the space between them.

"Does choosing this dream mean I need to let go of the other? Of the one filled with monsters and magic and angels and demons? Does choosing this man mean I pretend, for the rest of my life, that everything I experienced never happened? That I step away from this magic and lead a normal life? Chris, Clair, and Sam will come back, and when they do… I don't know if I am ready to let this go."

Dotty lifted her chin, staring at the girl before her. She knew what it was like finding out about magic and angels. She would never forget the day James revealed who he really was to her, and the pain – oh, so much pain, and loss along with it—but so much joy, and love, and adventure. That had been Dotty's own choice and now Emily needed to make a choice for herself.

"This world," Dotty began, "is as magical as it is deadly and not all deaths are final. You know about magic and angels, but you are not of the magic and angels. It's a hard walk filled with joy but also pain. I chose to know, I chose to stay. Your choice must be your own, but know this," Dotty said, leaning forward. "When you do choose – when you do finally decide, in your heart, what you want – it's forever. There is no going back."

Emily looked confused. "What do you mean?"

"I mean," Dotty said, "That if you choose to separate yourself from this magical life, I will make you forget it exists."

Emily stood up from the table so fast the chair crashed to the floor. "You can't!"

"I can and I will," Dotty said, leaning back and casually sipping her tea. "I have protected Clair through everything in her life. As much I like and respect you, Emily, I will not have a loose end walking around in the world who could possibly endanger her. Nothing has ever come before my family and nothing ever will."

Emily stared down at Dotty, fury, pain, defeat, and sorrow on her face. "So that's it. If I choose Mike, I lose everything else."

"Well, now," Dotty said with a smirk. "I didn't say that."

EMILY

She stood at the center of the field.

It was so plain. No flowers or shrubs and bereft of trees. Singularly open and blank. There was nothing here to mark that this place, out of all the places in the world, was special.

Or had been special. Just a field surrounded by hills.

Everything that had once made it special was gone. Everything.

Even the people.

Emily could not help but resonate with the field where the Gate had once stopped. It was like looking into her future. Empty. Boring. Something that was left behind while the magic moved on.

Emily sat, running her finger through the dead tan grasses, staring at the thin trees, feeling her heart reel at the loss.

There had been magic here. So much magic.

And magic was...

Magic was everything.

Fate.

It was an act of fate that had brought Clair back to town after she graduated college. Fate that Emily and Clair reconnected. Fate that Emily pushed until she learned the truth about angels, and magic, and evil. Fate that Clair returned after spending so long in-between worlds. Fate that Chris had also returned and led Clair to the Covenant.

It was fate that had stepped in and turned her ordinary life into something extraordinary.

She laughed, remembering how aggressively Sam had pushed her and Clair through workouts. All the running, all the meditating, all the stern remarks and snide comments. Yet underneath it all, his fierce protectiveness of not only the secret of Clair herself, but magic – an undeniable love of magic. A love Emily shared.

She remembered Chris, who was another type of magic all his own. Emily thought constantly about what type of person was given a second chance after choosing death. She wondered what kind of person Chris had been before he became a minor angel. She thought about Clair's constant fear for his safety, of her intense love for him. Chris, the constant pacifist among them all. He was always playing peacekeeper.

She sighed, remembering Clair fly for the first time. She felt the air that night as it pushed against the ground. Felt the power around her as it poured from Clair and into the earth.

Emily dug her fingers into the ground, feeling that same earth scratch between her nails.

It was magic. It was life itself, given form. It was extraordinary.

Though she did not have any magic herself and she was not an angel, Emily could not help but feel like she was supposed to be a part of it. Even now, after she had been left behind.

When Emily stood, she made the decision.

Emily got to the bar-turned-restaurant a little after noon.

It was quite possibly the worst time to be bugging Mike. He would be dealing with the barrage of tourists and the lunch regulars. The business had been so successful that Mike had hired a couple of staff members to help run the place. He preferred to stay behind the bar, while also managing the business of the Brown Bear.

Emily needed a plan.

She sat in her car, staring at the building and thinking. She needed Mike to be her ally in this. She needed him on her team. If he wasn't, she would need to decide between him and magic, and honestly, she was not sure which one would hurt more to give up.

She loved Mike and despite everything they had been through, they somehow fit together like they were meant to be together. She loved being around him and he uplifted her. He had even encouraged her to eventually go back to school, get her degree, and become who she wanted to be.

If Emily was being honest with herself, she had no idea who she wanted to be anymore.

When she came back to Healdsburg to take care of her parents, she had only one goal in mind: keep the family together in the family house.

But now?

Now she was involved in something so much bigger – and she did not want to let it go. Emily was smart, she knew she was smart. She would find a way to have magic and Mike.

Ha. Magic Mike. Emily actually wished she and Clair could have gone to see it together during the summer. It was really too bad her best friend was a seraph busy saving the world, though she supposed if Clair saved the world, maybe there would be a sequel they could see together.

Emily thumped her head on the steering wheel. She really did need to start sleeping more.

Maybe she should move in with him.

After he proposed, Mike asked her to move in and created space for her in the one-bedroom apartment attached to the bar. He had completely redone it after losing Joe. Mike had poured his inheritance into fully refurbishing the bar and the living space.

Now that Emily was planning to practice magic, she would need a space away from her devout Catholic parents. As right as it felt for Emily to bring Mike into the magical world, it felt just as right to keep her parents from it. They would never understand.

Emily knew in her heart that Mike would.

She exited her car and headed into the Brown Bear.

Mike was behind the bar, preparing drinks – mostly sodas at this time of day. There was a heavy lunch crowd, and Emily gave him a small wave when she entered.

He briefly looked confused to see her and stepped away from his work to come to her.

"Are you okay? What's going on?" he asked, flinging the towel he was carrying over his shoulder and eyeing the three couples waiting near the host station.

"Everything's fine," she said, glancing toward the bar. "I just wanted to talk, but it can wait. Mind if I sit at the bar until things die down?"

Mike searched her eyes for an explanation. He knew something was not fine. Emily feared he was coming to the wrong conclusion – that she was not fine about them being engaged or his offer to cohabitate.

"Mike," she said, leaning in and touching his arm. "I am fine. I do want to talk, but it's nothing bad. I promise. It can wait. This is your business – and I could use a beverage." She smiled at him, and he nodded, before walking her over to the bar.

"What're you in the mood for?" he asked, pulling up a glass from underneath.

"How about a lemon iced tea, please?" Emily asked, getting comfortable on the barstool and pulling out her phone. "I am just going to read a bit until it's less busy."

Mike made the drink and passed it to her before nodding once more and going back to tending to the customers.

Emily, instead of reading, opened the notes app on her phone and began listing out talking points.

In what felt like no time at all, the lunch crowd was dissipating and Mike was instructing one of the staff to take over management for a bit. He walked over to her.

"Should we talk in my office? Or is this a back of the building conversation?"

Emily snorted. "Well, it might be more back of the building, but I think your office is the better place."

"Alright," he nodded, holding out his hand. Emily placed her smaller hand in his.

They walked through the double doors and past the kitchen into a small office with a door located off the main hallway. Mike shut the door behind them and instead of sitting behind his desk, sat on the little couch to the right of it. Emily sat down next to him and turned to face him.

She took a deep breath, but before she could begin Mike cut her off.

"If this," he said, holding up his hand and pausing. He looked skyward for a minute, and then back to her. "If this is about us, and about you not wanting to be with me, if it was too sudden – I understand. I will understand. I'll be crushed, obviously, because I love you. You're better than I will ever deserve. But I will understand why you aren't choosing me."

Emily stared at him.

"I made a lot of mistakes," he said, running his hand through his hair. "A lot of mistakes. And I can't take them all back. Any of them back. I think back on that time in my life and I don't recognize the man I was, and that's no excuse, but it's the truth. You were always too good for me, you will always be too good for me. If it's a matter of time, you can have it. Just let me know. If you aren't opposed to me, you're just feeling rushed, we can take our time. You don't have to move in, we can date again. We can get to know each other more. We can wait to get engaged and get married. But you need to know, you're the endgame for me, Emily. You're the one. There's no one else for me."

Emily felt tears growing behind her eyes. He was staring at her, breathing hard, waiting for her to reply.

She said the only thing that made any sense.

"Dotty is a witch."

She watched his eyebrows scrunch together. "What?"

"Dotty is a witch," Emily continued, notes app with fully laid out plan to execute be damned. There was no way that this conversation was going to go well no matter what planning she did, so she just started talking.

"Dotty is a witch and Clair is an angel. Chris, the one we all said was Clair's cousin, is actually an angel. A minor angel, to be exact. And Sam, who is around with them all the time is an angel, another minor angel, who has been alive for centuries. Dotty is a witch who married an angel and had Clair's dad, who had Clair."

She could tell Mike was listening. She could see the gears turning behind his eyes, the way he was now fully checking her eyes to see if they were dilated. She let him look at her, scrutinize her. She needed him to know she was not on drugs. That she was not making a joke.

"I know it all seems crazy. It seemed crazy to me too, but I've seen it. I've seen magic. It's…" Emily trailed off, lost in thoughts. Sam moving the earth, Clair flying, Chris creating a fireball. Dotty and the books. "It's amazing, Mike."

"Okay," he said, taking a deep breath. "So…" Mike blinked. And blinked again. "You're telling me that magic exists?"

"Yes. I believe in magic. I've seen it." Emily ran her hands through her hair. "But we aren't supposed to know."

"We aren't?"

"Well, yes, Sam made that very clear. If the Covenant ever finds out we know we could be in trouble."

"The Covenant?"

"The governing body of angels on earth. Apparently, there are a ton of different types all over the world all run by one secret organization. That's where Clair, Sam, and Chris are right now. It's somewhere in remote Russia, but humans aren't supposed to know about angels and magic existing."

Mike stared at her, then stood up, then sat back down, all while running his hands over his face. He looked back at her, into her eyes.

"Okay," he finally said.

"Okay?" she asked, her heart pounding. Did this mean he was ok with magic? That he understood? That he believed her? Or was that "okay" just some metaphor for him thinking she was crazy, and he wished he had a panic button in his office?

"Yes?" Mike said, sighing. "Well, yes, I mean…" He rubs his fingers in circles on his temples. "It's weird, okay, but also, everything's weird."

Emily coughed a laugh. "What?"

Mike sighed, shaking his head. "The whole world is weird. Life is weird. There are things we cannot explain. There are things we try to but don't come close. I guess I always assumed some type of magic existed. I mean…" He stood and started pacing. "I believe you. I trust you. If you say this is true, and you'd have no reason to lie to me.

There are easier ways to make me look like a fool if you wanted to get revenge on me for being such a shitty boyfriend when I was high."

Emily laughed. "True, I could definitely think of at least eight easier ways to get revenge that don't involve convincing you I am crazy, getting you to believe in magic, and then humiliating you."

"Exactly," Mike said, chuckling and pacing. Emily wondered if it was a distinctly male thing to need to process new information while moving. He sighed, stopping and sitting next to her again, but this time closer. He grabbed her hands.

"I think I am so okay with this because everyone needs something to believe in," he said, rubbing small circles into her knuckles. "I turned to religion because they offered the AA program to help get me out of my addiction. Everyone needs something to connect them, to make them feel like they are a part of something. For me, I need that group to help me stay on the wagon. But as for connection," he said, gazing into her eyes, "you are the only person in this world who makes me feel right. I would go anywhere, do anything, be anything you need in order to be with you and be part of your story, Emily. If you say magic and angels are real, then I believe you."

Emily let the tears fall. "I love you."

Mike smiled. Emily removed her hand from his and pulled out the ring from her pocket. "I want to marry you, I want to move in with you, I want to practice magic with you. I want both of us to be a part of this new adventure I stumbled into. That's why I came to you today. Dotty made it clear that I need to be all in or I need to get out. I can't be all in without you."

Mike gently grabbing the ring, turning it to catch the light. "This is the most connected I've felt in months," he said, looking into her eyes.

"Same," she said, before leaning in and capturing his lips with hers. It was more than a kiss; it was a promise. They were in this together. They would explore this new world of magic together.

He placed the ring on her finger.

KIOKO

he flight to Athens was short.

The dinner with the dignitary Augustus had arranged was painfully long.

Bellen Georgiou was a plump, middle-aged, balding man whose love of food could only be rivaled by his love of hearing himself talk.

Prone to prose like many Greeks, Bellen had spent half the dinner regaling all of them with his stories about expensive vacations, designer yachts, and his insatiable taste for everything edible under the sun – as long as it cost more than the average human made on a living wage in a year.

Kioko, the unfortunate angel seated beside him all night, spent the bulk of her evening pretending that his sly touches under the table did not make her want to throw up the delicious lamb she had just eaten into her expensive champagne.

When the dinner finally ended, her team had excused themselves to their private seaside villa for the evening. Bellen had hinted that Kioko was to join him for the evening, but Kioko had simpered that she was much too full from all the delicious food to stay awake another minute.

Lies. All lies.

She was full, of course. It was a great dinner. However, Kioko had other plans.

As soon as it grew truly dark, she donned her evening jacket and slipped across town, back to Bellen's estate. He had a small, secret art collection that she needed to peruse without him watching. It was, of course, the only reason why they had paid him a visit. Kioko had gotten a quick lay of the land, Erik had downloaded the security keys remotely during dinner, and Clair and Chris had played the angel visitor part perfectly – they just did not know they were playing a part while everyone else was working.

She made it into the painting room easily enough, but found Bellen already there, drunk off his ass and wanking to a portrait of a nude woman. Kioko had easily knocked him out. He was currently on the floor somewhere behind her.

Kioko scoffed to herself and looked back up at the wall of paintings. Somewhere in this room was the key they needed to find the next location.

"Why is it always a fucking painting?"

Kioko whirled around. Clair strode up to her, dressed in the red lace gown from earlier, her heels replaced with a pair of shabby flats.

"What are you doing here?" Kioko hissed, moving away from the wall of paintings to block Clair from coming any closer. She had snuck into this specific part of the mansion on her own, slyly, she might add. How did Clair even get here?

"I was wondering where you were headed off to," Clair said as she looked down at the body of the dignitary. "Good job with that one. I heard what he was saying to you at dinner. Men like that don't deserve to live."

"I didn't kill him," Kioko said, glaring down at the grotesque man. "He's only knocked out."

"Oh," she said, cocking her head while her eyes reviewed the body. "Maybe you should."

Kioko could not believe this was happening. This was not how things worked in her world. She completed jobs alone. Especially this part of the job – the part that required intensive training. Clair was not fit for this. "Clair, you need to leave. Go back to your room. Go anywhere. You shouldn't be here."

"Neither should you, yet…" Clair glanced at one of the paintings in the far, right hand corner. "It's always a painting. Why is it always a fucking painting? I mean it. It's ridiculous how many times angels use art to 'hide' their secrets. It's so painfully obvious."

"What in the world are you talking about?" Kioko whisper-screamed. She could feel a headache beginning at the base of her skull.

"I'm talking about the orb," Clair said, gesturing to the painting she was staring at.

"Where do you see the orb?" Kioko looked back at the paintings. Pausing on the small one Clair was staring at. It did not look like much – jungle and vines wrapped together in an abstract way and it was small, maybe only six inches wide. It was not even behind glass like some of the others. She could not see any clues in the painting, and she did not see an orb. It was all greenery and browns. There was nothing in the painting that even resembled an orb. "I don't see it."

"No, you don't," Clair said, walking over to the painting. She reached up and touched the space between the vines and the spot began to glow. "That's the thing, it wasn't meant for you to be able to see. It was left for me, or someone like me, because I can see it without touching it. What does that mean, I wonder?"

The glow continued to spread from where Clair touched the painting, covering the entire canvas before settling into a dome shape between the painted trees and vines.

Kioko was transfixed. "Who would leave a clue for only a seraph?" It was all starting to make sense now. Augustus was not a stupid man. He had sent Clair on this mission because he knew she was the only one who could find what he was looking for. It appeased Kioko, somewhat, to know that Clair was not on this mission as some type of support system or even a charity case. She was here because he needed her to be here. She wanted to make sure Clair knew.

"That's why he sent you," she said, turning back to Clair. "Because you are the only one who could find this clue. You're the only one who can help us figure out where the orb is hidden."

Clair removed her hand and the glow disappeared like it had never existed. "Excuse you?"

"That's why Augustus let you come on this mission. He needed you to unveil this part of the puzzle for us, something only a seraph could do, which is why this mission even exists in the first place. He couldn't find it without you."

Clair's eyes narrowed. "You think the only reason I was sent out on a mission with you was to help you find a clue? And then, what? Go eat bonbons on the beach with Chris?"

Kioko just stared at her.

"You do! You think I am going to let you continue on and leave me here? Are you crazy? Do you even know what I am?"

"Of course I know what you are, we all know what you are," Kioko spat. "Mighty seraph, leader of all angelic kind, keeper of the power of heaven and might of evil." Kioko could feel she was pushing her luck with Clair and her temper but she did not care anymore. She was sick of everyone pandering to this girl. "You are an untrained, uneducated child who happens to have power and nothing more. It brings me great joy to realize that while Augustus has never been clear with any of his mission choices, *this* choice," she gestured at Clair, "at least makes sense because you have a *use*."

The room held its breath as Clair stared at Kioko. She knew she stepped over some invisible line when she felt the hair on her arms rise and her heartbeat pick up speed. Clair was leaking furious power into the air and all that rage was directed at her.

When Clair spoke, the ground trembled, and Kioko was struck dumb.

"It's about damn time I saw the real you."

As quickly as the energy had formed, it disappeared, and Clair relaxed back into her regular slouch while Kioko tried to slow her heartbeat.

"We don't have to like each other to do this job, Kioko. Hell, we don't even have to get along for all I care. I am here to complete a mission that apparently, I am a key part of, whether you or anyone else likes it or not. And I have been trained by one of the best angels I have ever met. Lucky for you, he taught me how to take a verbal punch better than anyone I know." Clair cocked a smile, placing her hand on her hip. "So, while it would be easy to start fighting with you right now over who has a bigger dick, I would rather get on with this clue collection so I can go back to my room and screw my boyfriend again."

It was so silent she could hear the bugs outside.

Finally, Kioko spoke.

"You know," she said. "I think maybe in another life I would have liked you."

Clair stared at her.

"I think maybe in another life you could have been me."

CLAIR

The clue in the painting had pointed them to a location in the jungles of the Misiones Province of Argentina. Erik had informed Clair that the small province was in the northeast of Argentina, flanked by both Paraguay to the west and Brazil to the north and east. The region was home to the Argentine side of the Iguazú Falls, the world's largest waterfall system, which stood nearly twice as tall as Niagara Falls. The next morning, the team would fly directly from Athens to Puerto Iguazú via one of the Covenant's private jets. Erik said it appeared they were headed away from the falls, but if they were lucky they might catch a glimpse just before landing. From there, they would charter an even smaller plane to drop them in the general area of the clue, and would continue on foot until they reached their destination.

Clair would think about all the ramifications of what Kioko said about her, Augustus, his plans, this mission, and her ineptitude tomorrow. It was all going to have to wait. As Clair quietly walked back into their dark bungalow, she saw Chris sprawled across their bed and all she could think about was him.

His mouth had fallen slightly open in sleep and his breathing was slow and shallow. He always appeared deeply relaxed to her when he was sleeping – like the whole world faded away and he could just exist. The moonlight coming through the open patio doors played against his smooth skin, slightly rustling the sheet that dangled low on his waist displaying his toned back.

No, right now Clair did not care about anything other than him.

She padded over, gently lowering herself onto the bed next to his side. He shifted toward her, even in sleep. She watched her hand as she slowly ran it down his back, softly tracing the muscles along his shoulders before flowing down his spine toward his hips before stopping and slowly making her way back up to his neck.

"You left," he said, his eyes heavy-lidded. She felt him wake as she touched him. No matter how light she was, there was a spark between them that could not be ignored when they touched. The bracelet on her wrist was growing warmer. The forever reminder of their losses and successes.

"I did."

Chris turned over, the sheet falling even more dangerously low on his toned hips, revealing the beautiful V-shaped muscles he had worked so hard to cultivate. He laughed. "If I wasn't so distracted watching you watch me, I would be mad with you for not telling me you were going."

She smiled, looking deeply into his eyes. He pulled his arms to rest behind his head as all men seemed to do when they are feeling smug and lying in bed naked. "You know what you look like," she said, gently slapping his six pack. "Sometimes I lose my train of thought. I didn't tell you because I knew you would want to come."

"Of course —"

"But I couldn't have you coming, because the person I was stalking was Kioko."

His eyebrows hit his hair. "Really? Why?"

"She went out on her own. I knew she would. I listened as she pulled information from that handsy Bellen this evening at dinner. We weren't just here to schmooze Augustus's benefactors. She was looking for something."

"That makes sense," Chris said, "at the Covenant, before I really knew her, there were rumors that it was part of her job. To get information from people, any way she could."

Clair nodded, looking off. "I assumed as much. She's beautiful and deadly, the perfect combination for a spy. And added bonus – she's an angel with powers no human would suspect. I bet she was great at her missions – is great."

"That doesn't bother you?" Chris asked.

"That she screwed men for information?" Chris nodded. "No. Women have screwed men for less. I don't like the idea that she was essentially being forced to do it for Augustus. But that gives me a better grasp on who *he* is, not her."

Chris smiled.

"What?" Clair asked.

"I think you two would like each other if you weren't always so angry at how the other operates."

She grabbed the pillow from behind his head and gently whacked him with it. "Of course I know that, you jerk, but I don't need to be reminded. She infuriates me. She had the audacity to insinuate that we would stay here while the rest of them continued on."

"What?"

Clair filled Chris in on everything that had happened, from stalking Kioko to finding the location of the orb.

"I feel like we get more and more questions and fewer answers. Who would leave that type of clue? And why? What is this orb anyway and why would Augustus want it?" Chris asked.

"I agree. Every answer always leads to more questions."

They both were silent for a moment, lost in their own thoughts.

"Although," Chris said, smirking at her. "I wouldn't mind just staying here with you for the rest of the trip. And by here, I mean *right here,* in this bed, preferably with you having fewer clothes on."

Clair laughed. She stood and unzipped her dress, loving how Chris followed her every move with his eyes. He looked at her like he would never be able to look at her enough, like his eyes would never get their fill of her body.

When she was completely naked, she rejoined him in bed.

She slowly swept her hand across his brow, down the side of his face, her thumb trailing against his lips.

"You looked beautiful tonight," he murmured, bringing his hand up to cup the back of her head, drawing her to him.

Chris kissed her tenderly at first, gently nipping at her lips before chasing her tongue with his own. He began kissing her as if he could not stop, as if enough would never be enough. As if the world was being reborn and recreated with their passion.

The fire within her soul stirred with every shared breath.

He kissed like a dying man whose only hope was her love.

She kissed him like he was the air in her lungs and the fire in her heart.

No more words were needed.

CLAIR

hey departed at six o'clock the next morning.

Clair would have been happy to stay in their little bubble forever, but Kioko was desperate to start moving.

Flying direct via one of the Covenant's Gulfstream 550s, it only took Clair's team about eleven hours to touch down at Cataratas del Iguazú International Airport, landing around noon local time. From there, a smaller cargo plane dropped them near the point on the map where the orb had indicated.

They had gotten some sleep on the flight, but with all the travel and time changes of the past couple days, Clair could barely keep her attitude in check. Luckily, Chris was still his bright and cheery self. Unluckily, Kioko was also her typical self.

Kioko had informed the team early on that they needed to travel on foot toward their destination since the local population had deemed the space sacred and therefore off limits to outsiders. Erik had thrown a fit about disturbing native land until Kioko pointed out that they were traveling with possibly the most sacred being currently on earth and they had elected to walk to minimize disturbances to the natural landscape. Unless they ran into a demon and had to fight for their lives, their impact would be minimal. The Covenant had deemed this mission net positive, so they would continue forward with the plan. Terri asked if Kioko thought it would be likely that they would run into demons, to which Kioko had only shrugged.

Kioko stood before the group with her hands on her hips and a steely expression on her face. They were congregating at the tree-line of a massive stretch of forest, already sweaty in the humidity and heat of the afternoon.

"Alright, listen up," Kioko barked. "We're headed into the forest. Squad positions. No one breaks rank. If you get into a shit situation, we all fall in around the seraph. If we get outnumbered, we fall back. Understood?"

They all nodded in consensus.

Clair thought this was all a bit much. It was a subtropical rainforest. Sure, a variety of big cats lived there, but this was Argentina, not the underworld.

Chris bumped her arm with his. "Our first mission. This should be fun."

"I'll just stick with you. You can keep me safe," she replied with a wink.

"You two, stop making eyes at each other and fall in," Kioko said sternly before turning toward the forest. "Eyes open." Kioko lit Augustus's beacon, the trail of light that would lead them where they needed to be.

Clair took a deep breath and brought her hands up into position, ready to produce fireballs whenever she needed. It had been her go-to offensive move ever since Chris had taught her the skill, what now felt like many years ago. She loved the way they felt in her hands. They helped her feel powerful and connected to her instincts, like she could do anything, defeat anyone.

They stepped through the trees and were immediately surrounded by sound, as if emerging from a great depth of water. Birds of all types sang, small animals ruffled the leaves upon the ground, and Clair could hear bug wings buzz and beetles chirp. The light played through the trees like fingers across a piano, smooth and fluid, as if it was dancing upon the ground.

Clair lowered her hands, observing her team members defensively point their guns in every direction, their heads swiveling from side to side as they scouted for danger while following the path illuminated by Augustus's beacon. Clair thought it was strange he had not chosen to travel with them. Men like him preferred to keep their own hands clean.

"This place is so beautiful," Erik said to Terri. "I am definitely taking notes on how to better program the artificial reality back at the Covenant. The way the light streaks through these trees is stunning."

"I've always loved watching the little angels," Terri said as she turned slightly toward Clair. "I like that you call them that. Hope you don't mind that I stole it."

"Not at all," Clair said, looking at the dancing specks in the shafts of light. "However…"

Terri and Erik turned to look fully at Clair.

"It's just," Clair began, and Chris sighed. He knew what was coming. "I don't really know if they're angels."

"Well, of course they're not angels," Erik said, laughing. "We're the angels."

"Are we?" Clair asked, deliberately looking up at the trees.

"What do you mean?" Terri asked, remembering to scan her surroundings.

"I mean, I don't know that we are really angels, at least not in the way that angels have been portrayed throughout history."

"What do you mean we aren't angels?" Erik said, forgetting to scan, and turning to look at Clair as they walked. "A massive amount of global theology has pointed to our existence and named us angels."

"I took theology classes in college so I understand the *concepts*," Clair stated, tilting her head toward Erik. "Understanding and believing are two different things."

"True," Terri said.

Erik stopped to face her. "You don't believe? You're an angel. You can literally *see* yet you don't believe?"

Clair stopped and surveyed the jungle ahead of them before turning to Erik who was still staring incredulously at her. "I believe we're here. I believe we're supposed to be here for a reason, but I'm not sure we're living up to that purpose. Nor do I think there's only one correct version of God. So, yes, we're 'angels.' We have powers, but it's just a title. A concept. A placeholder we use to classify ourselves. Nothing more."

She smiled wryly at her own reference to the Covenant's ridiculously flawed ranking system. Erik turned away from Clair, resuming his inspection of the forest and they began walking again.

Clair could almost imagine what it must be like to be someone like Erik. Someone who was not born, who simply began existing. She could imagine the absolute certainty of his existence – his belief in exactly who and what he was. She could almost see herself in his shoes, with nothing and no one behind her, and nothing more in front of her than the next breath, the next order. But Clair would never be ordered. She would always be a leader, always be the one ordering people to their lives or to their deaths.

She almost envied him in that moment. His easy life.

Then she thought of Chris. She needed him. To keep him, she needed her power.

She let go of the fantasy of being someone else.

"I do love them," Clair said, looking back at the little angels scattered within the light. "They are the angels' purest form. Unlike us, they don't think before doing, they just act. It often baffles me that the Ultimate Good gave us feelings."

Erik glanced at Clair, an unreadable expression in his eyes, before he turned back toward the rest of the group.

Chris walked closer to Clair, brushing his mouth against her ear. "But where would *we* be without our feelings, Clair?" He chuckled before focusing back on getting through the jungle.

She smiled.

They walked for hours.

They spotted a tapir once, its snout snuffling along the ground in its quest for food. Clair loved when the birds would swoop from the trees, their bright wings a flash of color among the deep greens of the trees.

Finally, the beacon brought them to a cave.

Clair sighed. So typical. Of course it was in a cave. She felt herself grow wracked with annoyance.

"Lights on," Kioko stated, tapping the switch of small light on her gun three times until it was blazing. "Stick together."

While the jungle was pure sound, the moment they stepped into the cave, they were greeted by deafening silence.

It was instantaneous, as if a barrier had been placed between the entrance and the rest of the world. No bugs or traces of dirt were in the cave, only rough rock walls and a slick marble floor.

"Who made this?" Clair whispered to Chris.

"I don't know," he said, shining his light at the walls. There were some drawings at random intervals, symbols or runes, Clair could not tell. "This isn't natural. Whatever made this place protected it." He moved closer to Clair, and she loved him a little more for it.

Clair alternated flashing her light at the walls to see the runes and to her feet, minding where cracks appeared in the polished surface. They had been walking for about thirty minutes when they began to see a dim glow ahead of them.

They followed the light to an opening which revealed a full-fledged dessert before them.

"This shouldn't be here. This doesn't exist," Erik said, frantically checking his phone and typing furiously.

No one dared to take another step as they took in the unexpected scene. The desert was dark and cold. When they had entered the cave, it had been late afternoon, but the dessert stood in a cloudless, starless night. Dunes spread across their field of vision to the horizon. Only the moon could be seen in the sky, but it was too large. Impossibly close. Clair had an ill-advised urge to try to fly up and touch it.

Kioko twisted her head to glance back at her team while maintaining her defensive stance. "Alright, team. We need to keep following the beacon. This is just another test. There are no baddies yet, so we keep pushing forward. Look for clues."

They shuffled forward as a unit, touching down on the sands. As soon as they had all stepped onto the sand, the world shook. They tumbled down a dune, tossed like ants in a kindergartener's maliciously shaken ant farm. When the shaking finally subsided, the cave had vanished.

"Squad one, up that dune. Squad two, you go to the other one. Find the cave," Kioko ordered.

They nodded and ascended the sandy peaks. When they reached the top, the squad leaders turned to each other, and shined their lights on their hands, signaling without talking. They nodded and each squad returned to the base of the dunes.

She turned to face the entire team. "We need to stay together and continue moving forward. We do not know what is ahead of us, but we can be sure magic is involved, and there is nowhere safe to take cover here."

The group surged forward, following Kioko's commands, and trekking through the dessert but seemingly making no progress for an indefinite period of time.

"Fuck," Kioko swore, pulling up the beacon. It was now pointing directly up at the sky. She rotated it back and forth, but no matter which way she turned it, it pointed up. She ran her hand through her hair and stared up at the moon.

"The beacon really seems like it's broken," Erik said after a while.

"Just take it, then," Kioko said, tossed it to him in frustration and instructed everyone to remain in formation. Her shoulders dropped and she returned to staring at the moon.

Most of the team stood at attention, waiting on further commands, as Erik fiddled with the beacon. Clair noticed Chris examining the dunes as if he could read the grains of sand.

She was surprised to find she was not upset at all. Normally she would be anxious in a situation like this, fretting that they were trapped in a never-ending desert at night with no way out. She peeked at Chris and took two steps away from him. She felt a slight trickle of anxiety hit her heart. She moved back toward him and felt an invisible wind move like a breath along the sand.

"In a real desert, it's blisteringly hot during the day and so cold at night that it almost makes you miss the heat of the sun." Kioko suddenly said. "Remember that one mission in Africa?" she asked, nodding to an angel whose name Clair could not remember.

"Hot and cold," Terri said, her eyes bouncing around expecting trouble. "'Be you hot or cold, not lukewarm.' Isn't that in a Bible passage somewhere?"

"Yes," Erik said, his brow pinched in concentration as he continued to twist the beacon in his hands. "It's from the book of Revelations."

"How is there sand here?" Clair asked of no one in particular. The hills they flown over had been forested and damp. How had they entered this vast valley of sand?

"It's magic, Clair," came Kioko's snide reply. "It doesn't have to make sense." She kept her eyes trained on the moon.

"For all we know," Chris interjected, "We could be going in circles, the land shifting and changing around us."

"Fuck." It was Clair's turn to swear. She did not like that thought. If they were in the same place they started, they could go around and around forever. Clair wondered if the Old Testament Hebrews wandered in the dessert for so many years because they, too, were just going in circles.

She moved back over to Chris's side and touched the gold chain draped around her wrist.

"What's wrong?" Chris asked, turning to her.

"Nothing," she said, looking back at the moon. "Except the never-ending dessert sand trap, of course."

She smirked and he scoffed. "Some first mission this has turned out to be."

Suddenly Kioko said, "The moon is moving. This could give us a way to tell time – it might even give us some sort of direction to follow. Erik, can you calculate it for me?"

"Right," Erik said, handing the beacon back to Kioko and pulling out his phone again. Clair laughed and everyone turned to stare at her.

"Sorry," she said. "In school they always forced us to memorize all these math formulas because they we wouldn't have a calculator when we needed one, and now we're literally stuck in a magical desert, but the phone calculator app works."

Terri laughed, Chris looked bemused, and Kioko narrowed her eyes before turning back to Erik.

"Well, I thought it was funny," Clair grumbled.

Clair sighed, closing her eyes and taking a deep breath. She needed a minute. She missed Dotty. Missed being home with Emily. She had talked to her right before leaving for the mission, but that was not enough. Like Chris, Emily grounded Clair. She helped her feel normal.

As she ruminated, Clair noticed the light behind her eyes growing brighter, but when she opened them, she was not staring at the moon, just dark sky. Clair turned back toward the moon. It had moved a little further down, but by the way Erik and Kioko were bickering it did not seem to hold the answers to their problems.

Clair looked into the glow of the moon and closed her eyes. She waited for the light, but it never came.

Trusting her instinct, she twisted back around and closed her eyes. The light slowly materialized. When she opened her eyes, she was facing away from the moon toward one of the dunes.

"Chris," she said, getting his attention. "Try something for me."

"Anything," he said.

"Close your eyes and stare at the moon,"

He did what she said. After a few moments she asked him to open his eyes.

"Did you see any light?"

"No," he said, cocking his head. "Weird."

"Totally," she said turning him toward her dune. "Now close your eyes."

He did as she asked, and she knew the instant he saw the light by the look on his face.

"Kioko!" he shouted, making many of the other angels jump. "Come here, I think we found something."

She walked over, examining the ground at their feet. "What?"

"Close your eyes," Chris instructed.

"What?" she asked, narrowing her eyes at them both.

"Just trust me," Chris said. "Clair's discovered something."

Clair gave Kioko a little credit in that moment. She did not argue and followed his directions to face toward the moon and then away.

"The moon," Kioko said. "It's a decoy."

"Faith," Chris said, his grey eyes shining in the darkness. "'Walk by faith, not by sight.'"

"What now?" Kioko asked, throwing her arms up in frustration.

"Sometimes this biblical stuff feels a bit sinister," Erik said.

"We need to travel blind," Clair whispered.

"What?" Terri asked, stepping out of line to face them. Everyone was staring at Clair.

"We need to walk by faith, like Chris said. I know it sounds ridiculous, but it's worth a try."

"And how will we know if we find the exit," Kioko said, "with our eyes closed?"

Clair thought a moment. They could pass the exit, or be attacked with their defenses down, but something told her that would not happen.

"We'll just know," she said to Kioko. Before she could reply, Clair continued, "It's like that scene in the Indiana Jones movie where they go to find the arc of the Covenant."

"That's actually one of the artifacts stored at the Covenant," said one of the angels.

Clair only raised her eyebrow before continuing. Nothing really surprised her anymore.

"Indiana had to walk out into the air to realize there was an invisible bridge there. It's at least worth a try." She looked around at all of the angels surrounding her.

"Alright," Chris said as he grabbed her hand and nodded to Kioko to do the same.

She shoved the beacon into her pocket as a signal to the team that she was fully on board. Slowly and at times reluctantly, everyone reached out to hold hands, forming a connected line of angels.

"Alright," Kioko instructed, "on the count of three, everyone close your eyes. If anyone feels anything that seems—"

"Magical?" Erik mocked.

Kioko narrowed her eyes. "Anything that seems off, let me know. You need to pay attention with your other senses." Erik was still unconvinced, but he nodded. Clair was relieved, because even as the seraph, she was not sure how much obedience she could command from this platoon.

"Alright," Kioko said, turning to look at the dessert one last time. "One. Two. Three."

Clair shut her eyes but it was not dark.

Glowing beneath her lids was a bright light floating at the periphery of her vision, just to her right. It reminded her of the shadows and flickers of light she would catch in the corner of her eye, most often at night.

"Are you seeing this?" Clair asked.

"Yes," replied Kioko, her voice clearly awed. "It's on the right."

Clair was glad to hear they were all being led the same direction. Kioko guided the group up a dune and as they summited, the light grew noticeably brighter.

Kioko sighed. "I think we're heading the right way."

Clair positioned the dancing bulb in front of her and walked across the darkness, clenching Chris's hand along the way. The group continued through the darkness, hand-in-hand for an hour, following the bulb as it floated left, right, down, and left again. The terrain had clearly changed from sand to something soft but firm. She could not be sure, but Clair suspected it was dirt. Just when Clair thought they were being misled, the light vanished. She heard someone in the group gasp and knew everyone had seen the light disappear.

Clair opened her eyes.

They were standing in a thick forest at the base of a hill. The trees surrounding them were larger than any Clair had ever seen, larger even than the giant redwoods of Yosemite. The landscape reminded Clair of her own hills, the ones that had looked down onto the Gate of Eden. Unlike the low hills of Healdsburg, the imposing mountains before them towered above even the trees and those in the center bore the distinct shape of three silhouetted men, all with their eyes faced up toward the heavens.

A valley of many faces.

"It has to be the middle one." Kioko was squinting through the night, the full moon casting eerie shadows across the trees. "It must be the leader, the largest face in the middle. There must be other access points to the valley or his tribe wouldn't be surrounding the larger one in a circle."

Clair twisted her heard toward Kioko, reminded instantly of Emily's quick thinking. "What?" Kioko asked, surprised at her expression.

"Nothing," Clair said, looking away.

"There are bound to be traps," Chris said, pulling out his khopesh.

"Well, then," Clair said, hearing the blades slide silkily from the sheathes crossed on her back. "Through the trees?"

The sun was starting to set as their tired feet crossed over the broken earth. Suddenly, all hell broke loose.

DOTTY

otty walked gingerly down the stairs, feeling the fluff of the carpet sliding between her toes as she descended.

Her bones were getting creakier by the minute, it seemed. Every day her body grew older while her mind grew sharper, more alert, and more ready to wage a battle against the constant and endless barrage of challenges thrown her way.

A low and melodic hum came from the couch in the living room. Seine stared at her from his perch on the armrest. His thick brown and black fur was long and unkempt. His large yellow eyes stared into her own.

Dotty had inspected him multiple times for anything out of the ordinary, but it appeared that he was just a cat. Just a cat who happened to feel extraordinary. Otherworldly. Magical.

Just a cat.

She had to keep telling herself Seine was just a cat.

"Hello, baby," she cooed, walking over to scratch his behind his battle-scarred ears. She did not know who he had been before he found her, the fights he had survived, but he was a sweetheart now. Cuddly, calm, and slightly terrifying.

She loved him.

"Make sure you go through the shop today," she admonished, fluffing his tail with her hand. "I saw some rather large spiders near the back area with the old books. Could be fun."

Seine meowed, acknowledging the request before he jumped from the sofa and strutted toward the shop.

Dotty had had a cat door installed between the house and the antique shop not long after Seine arrived. There was already a cat door built into the back door of her house. She liked that he was able to come and go as he pleased. At first, she had not liked that he would go outside to hunt mice, but then she realized he must have lived on the streets long before her. He would either be fine or not. She had come to terms with life being out of her control.

Dorthea sighed.

Out of her control, indeed.

Sam had messaged her that Clair was going to Greece. He had reiterated that he did not want to go on any mission involving the Covenant. It was not his place to step into the Covenant's business, he did not want to get dragged back in, he felt confident that Clair would experience a mission, become bored, and want to return home, blah. Blah. Blah. Sam was trying to justify his choices to her, again.

But Dotty hoped that was true. That Clair would come back free and ready to settle into her life.

The Covenant was alluring in many ways but James had always warned her it was dangerous. He said they operated outside the realm of the Ultimates. This was why Dotty had been so determined to keep Clair's powers subdued and secret. She did not want them coming for her.

Her husband had just disappeared one day without a trace before she knew she was pregnant. She had raised Elijah entirely alone and then lost him, too. She did not want anything to happen to Clair. She could not bear it.

Dotty grabbed her purse from the rack, checking to make sure she had her phone and keys, slipped on her walking shoes, and exiting the house.

She loved this town. It was tucked away and quiet. Well, it was quieter before it became a wine destination, but wine and antiques tended to go hand in hand.

Peace what she wanted most after her life of adventure. It was what she had tried to build with the love of her life, James, the seraph. He was an angel who was more human than most. He made her laugh and think. He was flawed and a magnet for the greatest good and evil in this world. He was beautiful, extraordinary, and kind. They had chosen each other.

Dotty did not grow up without means. Her family was well-established and she was a beloved only child who never went without. Her father was an early technology industrialist, a shrewd businessman with stocks and investments that vested early into the tech boom. Her mother called herself a home engineer. She managed her family's lives with panache, filling their days with fun and marvelous food. She would lend her talents to non-profits when she was not busy coordinating Dotty's father's illustrious work parties. Dotty vividly remembered the New England winters of her childhood, when snow would cover the ground and smother all the life that spread out as far as she could see from her bedroom window. She remembered her awe at the rebirth of spring every year. She enjoyed her upbringing and valued her parents' ability to provide for her dreams. She travelled, she partied, she learned. She was privileged and she knew she was lucky.

Dotty believed you could not have everything, that there was a give and take in life that could not be denied. She had been given so much good and so much pain.

She met James in France, along the river Seine. He had locked eyes with her, and she knew in her bones they were meant to be. From that moment on, it was them against the world. She became a part of his story and he amplified hers. They were two halves of the same soul, finally reunited across time and space.

Dorthea's parents had passed a few years prior to her meeting James. Theirs had been natural deaths. They were older when they had finally became pregnant with her, and it had taken her time to find herself and then him.

James became her family and then Elijah.

Then Clair.

She had become a grandmother, but also a mother again.

Life had demanded many things of her, but raising Clair was something she would choose to do over and over again.

In Dotty's mind, Clair was perfect. Her grandfather had been the highest-ranked angel on Earth and her father had spent his life torn between his two identities, the human and the angelic. Clair, however, was the most beautiful balance between magic and humanity. She was the best of both worlds.

Dotty turned the corner onto Main Street, heading toward the flower shop. She would need to get some groceries after her visit with Jean, but not so many that she could not carry them home.

As she neared the shop, Dotty was struck by a smell she knew all too well. Eden. James used to disappear for days at a time and come home reeking of it. They never really spoke of it, but there were moments in their marriage when the reality of their situation would hit her out of nowhere, making her heart race and her mind spin. She was married to a powerful angel who routinely traveled to Eden. At least, until the day he had disappeared.

After James, The Gate had continued its random disappearances and reappearances in Healdsburg over the years. Dotty had sensed its presence like a shadow in the corner of a room that can only be seen out of the corner of one's eye.

She wondered if Elijah had ever visited during his too short life. The Gate had waited for Clair. Did it ever wait for Elijah?

Dorthea had seen and experienced many wonderful things in her life, but she knew she would never understand parts of this angelic puzzle.

She entered the shop and walked into a wall of magical fragrance.

"Dorthea! Good morning," Jean greeted Dotty. Jean's apron was covered in dirt from her morning repotting. It looked like she had smeared a little dirt across her cheek. They were close in years, but Jean seemed to be aging backward, becoming more vibrant each day.

"Good morning," Dotty replied, looking at the dozens of pots of lilies scattered around the store. These were not just any garden-variety lilies. They were Eden lilies. Well, technically they were hybrids Jean had created from an Eden lily. Clair had brought the lily to Jean after Dotty had stomped on it in a rage, trying to keep her away from The Gate. Clearly, things had not gone according to plan for Dotty. These lilies may not have been entirely of Eden, but the blossoms were so eerily similar that Dotty felt suffocated by the magic of the flowers.

"Aren't they lovely?" Jean asked, turning toward the nearest lily. "I used the pollen from the lily Clair brought in, and the lilies I already had took to it better than I even dreamed! It was astonishing. I grew dozens of flowers from that one stem. They've been selling like mad."

"They are beautiful," Dotty murmured. She reached out to touch a soft petal between her fingers and the scent intensified.

"What brings you in today, dear?" Jean asked. She wiped her hands on her apron, rubbing the material between her grimy fingers, before picking up a discarded pencil to write a quick note on her desk.

"I just came to pick up a few of these," Dotty said, grabbing a handful of seed packets. She needed to check on Chris's backyard.

When Chris had first disappeared, Dotty had taken over tending to his garden and it had flourished. Dotty had always had a green thumb, but her talents had grown exponentially since her time with James. Her capabilities were now well beyond those of the average human. Dotty had magic in her. Her fear of evil finding them ran so deeply that by the time Clair was an adult, she had stopped gardening entirely.

"Ah, wonderful," Jean remarked, refusing payment for the seed packs. "You're probably about due for more soil, too, if my timing's correct. How is the backyard garden going?"

"Well, thanks," Dotty said, dropping a five on the desk despite the look Jean gave her. "I'm glad you convinced me to plant so many fruit trees. They are finally starting to become viable."

"Oh, yes," Jean said, leaning against the counter. "Lots of patience required with those, but the payout is worth it."

Dotty understood that. "How are things going with you?"

"Me?" Jean asked, eyebrows rising. "You don't normally ask about me. We talk about our shops, and plants, and the weather, but never just ourselves. Is that now fair game?"

"Uh," Dotty found herself at a loss for words.

Jean laughed. "Don't worry, Dorthea," she said, eyeing her. "I won't pry. I know you are private, always have been, but I wouldn't mind discussing magic when you have the time."

Dotty froze. "What?"

"Oh, you know," Jean said, stepping away from the counter and walking over to a disorganized stack of papers. "What spells do you use for your garden? Are you into runes? Or are you a purist, more of a full-moon-and-new-moon ritual witch?"

Dotty let out the breath she was holding and laughed. "I am not a witch!"

Jean's ever-present smile faded into a small frown, and she looked directly into Dotty's eyes. "Do not lie to me. I recognize magic when I feel it and I feel it with you, with Clair, and with this strain of flowers. I won't press you for more than you are willing to share, but we witches must stick together."

Dotty stopped laughing and looked at the woman. She had not had a real friend in years. How much could she share without being too exposed? What would be appropriate? What was believable? What did Jean truly believe?

"Well," Dotty said, leaning into the decision. "I've never done a full moon ritual. Have you?"

Jean brightened, the tension in the room disappearing like a popped bubble. "Oh, yes. You will have to join me for the next one. There's a few of us who get together – it's quite fun."

Dotty found herself agreeing to a full moon ritual with a group of people.

Hell must be freezing over.

EMILY

The sunlight glinted off the diamond on her finger as Emily shuffled the stack of books from one arm to the other, trying to open her car door without dropping them.

She was not sure why she was surprised when the first thing Dotty told her to do was pick up a large quantity of books, but Emily was not complaining. She felt like she had a mission again. It was the same feeling she had when she was researching for a school paper, that single-minded determination to succeed thrumming through her veins.

Emily had found some of the books at the library, some used on eBay, and others she had to buy new at their local book store. She figured she could scan any pages she would need to keep for reference from the library books so that all of the information she needed would always be on hand.

She planned to store the books in her car, since she was not about to tell her parents that she was looking into magic and witchcraft.

Mike had offered to let her store them at his place, but she wanted to be able to reference them whenever she had time between clients and at night. He had been hinting at her being allowed to leave things at his place for a while now, clearing a drawer in the dresser, half the closet was now empty. He wanted them to get a new place together, but until that was possible, he was making room for her to feel at home. She was over there all the time.

"Did you bring the books?"

Emily hauled the tote bag on her shoulder into Dotty's antique shop. It was evening and the shop was closed. The light outside had faded into that beautiful orange the shone before the grey of night consumed the world.

"Yes," she said, dropping the tote on the ground next to a table full of odds and ends. "I got every single one. I even had to order that really small one used from eBay."

"Give it to me," Dotty said, extending her hand.

Emily leaned down and sifted through the books to find the right one. It was petite and covered in worn, brown leather, with no labels to hint at its contents. Emily placed it in Dotty's hand.

"I peeked around in that one, but it just seemed like an empty journal to me."

Dotty opened the book and laid it flat on her left palm. She then rotated her right hand above the book in a circle three times. After the third rotation, she stopped and waited, staring at the book. Emily leaned closer, trying to see if words or shapes would appear upon the cover. Nothing happened.

"Good," Dotty said, snapping the book closed and placing it on one of the nearby shelves.

"What did it do?" Emily asked.

"Nothing," Dotty said, pulling the chairs away from the old dining set and placing them against the wall.

"Then why do I need it?" Emily asked, moving to do the same with the chairs closest to her.

"You don't," Dotty said, waiting for Emily to finish her side. "I needed it, but I had to make sure the witch who owned it before hadn't put a spell on it."

Emily stared at her. "You had me order you a book that you just wanted?"

"Yes," Dotty said, smiling. Emily huffed. "Now," Dotty said, rolling up her sleeves. She was whispering something under her breath. She raised her hands and all of the items on the table began to rise and slowly float away to the corners of the room, clearing the table.

"Holy hell!" Emily shouted. "I didn't know you could do that! Can I do that?"

"Doubtful," Dotty said, sweat on her brow. "I can only do that because I've lived my whole adult life around high-level angels and I have an affinity for magic. That's what we are going to figure out for you – whether or not you have an affinity for it. I need you to place all the books on the table now. We will start by going over where you should focus your research."

After only half an hour, Emily felt like she was back in college. The books Dotty had recommended were of all varying levels of study – botany for beginners, foraging, divination, green witch practices, books to see the unseen, and much more. Dotty assigned a variety of passages from each of the books. They discussed the meaning behind the selections and what Emily should look out for when she was reading, paying special attention to any small pull or feeling she might experience.

"It doesn't have to be significant," Dotty stressed, watching Emily jot down notes on her every word. The only break had been when they bickered about dog-earing the books. Emily had been indignant with Dotty. She sold antiques, for goodness's sake. Dog-earing damaged the books, plain and simple. Dotty had merely shaken her head and insisted that it was the content of the books that mattered, not how they looked. Emily wanted to scream but reined herself back in, instead focusing her energy on effectively structuring her notes, a skill which had helped her get into Stanford all those years ago. "Anything at all. A small fluttering of your heart, a warmth in your fingers, even hiccups. Note down anything random and what you were reading when it happened."

Dotty said that it took her decades to manifest, even thought she had spent a lifetime around angels.

Then she pulled out the crystals. There were ten of them in all different shapes, sizes, and colors. Emily had never seen such beautiful rocks. Dotty sat across from Emily, lining up all the crystals in a row.

When she finished, Dotty steepled her hands and surveyed her work before glancing at Emily and looking back down to the rocks. She sighed.

"Wait here," Dotty instructed. She went into the back office and Emily could hear her rummaging through her desk. "They must be inside," Dotty said, her voice fading further away. "Stay there, I'll be right back."

"Okay," Emily shouted so Dotty could hear her. Emily looked down at the crystals in front of her. They were pretty, but none of them were calling to her or making her feel anything. They all looked like they should make her feel something – they definitely had a witchy vibe. Emily wondered if soon Dotty would pull out a crystal ball.

"Maybe that's what she's going to get," Emily chuckled to herself. In her mind, she knew this was crazy– her being trained by a witch– but in her heart it felt right.

Emily realized that she had not been in this room since they had figured out what was hunting Clair and the Gate, over a year ago.

Emily took a moment to survey her surroundings.

The first thing that always hit her was the smell. It was musty and old, like mold was waiting within the pages of the books or the cushions of the tufted furniture. The scent was somehow comforting, as if breathing in a quicker death somehow eased the whole situation.

Next came the sheer volume of objects filling the room. Rows upon rows of books and antiques twisted and turned, making the space feel somehow larger, despite the looming, tilted stacks of items that felt like they like they could topple onto her head at any moment. Most of the time, she could barely find the path through it.

Emily took a deep breath.

She missed how lively this space had been when they were all together. The energy of the collective group had filled her with a sense of determination and purpose.

Emily tilted her head suddenly.

There was something…

She stood up from the table slowly.

Something was making a sound. It was an incredibly soft noise, like a gentle breeze whistling through the trees. So quiet it was almost non-existent.

She followed it.

She tilted her head back and forth to better hear it, following the sound as it led her from room to room, finally stopping in front of a bookshelf. The whistling guided her eyes to the top, where she spotted a midsize jewelry box. Emily pulled the box down onto a lower level of the shelf. The box's wood was a deep mahogany color and it was covered in painted flowers that had long since been scratched and chipped. When she lifted the lid, Emily expected to see the embedded machinery of a music box, but instead she was greeted by some old photographs and a leather-bound journal. When she touched the journal, the whistling faded into nothing.

"Good," Dotty said, from right behind her.

Emily started, twisting around and grabbing her heart. "Oh my god," she exclaimed. "You scared the shit out of me!"

Dotty merely smiled at Emily as she regained her breath.

"Good?" Emily finally asked, looking down at the book in her hands. "It's magic." It was not a question. Emily could feel it in her bones.

"You can teach someone about anything, dear," Dotty said, taking the book from Emily's hands. She flipped to a page near the back and held it out to Emily, who noticed clusters of symbols she had never seen spread cross the pages. "You can teach them how to do something, but you cannot teach them how to *feel* it. You can't teach them to *care* about it." Dotty handed Emily the book. "This is the spell you will need to be able to do before we are done."

Emily looked back up at her. "What do you mean, before we are done?"

"If you cannot make this, you are incapable of saving yourself." Dotty said. Dotty's eyes in this moment would haunt Emily for the rest of her life. The intensity that radiated off her was like that of a black hole that would consume the world. This moment was being imprinted upon her brain; this conversation, this experience, this feeling.

"What?" Emily breathed, quiet even to her own ears. "Save myself from what?"

Dotty broke eye contact, looking back down at the book. "Once you have truly tapped into the part of yourself that can manipulate magic, the part that feels it and can identify it at any turn, only then will you be able to do this spell. It is the only thing that matters to you now. Devote yourself to it. Live it. Breathe it. Learn how to do this spell and you will save yourself."

"Save myself from what?"

Dotty turned away, walking back toward the crystals on the table.

"What's coming."

KIOKO

Clair moved like death.

That was all Kioko could remember thinking as they neared the largest mountain in the valley. They each led a squad, Kioko's taking the left, Clair's the middle, and Chris the right. The shadows came upon them quickly, dark shapes emerging from the ground like corpses.

They *were* corpses.

Hundreds of them.

The furious bones of the buried indigenous people who used to inhabit the valley rose from the earth in magical, shadowed bodies.

At least they could not be classified as human, which made them fair game.

Kioko destroyed her share but felt the fear seep into her bones as she watched Clair fight through the throng like a shadow herself. Her eyes glowed like lightning as she cut down one after another, their dark blue blood spraying all around her like wings of blood.

She was enjoying this.

The thought stayed with Kioko until they reached the top of the hill leading to the central mountain and came face-to-face with the largest shadow they had encountered yet.

It had the head of an ox with the eyes of a snake. Its body was half-man, half-horse, with talons for hooves. It yelped a terrifying shriek.

Behind the creature shone a glowing ball of light, illuminating the valley at least a mile of in every direction.

They were on the right track. This must be what Augustus had sent them to collect.

They just had to get through one last obstacle.

CLAIR

Clair sprinted behind the beast and sliced its back legs with the khopesh, then bolted for the orb.

Clair found that if she concentrated, she could turn off the part of her brain where she was actively in control. She was still present, still her, but she could let her instincts take over. Her mind processed the moves before she ever had to think about them. It was just like everything else with her newfound level of powers – it came easy to her, like breathing.

She became death.

Clair heard the shadow's dying breath and turned to see the rest of the team coming up to join her at the orb.

It was like a giant snow globe. A towering, round glass jewel in the heart of the forest. The light from within was almost blinding, bathing the ground in blue and purple light while pulsing with white hot energy.

The angels walked up to the glass, squinting as they peered in, trying to make sense of the scene before them. It was slightly hazy, like watching fish through water. Clair could see six bodies lining a walkway to a glowing cave with one lone figure stood in front.

Kioko pushed on the glass, but it would not budge "I don't know this magic," she breathed, deftly running her hand along the smooth edge. "But it's wondrous."

It was unusual to see Kioko enthralled by anything. Clair thought it must take a lot to impress her and snap her out of her boredom, Kioko had seen more than most.

Clair touched the dome. It was smooth and warm, like a freshly washed glass. Suddenly everything around her began to spin. She watched the world fly by around them, and she instinctively knew she was losing mortal time again. She was always losing time. She pressed her palm further into the surface and watched as her hand fell through.

Don't.

Clair paused, sucking in a breath. It had been so long since she had heard the voice. Why now?

She yanked back her hand in frustration and folded her arms, then let out a huge sigh. Chris came up beside her.

"Be careful," he said, his grey eyes bright in the light. She smiled at him and faced the orb.

Slowly, like walking through gelatin, Clair felt the barrier allow her to pass. Inside, the air was crisp and still. The dirt beneath her feet did not crunch. She realized that the space was soundless. When she looked back at her companions, Clair gasped.

The earth was spinning around the orb, time flying by outside of it. In under a minute, the night sky had turned into day. Kioko must have ordered the angels to touch the wall, because a number of them stood there, hands pressed against the wall, watching time fly around them.

Great. Another event stealing precious human time from her. Clair turned back toward the stationed guards.

Seven people stood before her, not shadows, but living, breathing humans. Three stood on either side of the path leading to the pulsing center, and the seventh stood in front of the cave door, his hands at his sides. They were all different ethnicities, ages, and genders. Clair assumed the man closest to the cave was their leader. They did not move, but stared at her with dark expressions, their skin smooth and their faces chiseled. They were clothed in rough-spun pants and white linen shirts, each bearing tattoos on their arms and thick leather boots. These were soldiers.

Clair turned around again to look at Kioko and Chris, who stood together with their hands pressed against the orb. The angels who were not touching the orb moved around them in fast motion. Chris must have yelled something to them, because they all touched the orb, finally on the same frequency.

Why could they not get in?

"They are not human."

Clair spun to see the leader staring at her, his position in front of the pathway unchanged.

She looked back at the angels, at Chris – that was true. After everything, she still held human blood. She felt the chasm between her and Chris widen in her heart – it was something they would never share.

These soldiers must have stumbled across the orb somehow, and were using this space separate from time to prolong their lives. But why? Why protect this cave? What could provoke anyone to guard something at the expense of time?

"Turn back, angel," the leader commanded.

She faced the leader, who stood silhouetted by the glowing cave door. He was definitely the head of the group. Clair walked toward him, passing the other sentries who followed her with their eyes, but did not move.

She had to get whatever was in there – information, object, whatever it was, she did not care.

"You cannot pass here, seraph," he said, standing tall in front of the path. "It is not good for you to be here."

How long had these men been here? By their attire, they looked to be a mix from the last few decades, except the leader. He seemed much older, ancient even, but that was impossible. Unless…

"The light force preserves us," the leader said, reading her thoughts again. "Time passes beyond the orb like the river flows down the stream."

Clair took one last look at Chris, who seemed perplexed, and at Kioko, who was shouting something that looked like her name and the word "human."

Clair turned back around.

"I've come here for whatever is in the cave," she said, stopping a few yards in front of him.

"Then you have come in vain," he said, his wise eyes molten in the light. "We have guarded the cave for many years, seen the earth spin and change longer than your lifetime. What dwells in the cave is no longer a thing. That was taken long before."

Clair paused. Augustus had said it would be here. Why would there still be guards if there was nothing in there?

"What is in the cave now?" she asked aloud, trying to see through the blinding white light behind him.

"Death."

Clair raised an eyebrow.

"Nevertheless, I need to get into that cave, please," she said walking toward the leader.

"That is impossible," he said, folding his arms just like his brethren. She stopped about three feet in front of him.

"There is no such thing as impossible anymore," Clair said, matching his stare.

"The knowledge you seek is not that which was asked of you. You were misled."

"Misled?" she questioned, prowling in front of him, looking for a way past him to the door. This must have been why Augustus insisted she go. Not for training, but because he knew she was the only one who could get into the orb.

"He did know. He knows more than he tells you."

"Stop doing that."

The leader only stared. She had to get past him.

Sensing the slightest hesitation in the air around him, Clair feinted left, and sprinted past the sentries and the leader, straight into the glowing door. She slammed into it and fell backward. Clair spit the blood from her mouth and twisted her head from where she lie on the ground to see all the soldiers maintaining their positions.

No one was going to try to stop her because she could not get in anyway. She stood up and placed a palm to the luminous door. It was cold like stone, like it was not magical at all. Clair turned to face the leader.

"How do I open it?"

"You don't," the leader said.

"But you can?"

No answer.

"Open the door," she said, her anger bubbling to the surface. She did not want to hurt these people, but she had had enough.

"No," he said.

"Open the door!" Clair shouted. She was next to him in a second, holding her blade to his throat.

She could hear Kioko behind her shouting through the bubble, louder than she had ever heard her yell before, her anger coming through. "He's human, Clair! Human! We cannot harm a human – do not break the pact of the angels!" She was screaming it over and over, while the leader remained stone-faced, arms crossed, the blade resting gently against his throat.

They had come too far to just leave.

But Clair was not a murderer. She could not kill an innocent because he would not comply.

Clair lowered her weapon.

"Open the door," she commanded once more, staring into his eyes. "I need the information behind that door. It's important for us. I need you to open that door. I need to see what is inside it."

"Your journey has been in vain, angel. There is no information that you were sent to seek. Return to your master and find another venture."

Clair bristled. Master? She had no master. She was here of her own accord. She wanted to test herself on a mission. But why? Maybe she *had* been tricked. Had Augustus used her so easily?

She started to walk back toward her companions when the leader spoke again.

"Good luck, angel. He wishes you well on your journey."

It was the wrong thing to say.

CHRIS

As soon as she stepped through the glass, Clair froze, her body moving so slowly it was an effort to track any movement at all. Chris placed his hand back on the dome and watched time fly by. It was disorienting, dizzying, to watch the stars move and the sun rise and set in minutes versus hours.

"Keep your hand on the dome!" Chris shouted.

"Hands on the glass!" Kioko commanded, and they all obeyed.

Suddenly, Clair was moving at her normal speed, but all around them time sped. The night turned to day and back again in a matter of seconds.

They watched and listened as Clair spoke with the leader and tried to get past him into the cave.

"Open the door," Clair said. "I need the information behind that door. It's important for us. I need you to open that door. I need to see what is inside it."

"Your journey has been in vain, angel. There is no information that you were sent to seek. Return to your master and find another venture."

Why would Augustus send them here if there was no information? Nothing to collect?

Clair was returning to them when the leader spoke again.

"Good luck, angel. He wishes you well on your journey."

Clair stopped and turned.

CLAIR

hat?" she asked, staring at the leader. He merely stared back.

"He doesn't want you here, Clair," the leader said, his watery, brown eyes determined.

"Who doesn't want me here? You?" she said, feeling annoyed.

"Your father."

Clair felt her stomach drop.

Her father?

Her father was here.

He had been here this entire time.

She thought he was dead. Dotty thought he was dead.

"My father," she said and the sword in her right hand hit the ground with a soft plunk.

Clair looked from the man to the light, and her face froze.

"My father..." she slowly repeated, staring at the light. She looked back at the rest of the angels outside before turning back to the light. "They couldn't get through, but I could. Because..." She stared at the light again.

Her mind could not catch up with her thoughts. Why was he here? Did he come here right after the accident? Why were they holding him prisoner?

"We are not," the leader said.

She looked at him again. "'You are not' what?"

"We are not holding him."

Clair let that thought sink in. Her father was here of his own will. He was not dead or working for the Ultimate Evil. He chose to stay here. Chose not to be there with her, with her grandmother.

Her grandmother, his mother. He knew his mother was alive…or maybe he did not.

She looked around at all the time passing around her. Maybe he did not know. But did he not care? Her father. She had to talk to him. She needed to know. How *dare* he? What had really happened to her mother?

Anger like she had never known filled her chest.

"I don't care if he doesn't want to see me," she said with calm fury, her hands in fists at her sides. "Open the door. Now."

"I cannot -"

"OPEN THE DOOR!"

The air around her shot from her body, throwing most of the humans off balance. The leader looked at her, his eyes sorrowful.

"I don't know the pain in your heart, but I will not willfully open that door."

Clair heard the words he was not saying. He was not saying he could not, he was saying he *would* not, and she believed him.

He was the only way to her father, and the anger inside of her would not allow him to sit like a coward, hidden away any longer.

She knew what she had to do.

Clair looked at the leader and saw the resolution in his eyes. He knew what she was going to do.

"You say you don't know my heartbreak," she said, the sorrow threatening to consume her, the anger radiating energy from her body. "Well, now you will. Death calls to death," she said as she plunged her hand into his body and ripped out his heart.

Chris

PEN THE DOOR!" she roared, inches from the man's face. Even from outside the glass Chris could feel her power flaring with her anger, the tendrils of her magic seeping out into the forest.

Distantly, Chris thought he could still hear Kioko yelling over and over to Clair, "He's human–don't break the pact!"

"I don't know the pain in your heart, but I will not willfully open that door," the guard said, sympathetically staring at her. But Chris could feel her rage building, becoming a living thing. Her face hardened.

"You said you don't know my heartbreak."

Her face went blank. Cold. Calculating.

"Well, now you will. Death calls to death," she said, before plunging her hand into his body, ripping out his heart.

Kioko screamed.

Clair, strode into the cave with a man's heart bleeding in her hand.

Chris did not know he was shouting until he ran out of breath and collapsed to his knees.

Clair had just killed a human.

CLAIR

Clair squeezed the heart, barely registering the body as it fell to the ground. She watched as the red drops poured down her hand and onto the blue light, corroding the sealed door like acid on wood.

It opened like a blanket catching fire – small holes burning into a larger holes until the barrier was completely gone.

Clair stepped through into another world.

Worlds upon worlds upon worlds. Why could one world never be enough for them? Clair would never know. She stepped into a dreamlike paradise.

She could hear the slow and steady gurgle of a stream nearby, flowing through the middle of the pristine, expansive flower fields. The scent that surrounded her was a mix of clean laundry and freshly felled mahogany. It completely contrasted against the eruption the of colors the flowers. Clair reached down and grasped a singular purple rose which sprouted from the ground like it was exactly where it belonged and not defying nature.

She plucked it, the stem pulling easily from the ground. When she brought it to her nose there was no scent. There were no thorns. It was blank – like its creator could not be bothered with the details of the illusion enough to care for the individual aspects, only the bigger picture. The overall effect.

She squeezed the rose, watching some of the blood from her hand imprint on the petals before she dropped it to the ground.

Clair gazed at the blue sky and fields before turning back around toward the entrance she had just stepped through.

It was gone.

Standing behind her near the stream was a man.

Clair had the fleeting thought that she should feel some sense of familiarity. That she should recognize him in her soul as her father.

But she did not.

She just saw a man, in frayed jeans and a black t-shirt, his legs slightly apart, his hands loose at his sides. He had piercing brown eyes, a slightly crooked mouth, and ears almost too big for his head. They had the same nose. Same skin color. His shaggy hair shared the same colors as hers.

No grey in his hair.

He looked closer to her age than what she imagined her father would look like if she had had any sort of normal life.

They evaluated each other, each weighing the quiet of the moment. Both of them knowing that whatever came next would shatter any peace in this haven she assumed he built.

That he built. Where he hid.

She stared at the man who had helped create her and she waited. She waited to see what he would say. Because Clair, Clair was finding it hard to find anything to say to someone so narcissistic.

"Clair," he said, his voice echoing in the space. She was instantly brought back to a dream she had months ago, before everything, before the Covenant. Of feathers covering her face, of an angel crying near a stream.

But this was no angel to Clair. She continued to stare at him.

"Clair," he said, his hand barely twitching to reach out. "What are you doing here? How did you –" his eyes flickered down to her blood-spattered hand. "Oh, Clair – no. Tell me you didn't—"

"Didn't what, *father?*" Clair spat, closing the space between them. She still remained a length away, but she was disappearing into that powerful place in her heart, the place that told her she was invincible. That she was better than this seraph, even if she was supposedly less powerful. Clair had been living while he had been hiding. She was not afraid of him or anything else. She would endure, and in the meantime she would put this man in his place. "Don't tell you that I killed your little human pawn? That I ripped his heart out and broke through your barrier?"

Clair scoffed, looking around the picturesque landscape that looked too much like a painting. Like Eden, but tangible, real. She sensed that time was not flowing as quickly as it had there. She could feel in her bones now. She knew what it was to lose time.

She was still losing time in the real world. Clair looked down at the grass beneath her feet and saw the red on her hand leftover from the man guarding this place. The red was shocking against all the greenery and flowers – against all of the false beauty.

Clair made a fist and looked back up at the man who was supposed to be her family who had abandoned her.

"What happened to my mother?"

He slowly closed his eyes, then opened them. "Hannah…" He ran his hands through his curly, shaggy hair. Pulling at the ends, his eyes darted to the stream and back to her. "She found out what I was. She saw things in you, in me… She knew something wasn't quite right, but I didn't want to tell her, I didn't want her to know. I didn't want to become some circus sideshow. All my life I had been gifted. All my life people were drawn to me. I knew why, mother told me why, but it was a constant battle.

"She tried to kill me, once. Your mother. When she found out what I was. She always thought there was something off about me, but she loved me and ignored it. It wasn't until you started showing powers as a young child, that she knew there was something very different about us. She confronted me about it. I didn't want to risk telling her so I made something up, but she knew I was lying. She started having these crazy dreams and visions. She was confused and worried about you, and she kept telling me that she saw a future for you where both of us weren't in it. I knew then that we were not supposed to walk the earth together, you and I. I knew that I needed to make an escape, but I couldn't. I loved you both so much I couldn't leave.

"So, I tried wiping her memories. I cleansed her mind. Every little thing she noticed that was different about me, every time she had questioned me, all the dreams… I took them from her. Then… Then I started having them. The visions. The memories. The dreams…"

He turned toward Clair, staring into her eyes.

"Her dreams, they kept coming for me – they would wake me in the night, screaming. Everything that I took from her started coming back in every dream. Even she started having dreams about the memories I took. She was questioning her entire existence. The dreams though, my dreams, they were too much. I had to get out. I needed to look for what was next, for something that would help. I told Mother I wanted to go to the Covenant, I wanted to find help. She said it was too dangerous. She said that was a sure-fire way to get put on display, to become a pawn, but I knew I needed to go. They didn't know I existed. Staying in one town for your entire existence made it easy for my witchy mother to hide us, but I knew something was coming, that we needed help. And then you manifested."

He paused and inhaled slowly. Clair did not move.

"You were with your mother. I had stepped out for a walk in the forest. You started glowing and objects started flying around you, and your mother freaked out. She ran to me. I told her I would explain everything in the car, but we needed to go. I knew if Mother found out about your powers she would suppress them with magic. You didn't need that. the oppression of growing up hiding who you really are… The spells, the constant drugging of our bodies with magic to dull our gifts. No one should go through that."

Clair narrowed her eyes at this man. He was blaming Dotty? Using Dotty as his excuse for why he left her? Or her powers? Because he didn't want them suppressed? Because that suppression was somehow worse in his mind than not being together as a family? How selfish was he?

"She didn't want to go, your mother. We were in the car driving to the airport, and she lost it. Said we needed to turn back and talk to Mother, get her to help you. That we couldn't uproot you. How could we protect you? We didn't even know where the Covenant was. She kept insisting I was wrong. Meanwhile, you were in the backseat crying and glowing, and the car – the car started turning on its own, pulled by your magic – and then we were flipping, crashing. There was fire and I couldn't get to your mother, but I got you and I knew right then. I knew I needed to leave you.

"I brought you to Mother's house. I left you on her porch. I knew she would bind your powers and I left to find someplace safe. I needed someplace safe to wait. I don't know for what. The voices in my head, they were too much, too loud all the time. They grew louder after your mother's death. I came to this forest looking for magic and made a sanctuary. This sanctuary. The voices, they can't get us here, Clair, we exist somewhere separate from time. Time will go on and on until it finally ends. Until all of it ends. But you, the best thing I could do was leave you. It was the best thing for you.

"I had just lost my wife," he said, tears streaming down his face. "I had lost my entire life."

Clair did not hesitate.

"You lost? You ran. You are a coward, hiding here for years in this pretty fantasy instead of facing what you did. Instead of using what power you had to make a change, you just walked away."

He was weak. A coward who ran from his responsibilities. Who ran from his potential. Who left his own child. He chose himself. They all did. Just like Augustus. And they were all going to pay for it.

"Oh, Clair," he said. "You just don't understand. You don't understand what it is to be a seraph. You don't understand the power and how it traps you and how it controls you and how it leads you. I couldn't face it, Clair, the power. It was too much. I couldn't face what I had done to your mother, I couldn't face anything. So, I came here and made this place – don't you feel it? The peace? The quiet? Don't you feel the time passing around you, while you are safe, protected, cocooned in this beautiful paradise? It's perfect," he said, gesturing around him to the flowers in the fields and the water in the stream in the quiet beauty.

Clair felt her blood begin to boil.

Who was this man who thought he could tell her what she did and did not know? He was never there for her. He killed her mother. He let her die. He left her. He didn't raise his own daughter. He left his child to his mother to raise on her own – all by herself. Alone. His pretty speech was nothing more than a narcissist looking at loopholes and pain to justify the injustice of his own choices.

Clair was a seraph in her own right, someone who could have used the guidance of an adult who knew what she was going through. Clair had her powers bound for almost her entire life and she had only discovered them by chance! Chance, it was all by chance. Chris, Sam,

Emily…it was all chance that created her. That made her whole. That brought her here, to this point, to stand in front of her father and find him unworthy. This man before her was not worthy of the gifts he had. He did not deserve the power that he had.

She was repulsed by him. Repulsed by his weakness.

Clair thought about all the time she lost in Eden, and how she hated it. And here he was, happily throwing away time.

In his eyes, she saw the truth.

A mother who was left for dead. A father who chose himself instead of facing their shared destiny. Two parents unfit to do a job that her grandmother never should have been forced to do.

In that moment, Clair felt no pity for him, only anger. Anger that he was still here on this planet, waiting for the end of the world.

He would realize what true power was and the world would be better without him.

Clair did not need the voices in her head to tell her what to do. Did not need the instinctual power of her mind to find the power she needed for this.

Clair stretched out her hands and felt for the barrier. With everything in her, she pulled, imagining the bubble around them. She imagined it popping, she imagined burning all of the pretty flowers, and drying up all of the rushing waters until nothing but dead earth remained. She imagined the bubble crashing down around them.

She saw his eyes widen in fear as he started yelling at her, begging her to stop.

But she did not. She would not. She could not.

She imagined her dream, of the man by the stream. She imagined the feathers of the myth they were both born from covering his hair, his arms, and his legs. She watched as her magic transformed him into a feathery mass, screaming in agony as he clawed frantically at the magic consuming him. The magic being pulled from him – into Clair.

He did not deserve it. He did not deserve to be a seraph, a father, a son. He did not deserve any of it.

She she ripped his world out from underneath him, she stared into his eyes and felt nothing.

CHRIS

hris?"

He could feel someone near him. It was a voice he knew but could not place.

"Chris, you have to wake up! We have to go!"

Go? Where did they have to go? They were doing something. Something important. Something was waiting for them, or they were looking for something, right?

"Chris! Oh, for the love of –" He felt a sting on his cheek and his eyes flew open.

"Hey!" he yelled, rubbing his cheek. "What the –" Chris looked around. They were standing in the bottom of a giant crater. "What happened?"

He stood up, looking around. The crater went on for at least a half mile in all directions. The ground was charred and burned and the rainforest at its edges looked like it had been sliced in all directions with a sharp knife. He was sickened at the sight of half of a wild boar, severed right down the middle. They were back in Argentina. Tossed back into the real world, away from the magic of the sphere. How?

"Terri," he said, turning back toward her. "What happened? Where's Clair?!"

He turned in a circle. The other angels were here, and Kioko was shouting orders. One of the angels he did not know, an earth affinity, was lying on the ground, his arms bent at odd angles, eyes bloodshot. He was breathing heavily.

"Chris," Terri got his attention. She was covered in dirt. "Something really bad happened. Clair went into the cave and then all at once, it all started crumbling. The bubble, the forest, the mountains. Luckily Jason was able to bury us all as deep as he could before the explosion."

Chris looked down at himself, expecting to see dirt, but he was as clean as he had been before the explosion.

"We couldn't get to you, Chris," Terri said, grasping his shoulder. "When everything started happening, your eyes went white, and a bubble appeared around you. We tried to wait but there was barely enough time to get underground. The explosion destroyed everything, even the world we had traveled through. I'm so glad you're okay."

"A bubble?" Chris looked down at himself. "What... I don't remember. I remember watching her walk into the bright cave, then nothing."

"She didn't come out, Chris," Terri said, patting his shoulder, tears in her eyes. "She didn't come out. It's all gone, all of it."

"No," Chris said, turning toward Terri. "She's alive. I wouldn't be here if she hadn't protected me, and I'd know," he placed his hand over his heart. "I'd know if she was gone, Terri."

Terri nodded, but he could tell she was unconvinced. Chris could not take any more of her pity.

"Kioko!" he shouted, striding over to her. "We need to get back to the base, contact the Covenant. If something happened and Clair isn't here with us, she would have gone back there. Something happened."

"What happened is the seraph lost it!" Kioko shouted, gesturing around them. "I almost lost an entire team, an *entire team* because she lost it, killed a human, and who knows why, but flattened a mile of rainforest. How do you think we are going to cover this up, huh? How are we going to hide this from the humans? You're damned right we have to get out of here, but not to find your precious Clair – we need to stay out of the media. I've already contacted the local base, but we're not going back there. A jet is coming to take us back to the Covenant."

Chris heard a jet arriving from overhead and watched as it touched down near their location.

He hoped Clair was back at the Covenant, waiting for him.

What had happened in that cave?

CLAIR

She lost time, again.

She was headed to the Covenant. To find Augustus. To rail and rage at him for knowing, because he had known. He had known what she would find. Who she would find.

She would destroy him for it.

But as she flashed out of existence, intent on appearing in the Covenant, she lost herself...

The power was too much.

She barely remembered what happened after she killed her father.

Suddenly she awoke. She was in the snow, standing outside the imposing castle, looking up at its gaudy towers. She had once stood here in awe of its beauty. Now she saw it for what it really was, a façade for just another corrupt cult.

She walked up to the gates, flung them open with her mind, and stormed inside.

CHRIS

he jet touched down right outside the Covenant's spell-locked borders.

Chris and Kioko were first off the plane. The castle was still standing, and in Chris's mind that must be a good sign.

As they entered through the back, they ran to the nearest servant, stopping her in her tracks. "Where is everyone?" Kioko demanded.

The servant's eyes flashed with shock and fear. Kioko did look fearsome in that moment, covered in dirt and blood from the mission. "Everyone is in the ballroom, ma'am. Augustus is entertaining dignitaries," the woman said before scurrying off.

Kioko and Chris headed to the ballroom.

Chris only hoped Clair was here, and safe, and ready to talk about what had happened.

CLAIR

She stormed through the hallways.

No matter where she went, she did not encounter another soul.

She wondered if they could feel her wrath and were avoiding her.

As she turned toward the ballroom, a man emerged from a room to her right.

Clair stopped dead.

"Cole?" she breathed.

Cole turned toward her, shock evident on his face. "Uh, Clair," he stammered, looking around the space as if someone would come to his rescue.

"You're here?" Clair was putting the pieces together. This was far from what she had ever expected to see in her rage, in her grief. Cole was a part of the Covenant. He had always been a part of the Covenant.

He was sent to spy on her in Healdsburg.

They manipulated everything.

Cole must have seen the murder in her eyes because he quickly retreated to wherever it was he came from, through a door and out of sight.

She let him go. He was not the problem.

Clair decided she only had one more soul to take today, and it would be the sweetest of all.

KIOKO

What an utter shitshow.

The whole damn thing. Everything since they had entered that forest and desert. Hell, everything since Clair and Chris showed up.

Utter. Chaos.

And now Augustus was *entertaining*?

He must have known what Clair would encounter sending them there on that mission. He must have known, at least in part, how unstable she would be. How she would react.

Why? Why would he potentially compromise their greatest asset? It did not make any sense.

And now he was throwing a soirée for his contacts? None of this made sense in her mind. None of it spoke to the calculating master she had dutifully followed all these years.

None of it.

Kioko stepped into the ballroom, Chris right on her heels.

It was jam-packed with angels and dignitaries. It looked as if Augustus had invited almost all his contacts from across the globe and brought in most of the Covenant's angels who had been stationed abroad.

He was standing in the center of the ballroom, speaking casually with some president or other, when he saw them.

He smiled.

"Chris, Kioko," he said, gesturing to them. People nearby turned to watch as they approached. "Back so soon?"

"Is Clair here?" Chris asked him, continuing to search the hall with his eyes. When he did not find her, he turned to look back at Augustus, who was smiling.

"Not yet," Augustus said jovially, grabbing an apple from the overflowing centerpiece of a nearby table. The Covenant loved dazzling people with its opulence. Augustus stared into Chris's eyes and took a bite from the apple, allowing some of its juice to dribble down his chin before pulling out a mulberry silk hanky and dabbing it away.

Kioko could tell Chris was on the verge of shouting at him when the doors to the hall suddenly blew open and were ripped off their hinges. People screamed. Some of the angels grabbed weapons.

In strode Clair.

Kioko rarely feared anything. She rarely thought of death as a potential in her immediate future.

But Clair...

Clair was death incarnate.

Her eyes were nearly white with power. The tattered clothes from the mission wafted around her in an invisible wind created by the power seeping out of her.

She stopped twenty paces from them.

"You," she said, staring at Augustus.

"Me," he whispered, a serpentine smile teasing the corners of his mouth. He took a moment relish her stare before turning to the crowd. In a booming voice he announced, "This, my friends, is the seraph! The only one alive on this planet. The most powerful angel on earth. She has come to usher in a new era! An era of the angels. You will be with us, or you will be against us."

Cheers went up. Glasses clinked. Kioko noticed many of the angels and human dignitaries laughing merrily together, delighted at the prospect. Fewer sat murmuring, leaning in toward each other, concern on their faces.

This was not the Augustus Kioko knew. War? With the humans? This was not the way they did things.

Kioko was stunned into silence. She felt like she was floating outside of her body, watching the scene play out from overhead. Her entire existence had centered around this man and the Covenant. She gave her body, her mind, her soul. Her entire life. And for what?

"Angels," Augustus continued. Clair glowered, the whites of her eyes glowing more vividly with every word. "It is time for a reckoning. It is time we take back the planet that we have so magnanimously defended from evil for all this time. We are the true rulers. We have the power, the skills, the resources, and the intelligence. It is time for us to make the world a better place. Now comes the time of change. Now comes the era of the angels."

He turned to Clair, still as a statue amongst the chaos.

"Starting with you," he said, gesturing to her. He waved his hand and chests filled with gleaming practice swords filled the room. "The first angel to land a blow on the seraph will be promoted to my rank and will work alongside me in the new world."

Kioko froze. The room held its breath.

What Augustus was offering was impossible. Unachievable. No one would ever rank at the same level as him. Even the other thrones angels knew they would never be on his level. To rule alongside him? Even Kioko was briefly tempted by the thought. The power, the authority. No more snide remarks behind her back. No more *whore* thrown at her by her peers.

Equality. He was offering equality and power.

But it was a death sentence.

One look at Clair and anyone could see it was a death sentence.

"What are you doing?" Chris shouted, and Kioko snapped out of it enough to see that some of the angels had grabbed swords and were advancing on Clair, whose face was like stone as she watched them approach.

"So, this is what you have decided?" she asked, her eyes never leaving Augustus. "Fine."

The angels advanced.

CHRIS

What was happening?

One minute, Chris was trying to find Clair, and the next, Augustus had declared war on the humans and then on Clair, the only living Seraph.

"No," Chris said, watching as the angels began attacking Clair, trying to get a hit on her. "Are you crazy? Stop!" he shouted, looking for Sam, looking back at Kioko who seemed, for once, completely lost as to what to do.

Chris watched as Clair took out the angels one by one. One by one, she knocked them all out, moving with that feral grace she had possessed in the forest. With every move she got closer to where Augustus was standing, near Chris.

Lightning flashed through the window, striking her, illuminating her as if she was the sun.

The leaders of the world stared down upon her greedily. Their dreams of controlling the world, of power, and of an angelic rule – it all centered on Clair.

All the while, Clair simply fought her way toward Augustus, and Chris could not help but wonder if anyone saw what he saw in her eyes – death.

Clair reached Augustus, who was smiling with maniacal glee.

"Clair!" Chris shouted, jumping in front of her. He sucked in a breath. Her eyes had turned a deep molten gold. She took three breaths in front of him, her eyes staring past him toward Augustus.

Her face contorted in a feral smile, a look Chris had never seen on her face before, as she raised her hand and pointed at Augustus.

"You brought this upon yourself," it said, before Clair disappeared.

Chris inhaled, realizing he had not breathed since it took over Clair.

"It has begun," Augustus whispered. Angels were running, the leaders were scattered. Chris watched as some of the angels began circling Augustus, praising his reign, ready to start the new world.

Terri ran up to Chris. "Chris, where did she go?"

"I don't know," Chris said, looking toward Kioko, who seemed torn between going with them and disappearing altogether. "Kioko, you always have a place with us if you want it."

Kioko did not respond, and Chris and Terri went in search of Clair and Sam. They had to get out of here. It was time to go.

Terri and Chris began running, looking through doors and down multiple hallways.

"Chris, are you sure she's still here? Shouldn't we find Sam instead?"

"She's got to be here," he said. "I've never seen her disappear like that before, but Augustus just declared war on her, on humanity itself."

Terri was right behind him as they ran down the next hall, when she spoke, her voice was quiet, but full of conviction. "Chris, maybe you should let her go."

"I can't just let her go, Terri!" Chris shouted as he whirled to face her. No one was in the hallway with him.

"Terri?" Chris felt a chill creep down his spine.

She was gone.

Terri was gone.

Chris could see a smattering of dust on the floor. He felt tears prick his eyes. He could not think about what that meant now. He had to keep looking for Clair and Sam. They would know what to do. They would know how to help him.

Chris ran past the laboratory. He saw Erik frantically throwing things into boxes.

"Have you seen Clair?" he practically shouted, looking around as if she would be sitting in a corner somewhere.

"No," Erik replied, slightly out of breath, barely sparing Chris a glance.

"Where are you going?"

He looked at Chris, not an ounce of panic on his face.

"I'm a smart man, Chris," he said. "Nothing good will come of all this." Erik looked around at all of his technology, all of the books, all of his centuries of research and files. "Anyone who stays, does so at their own risk."

"I don't understand."

Erik looked back at Chris, eyes showing his years for the first time.

"You will."

"You have a space with us, if you want it," Chris said, not waiting for an answer before he sprinted from the lab.

Where could she have gone?

Chris was running through the upper levels of the Covenant, down every hall, pushing open every door trying to find Clair, hoping she had returned to the mansion where they had resided in bliss mere days ago.

He ran past all the art, for once not appreciating anything about this place. Anything about the Covenant. He wondered how he ever thought this organization was doing anything good for the world. How he thought they were right and just. It was all a lie.

Chris heard whispers coming from the door on his left. He flung the double doors open.

Four men he had never seen before were in the room. They turned to stare at him as he came in but said nothing. Two were seated, one was leaned against the wall, and the other had stopped mid-pace.

"Have you seen Clair?" Chris asked the man nearest him, the one who had been pacing. The man's eyes widened and his brows creased. He blinked deliberately, as if to clear his head, before speaking.

"You must protect her. You are the only one who can stop what will come." His voice was like an echo, as if it was being sucked into the room around them. The man started to blur before Chris's eyes, like a mirage in the dessert.

"That's what I am trying to do!" Chris yelled. "Where is she? You mean war? That's what's going to come?"

"Home," the man said, turning to Chris. "She went home."

Home.

"Thank you," Chris breathed, looking at each of them once more, memorizing their faces. They looked so familiar, yet he knew he had never seen them before. "Thank you."

Chris nodded and he ran back out to look for Sam.

As the doors began shut, the four disciples started to disappear, and a whispered sentence could be heard on the wind.

"Good luck, boy with the loaves and fishes."

SAM

I t was pure fate that Sam was in the hall for the feast when Augustus declared war on humanity.

He watched as Clair lost it. Something had happened on that mission, something bad, and Sam knew that Augustus had planned all of this, had known that this was going to happen. He knew Clair would come back enraged and broken.

He could not get to any of them during the chaos. He was too far back, too overrun trying to stop some of the angels from going after Clair. After she disappeared and Chris ran out, Sam walked up to Augustus in the hall.

Augustus nonchalantly sipped his 1841 Veuve Clicquot champagne as if the seraph on earth had not just threatened his life, as if most of his angels were not running from him. As if the Covenant was not crumbling.

"Ah, Sam," Augustus said, all pretenses gone. "Come to finally say your piece?"

Sam punched Augustus in the face. The crack echoed in the room and Augustus fell to his back on the floor.

"You knew, you bloody bastard, you knew this would happen!"

Augustus was laughing as blood poured from his nose, making him look all the more deranged.

"It has begun, Sam," Augustus intoned, the blood cascading from his nose into his mouth staining his teeth a violent red. "It has begun. Finally, the earth will fall, and we will rise. No more hiding in the shadows." He stood, facing the remaining angels in the room. Those who had not fled watched Augustus with a kind of fervent idolatry.

"We are no longer slaves to the shadows, my friends. Join me. Join me and we will rid the world of humans. We must strike against the mortal world – the seraph in the lead. We must strike now before we are too late!"

Sam backed away, shaking his head. "You are a fool. You cannot go against humanity. You will bring us all down with you!"

"No, Sam," Augustus said. "I have brought the devil into the world. I have brought him here to destroy everything so that it may be rebuilt."

Sam thought of Clair, of the way her eyes had glowed golden.

"Yes, Sam," Augustus said. "You know what is to come. You know what she is capable of now, what she will do with his strength guiding her."

Sam could not breathe. He bent over, willing air into his lungs. She would not become that. He would not let her. Chris would not let her.

"You cannot save her, Sam, she is lost. Join me," Augustus said as he was prowled toward Sam with a bloody hand outstretched. "Join me as we usher in the new world."

"No."

Sam ran to find Chris.

DOTTY

otty was pretty sure she had been dreaming of soft words and gentle touches.

She woke with a start when she felt Seine jump onto her stomach.

"What?" she coughed, sitting up. "What on earth?"

Seine just stared from her to her window, and back again. His large yellow eyes shone brightly in the soft light of the moon.

Dotty felt compelled. She stood, walked to the window, and looked out. It was dark, but she could make out a figure sitting on her porch.

She felt her heart squeeze.

Grabbing her robe, she ran as quickly as she could down the stairs. She threw open the front door.

Clair was sitting, her head in her hands, on the top step of the porch.

Dotty ran to her. "Clair! Oh my, Clair. What's happened, dear girl?" Dotty sat down next to her, pulling the girl into her arms. In that moment Clair seemed so small and frail that Dotty was reminded of when she was a toddler – bouncing around the property, sometimes scraping her knee or getting a splinter from one of the many trees she tried climbing.

"I'm a monster," Clair breathed, sobs wracking her body. Dotty held on tighter. They were not normally physically affectionate, but they loved each other.

This was her Clair, her granddaughter. There was nothing she could do that would push Dotty away.

"Oh, Clair, I am sure it –"

"I killed him," she whispered, freezing in Dotty's arms. "I killed him. I didn't even hesitate for a second. I just –"

Clair turned her reddened eyes to Dotty, they glowed softly in the moons light, almost like Seine's. Clair was thrumming with sobs and power – Dotty could feel it now that her shock had worn off. She could feel immense power emanating from Clair. Out of the corner of her eye, she watched as the roses she planted only last week began to grow, quickly becoming bushes with buds and then flowering right before her eyes.

Dotty turned her full attention on Clair.

"Clair," she said, "It's going to be okay. Whatever happened at the Covenant, it's going to be okay."

"It wasn't at the Covenant," Clair said, tears streaming down her face. "It was the mission. Augustus knew what was coming… Augustus knew he was there. He sent me there to find him, he knew what I would have to do, what I would become. He couldn't get in. It had to be me."

"He couldn't get in? Who did he send you to find, Clair?"

"Elijah," Clair breathed.

"Elijah?" Dotty whispered. She felt lightheaded. "You found Elijah?"

Clair nodded.

Dotty took a deep breath, turning her face toward the moon. Her son. After all this time. He was alive…

She turned back to Clair.

"I killed him."

Dotty stopped breathing.

"My own father. I killed him. One second, we were talking, and the next…"

Clair stood so abruptly that Dotty fell back onto her hands, breath seizing into her lungs, splinters digging into her palms. Clair began pacing back and forth. "He was just there. He had created this space for himself, where angels couldn't get in. He'd trapped men in there with him, while time sped by outside – it was like being in Eden, it was going by so fast. He was just there the whole time – not dead, not hurt, not *gone* like James. He was there, Dotty!"

Clair screamed, pulling at her hair, and some of the power flowing from her snaked up the closest tree, aging it, killing it. Its branches began to snap and fall. Dead.

Elijah was dead.

Dotty brought her hands to her face. They were bleeding. She got blood on her face. Small rivulets ran from her fine wrinkles onto the porch.

Elijah was dead.

Her son was dead.

Clair had killed him.

Clair had killed her father.

Clair was not paying attention to Dotty, she just kept talking. About the dome, about how she was part-human so she could get in, about the men guarding the entrance. About a bleeding heart. About Elijah. Unapologetic Elijah who had confirmed that he had killed his own wife. Sweet Hannah who had wanted to come to Dotty for help, who did not want to go to the Covenant, who was okay with Clair being an angel. Clair ranted that Elijah was going to wait until the world ended.

He was waiting for the world to end.

He did not want to come back for either of them.

He would not come back for either of them.

And Clair…

"I was so angry," she continued. "I was so angry. I saw this beautiful little bunker he had created for himself, willing to just wait everyone out. Willing to just watch the world burn. Willing to choose himself. He chose himself. Even when I was there, standing in front of him," Clair stopped moving, looking up at the moon. "Even standing in front of him, he chose himself. Said I needed to leave. Said it was too much, that I didn't understand. I lost it," she said, crumbling to her knees. "I wanted to break it – all of it. I wanted him to suffer for his choice. I wanted him to be forced to feel the consequences of his abandonment like I had my entire life."

Clair stared down into her hands. "I pulled it all into me, all of it. The dome, the sanctuary, his power."

She looked up at Dotty, haunted. "I pulled his power from him. All of it. It came to me, willingly, like it was waiting. Like it wanted to be free of him. I didn't even know it was possible, I just wanted him to suffer and…"

He was dead.

"And I'm…I'm sad for you, Grandma. And I feel dreadful for the pain this must be causing you…" her face hardened, nothing of the girl Dotty had raised left in her eyes. "But I'm not sorry he's dead. I'm not sorry he's gone. He didn't deserve it, any of it – or us. He chose wrong."

They stared at each other, the silence deafening.

"It's…" Dotty cleared her throat. "I'm glad you're okay, Clair," she said, speaking the only truth she had in the moment.

Clair closed her eyes and Dotty watched her entire body deflate. When she opened them again, Clair looked like she had aged a century, like she was shouldering all the weight of the world.

They stared at each other for what could have been a couple more minutes or a couple lifetimes, both lost in their own thoughts, before Clair stood and said she was going to take a shower.

Dotty heard the door shut. She looked back down at her palms.

They were no longer bleeding. Clair must have healed her, without even thinking about it.

She wiped the leftover blood onto her robe, stood from the porch, and walked into the antique shop.

She sat down at her desk in the corner of the shop, the one she rarely used, and opened a locked drawer in the bottom right cabinet.

From the cabinet, she pulled out a small photo album.

She opened that album and cried.

She cried for the baby she had birthed, the baby she had raised. She cried for the boy who had been so special, so enchanting. She cried for the man he had become, and the man he could have been. She cried for her husband, for the family that never was supposed to be.

Finally, she cried for her granddaughter. For all the things she had done, and all that she had yet to do.

Dotty cried for all of them.

Then, she shut the album, locked it up, and went back upstairs.

SAM

T

That was Dotty," Sam said, pocketing his phone. "She said Clair arrived at the house late last night."

Sam looked over at Chris who remained unresponsive. He had not spoken since they left the Covenant. They were sitting in a Russian airport, waiting for the flight back to California that Sam had booked on his credit card. He looked out over the angels who were coming with them, grateful he had amassed so much money over the years. Kioko, who like Chris had been silent during the entire rush to the airport. A couple other middle order angels he did not know. Almost ten minor angels, all of whom had followed Chris when the pandemonium ensued. Erik, the tech guru who Sam was sure would be worth his weight in salt over these next few…days? Weeks? It could be months. Years even.

Sam looked down the barrel of infinity, surrounded by angels, pushed into a situation he did not want.

No matter what he wanted, they needed him.

They were all so green.

"Flight is on time," Kioko said, flopping into the seat next to him.

"That is one good piece of information," Sam retorted, watching Chris slip his headphones into his ears, ignoring both of them.

Kioko glanced across at Chris before turning back to Sam.

"What can we expect when we get to your base?"

"It's not a base, it's a home," Sam corrected, running a hand through his hair. It was getting too long. He needed to cut it. He barked out a laugh. Kioko raised a brow at him. "I was just thinking I need a haircut."

She cocked her head. "Yeah, you do."

"I have not had any time to think about such simple things and I probably will not even have time for it when we get home. What a time to even be thinking about something so hideously inane."

Kioko took a deep breath, scanning the airport. "There's never enough time, Sam. You just have to make it."

He leaned over, resting his head in his hands, knowing she was keeping a lookout for danger.

"I was so close," Sam said, rubbing his face. Kioko remained silent, waiting for him to go on. "I was so close to being done. I thought getting Chris back, training Clair, would be it for me. Then there was the Covenant and Augustus. He had planned this mission from the very beginning," Sam said, sitting up and crossing his legs, outwardly composing himself though internally he was perhaps the messiest he had ever felt. "He knew what would happen to her, whatever it was. He knew she would snap."

They both paused in reflection. Each had a long history with Augustus. They may know him better than anyone in the world.

"Whatever happened," Chris piped up across from them, "we'll make him pay for it."

Sam swallowed and Kioko grinned.

"That," she said, "is a promise I can keep."

CHRIS

The Covenant was in chaos.

Clair had disappeared after the fight with Augustus. Many of the angels were abandoning ship, no longer believing in the mission, in Augustus. Some saw his choice as the right step. Bringing down the human race would pave the way for angels to rule earth.

Zealots. All of them.

The rest were scattering.

Kioko and Erik had decided to join Chris and Sam back in the states.

Sam, even though he hated the idea, was going to establish a base there for any who wanted shelter.

Clair had destroyed most of the technology in the Covenant before she left, immobilizing them until they could be fixed or replaced. Without Erik, their recovery would surely be even slower.

It did not give them too much of a lead, since they were going to be operating with less resources and personnel, but it would give them a head start to get established before Augustus and his crew came after them.

Chris resented bringing the fight back to Healdsburg. Healdsburg was his home, Clair's home. If they had a future together, that is where Chris had always envisioned it.

Sam was seated beside him on the plane in coach. It was very different from the posh jet the Covenant had sent to pick them up in Argentina.

Sam's eyes were closed but Chris knew he was not sleeping.

Chris wanted to scream, "Why? Why would Augustus do all this? Why would Clair kill her own father? Why even send her there in the first place? What was the point of it all?"

But he knew. He knew why Augustus did what he did, and as for Clair…

He could imagine her shock, he could imagine her pain, but never would he have thought she could kill an innocent. That human guarding the door. She had been so ruthless. So out of control.

Kioko had ranted ferociously the whole trip back to the Covenant, screaming about losses and human life and cover-ups, but mostly about control.

Kioko did not think Clair was stable. A bomb waiting to go off, she had said. Chris suspected part of the reason she was coming with them was to monitor Clair.

Kioko thought Augustus was a threat, but that Clair was the real problem.

"She's either an asset or a liability, Chris," Kioko had said. It was clear Kioko felt she was the latter.

But this was Clair, his Clair. He would never make assumptions about her, about what happened… He needed to hear it from her.

As Chris ran through every possible scenario for what could have happened, he clung to the hope that Clair was okay. That they were okay.

DOTTY

When the full moon finally rolled around, Dotty was more than ready to be alone.

The Covenant refugees had taken up every available space in her house, and even though she knew it was the right thing to do, she missed having her own space. She was feeling her age more and more these days.

Especially since Clair returned.

Clair was broken. Dotty could see the trauma in her eyes. A trauma like the one Clair had barely survived in high school, when that religious group had taken everything from her. Her poor granddaughter had been, ages later, traumatized by yet another zealot.

In some ways, Dorthea was grateful that Clair was as powerful as she was, that she could protect herself.

Even though…

Dotty paused in her walking, forcibly stopping the tears from coming. It was done. It was not right, but neither was what her son had done to the three most important women in his life.

Dotty refused to process it.

It was too much and wallowing in her grief would not make a difference. She knew better than most that you cannot change the past, as much as you may wish for a different outcome. Those who were gone, were gone. There was no going back.

Dotty continued walking to the spot where she would be meeting Jean for the ritual.

She had thought about inviting Emily. The young woman was doing well in her training. Emily had been introduced to the new angels, but she was keeping Mike away from them. She was still practicing, progressing in her training much faster than Dotty had anticipated. She had a lust for the magic – the knowledge. Dorthea chuckled a bit to herself as she walked. She had definitely motivated Emily to strive for greatness.

It had not been an empty threat.

She would have erased her memories.

Dotty sighed.

She truly had wavered about bringing Emily, about asking Jean if she could come. She wanted to tell Jean about Emily, but Dotty needed something right now that was only hers. It might be childish, but she had the right to be selfish. She was being selfless enough allowing her home to be invaded by angels in her time of grief.

"Dorthea," called a perky voice. Dotty spotted Jean at the entrance to the trail. "Welcome, welcome. Glad you could make it."

"Of course," Dotty said, gesturing to the basket in her hand. "I brought the supplies you suggested."

"Oh, wonderful!" Jean was wearing a simple tufted long-sleeved jacket and loose-fitting pants. "The rest of the girls are already there. I wanted to wait for you. I am glad you came."

"Me, too," Dotty said sincerely. "I haven't ever done a full moon ritual."

"Really?" Jean seemed genuinely surprised. She gestured to the trail, and they began walking. "No matter, it's all very simple."

"Oh?"

"Yes," Jean said, hoisting her own basket higher on her arm. "The New Moon is for manifesting our desires and wishes. A Full Moon is for releasing what doesn't serve us. Be it emotional, mental, or something physical. It's a time to release our emotions into the earth and let go."

Dotty considered this. "I think this will be exactly what I need."

"We all need it, once a month, like clockwork," Jean said, chuckling. "I haven't had my menses in years, but it feels a lot like that. Like a necessary and biological purging of the spirit."

Dotty watched the ground as she walked, being careful not to trip, and thinking about what Jean said.

They reached the group in no time. There were five other women gathered who Dotty thought she may have seen around town at some point or another, but who she did not know. They all seemed to know her though.

"I've seen you walking before," one said.

"Been to your shop," said another.

Dotty did her best to be social, friendly. She was surprised at being so known in the town. She thought of herself as a person who faded into the background, a recluse. These women knew her, looked for her. She felt seen. Not as Clair's grandmother, but as Dorthea.

It had been a long time since she felt seen.

They formed a circle on the cold ground, lighting the candles they had brought, and placing them on either side of their knees as they sat cross legged.

To her surprise, Jean led them.

"Welcome, all," she said. "It's so good to see so many returning faces, and some new ones." She nodded to Dotty, a smile on her face. "We are not a coven of many words, especially tonight. Tonight, we have come to think, to search our souls and see what no longer serves us. To let go."

Dotty took a deep breath.

"Let us begin with a few moments of silence. Look at the moon, search your hearts. When you are ready to let go, give it to the moon. She does not judge."

Dotty looked up at the moon through the trees. It was full and bright, no cloud cover. Dotty let her mind wander and then empty.

As she stared at the moon, she felt thankful for the first time in a long time. Thankful that for some strange reason, looking at the moon seemed to ease her mind and her heart. It was such a striking moment of reprieve from all the chaos and emotions coursing through her, that she felt herself begin to cry.

She cried for her son, for her husband, for Clair, and for Clair's mother. She cried for the angels, broken and confused, in her house.

She cried for Sam, who had spent too many years searching for something he had yet to find. She cried for herself. For her trials and tribulations. She cried for her heart, which felt as if it had been tested beyond her limits. She cried for the future she could so clearly see reflected in the heart of the moon. She cried for the end of the story she felt coming soon.

As the tears flowed in gentle streams down her cheeks, Dotty stared at the moon and let all her emotions and heartbreak flow from her.

Dotty gave them to the moon.

The moon received them.

SAM

Sam was officially put in charge.

The angels had convened in the antique store. They referred to themselves as the New Covenant. Kioko had spoken first and loudest. She asserted that because Sam was the oldest angel among them – despite whatever classification or ranking the Covenant may have assigned him – and because he was funding their endeavors, that he should be in charge.

Unfortunately for him, no one objected.

"Alright," Sam said. "Erik, what have you found?"

Erik stepped forward, placing a laptop on the old pool table they were using as a command center. "So far, not much. There have been some blips of activity near the original base, but nothing huge. No news outlets are reporting any major shifts among any of Augustus' contacts, religious or political. I was able to hack into the old minor angel tracking system, and offload it onto a new secure server, so we have access to that."

Erik flipped the laptop around so everyone could see. The screen displayed a digital map of the world. Every few seconds, a red dot would randomly appear. "Those red dots represent the minor angels popping into existence," Erik said. "And as far as I can tell, no one is assisting them."

"They're just going into their new lives blind?" Kioko asked, her arms crossed over her chest as she learned against a nearby bookshelf.

"Essentially, yes," Erik said, cringing as some of the minor angels in the room began talking with each other. Most minor angels were located by the Covenant when they popped into existence. They would wake to find brief instructions, a passport, and a little money left for them by the Covenant. The new minor angels popping up on the screen had nothing. No information, no identities, no support.

"Okay," Sam said. "This seems dire, but before the Covenant started doing this – for example, when I popped into existence – we figured it out."

"No offense, Sam, but you appeared during the High Middle Ages and things are completely different now," Erik said. "Sorry, but it's true. Modern tracking technology is has wildly changed things from the olden days. A bunch of random people starting to pop up with no identity and no memories is going to catch the eye of some government agency."

Sam sighed and pinched the bridge of his nose between his thumb and forefinger. "Okay, so is helping minor angels our first priority, or finding Augustus and trying to stop him?"

"Augustus," Kioko said, venom dripping from her words. "He has to be the priority. We take him out and the rest of the zealots will back down. There will be no one else to follow. Then we can fully retake the Covenant."

"But," one of the minor angels spoke up. "Those poor angels. Shouldn't we divide our efforts?"

"We're already divided!" Kioko shouted. "Look at us. We're a veritable ragtag fringe group at this point. We barely have the equipment to go after Augustus. We can't go traipsing all over the world trying to save random angels. Sam might be rich, but he's not limitless."

"True," Emily said, somewhere on Sam's right. In truth, he had forgotten she was in the room until she came to stand next to him. She pointed to the screen where a new dot had shown up. "What if we just focus on our state for now? We still prioritize Augustus, but we utilize our resources locally for those we can help."

Kioko immediately taken a liking to Emily, which Sam thought was interesting. She stared at the girl, before nodding. "I agree, that could work."

"I have relationships with various angels all across the world," Sam said, shocking some of the people in the room. "Not all of them will want to help, of course, but some will."

Kioko sighed, Emily watched the little red lights flick on, and some of the minor angels discussed what the new angels would need.

"Now," Sam said, changing gears. "How do we go about finding him?"

"So, we're doing this again?" Clair stepped into the room and Sam felt his hackles rise. Ever since destroying her father, Clair's power loomed like a black hole around her – infinite, endless, and consuming. He could feel it whenever she was around, compounded with the attitude he could no longer stomach. Sam was not afraid of Clair, but the same could not be said for the minor angels who he watched scurry out of her path.

"We're doing this planning thing again? We've already done this before. Remember Eve? Aren't we over going round and round doing the same things? Let him go," Clair said. She turned to face Emily and extended a finger in her face. "And *you* need to stay out of this. This is their problem. They chose this. You're going to get yourself killed."

"Clair," Emily admonished, standing to her full height. "The last time we made plans like this, it was to protect *all of us* from Eve. We made a good team. You and Chris made your own plans to run off without us, leaving us completely in the dark. I remember how that ended with you going missing for seven months and Chris joining the Covenant. This time, we are fighting this fight *together*. This isn't just their or your fight. Augustus wants to erase humanity. That's me. That's Mike. That's Dotty. We can't just do nothing."

"Where is Mike?" Clair asked cuttingly, watching the blush creep up Emily's face. "Oh, yeah. That's right. You let know about magic but not enough to help you plan. No worries, though, you have Sam to be your angelic partner." Clair glanced between Emily and Sam, and Sam felt his own neck grow hot. Nothing was going on between them. Nothing would ever go on between them, but the insinuation was clear, and Clair had just put a target on them in front of the other angels.

Clair sighed and turned for the door.

"Fine, do what you want. But Chris goes nowhere without me."

With that, she strutted from the room, slamming the door behind her.

EMILY

mily went home to the apartment she now shared with Mike that night and told him everything. She told him about Clair coming back and the angels at the antique shop.

She warned him about Clair and how volatile she had become. She made him promise to get involved with magic with her. She was already working on his own pendant like the one Dotty taught her to make for herself.

The night was crisp but bearable. Emily stood on the porch of the Brown Bear, staring at the forest. Mike had gone inside to make them both hot chocolate and Emily could not stop the tears that began tracking down her face.

Clair would never be the same. The mission had fundamentally changed her. Clair had come home fueled by boundless rage. Emily missed her friend and wondered if her friend would ever really come home from that mission.

Emily remembered the terror of Eve. The first time she really fully understood the danger of being connected to magic. She remembered the long hours she had sacrificed researching. She had never been so tired… until now. Though she didn't regret her decision, sometimes the reality of the situation would hit her. The gravity of her choice to be involved, to get Mike involved. The painful memories…

"Em?" Mike came up behind her. She recognized the familiar rhythm of his feet hitting the ground, as familiar to her as her own steps.

She turned to him.

"Are you okay?"

He looked concerned. He was always concerned now. Concerned for her, never himself. He had been great. He was planning on helping the angels to fight a war they both had no real place in, but he did not know.

He must have seen something in her eyes because he waited, watching her. He knew she had something to say, something important. She could feel the weight of the words she had held back for too long thickening the air between them. She could not let him continue without knowing. He deserved to know. She just wished she did not have to be the one to tell him.

"There's something I need to tell you," she said, stepping closer to him. Wondering whether this would be the last straw for him – the final thing to break them. The final burden she would place upon his life and his mental health.

Emily took a deep breath.

"I need to tell you about Joe."

CLAIR

lair was crying.

The tears flowed down her cheeks, dripping onto the earth, becoming rivers set to drown the world. She could not stop, even as the world began to drown in her sorrow.

Even as she watched it all die.

She wished she could drown with them.

She watched as they were all washed away…

It was just a dream.

SAM

Sam read the text from Emily.

Sam, please come over this evening. We need to talk.

He was getting used to texting. It definitely had its uses – simpler than a call, faster than an email. Certainly faster than a pigeon, although he missed the sounds they made. All the cooing and feather ruffling. They were always so fat and round. He had never seen a scrawny pigeon.

Those animals know how to survive.

Texts were much less informative than a telephone call. There was no inflection, no ease with which to hear emotion in the words. Sure, there were emojis and punctuation, but Sam kept running his hand through his hair all morning, wondering what it was that Emily needed to talk with him about.

It might be about Clair. Everything seemed to be revolving around Clair, or the disbandment of the Covenant, or some sort of business around saving the angels of whom he had found himself the main beneficiary. But if it was that, she would have just come to the antique shop. Instead, he was walking toward her apartment over the Brown Bear.

As he walked, he ruminated.

Emily was different. She was not...

She did not *need* him like everyone else.

Especially not since she had begun her studies of magic with Dotty. Emily was a force to be reckoned with.

He arrived at her home that evening, the apartment she now shared with her fiancé, Mike. Sam wondered if Mike would be home. Sam knew Mike knew about the angels and about magic, but Sam had never met the man.

He knocked.

A man answered the door. Tall, almost Sam's height, with blue eyes and dirty-blonde hair that was cropped short. He was muscular, with thick arms and thighs and a tapered waist. Mike was as beautiful as he was masculine.

"Hello," Sam said, extending his hand. "I'm Sam."

"Mike," the man said, taking Sam's hand and issuing a perfect handshake. Not too hard, not too soft, not too limp, and not sweaty. No callouses, but rough. "Thank you for coming."

"Of course," Sam said, linking his hands behind his back. He found himself a bit nervous. "Emily invited me, she did not give a reason."

"Oh," Mike said, rubbing the back of his head and glancing behind him. "She actually didn't invite you. I did."

Sam felt his eyebrows climb onto his forehead. "Oh?"

"I stole her phone," Mike said, no remorse in his voice. He stepped closer to Sam, invading his personal space. Sam could smell bergamot and cloves and feel the heat radiating from his body before Mike turned to close the front door. "I'd actually like us to head to the Brown Bear. I've closed it for the night."

He did not wait for Sam to respond. He began walking around the building, expecting Sam to follow. For a human who was aware of Sam's powers, he was mildly impressed with Mike's gusto.

Sam followed.

Sam had been in the Brown Bear on many occasions, but without its patrons it felt eerily empty.

"I don't like it like this," Mike remarked, going behind the bar and gesturing to a seat in front. "Quiet. Cold."

Sam sat in one of the chairs in front of where Mike was standing, and admired the bar top. He loved the wood frozen beneath the veneer. Mike bent down and opened a cabinet in the bar before pulling out an unlabeled glass bottle with amber liquid.

"Joe made this," Mike said, procuring two glasses. "The last batch. It's like moonshine, but stronger somehow." He chuckled, the sound somehow both playful and deep.

"I did not know your uncle," Sam said. "But from what Clair said, he was a good man."

"Yes," Mike said, glancing at Sam and uncorking the bottle. "He was better to me than I deserved."

"He would be proud of you," Sam said. He could smell the liquid already, a pungent biting scent filling his nose. It was definitely strong. He looked back up at Mike, who was staring at him. "What?"

"No one's ever said that to me before," Mike said. "Of course, Emily has said it loads of times, but she's always seen the best in me. But my family, even after everything I have done and all the steps I have taken to get here, will always see me as a good-for-nothing cocaine junkie."

Sam stared back.

"People…" Sam started, taking a deep breath. "People do not like change. Even good change. They do not like not knowing what to expect from someone. Even if that person changes or grows into something better, when they cannot predict that person anymore or control them, it… scares them. Because it means that they, too, need to look at themselves, and doing that would require work. Change may require sacrifice, and most people are not ready to sacrifice what is necessary for what is right."

Mike inhaled slowly and poured Sam a glass, then filled his own with water from a procured decanter.

"I can see why Emily is in love with you."

Sam choked on air and exclaimed, "What?"

"She's in love with you," Mike said calmly, placing the glass in front of Sam and taking a sip of his own. "Hell, I'm half in love with you already and we've barely been in each other's presence for ten minutes."

Mike chuckled at the look on Sam's face. "Don't look so shocked. You can't tell me that in your long life you've never been with a man before?"

Sam felt his cheeks grow warm with something that felt oddly like embarrassment. Mike laughed. "Anyways, I thought it would be good for us to spend some time together."

Sam was speechless. He shook his head.

"I—" he looked at Mike. "I am not in love with her."

"No," Mike said, leaning onto the bar. "But you could be, if you ever set aside your self-imposed unhappiness."

Sam felt his mouth pop open. "I do not–"

"Look," Mike cut in. "That's not why I brought you here. Well, not all about why I brought you here. Why don't you sit back down?"

Sam blinked, he had not realized he was standing, and sat on the stool.

"I want to talk about Joe."

"What about him?"

"I know about what happened to him."

Sam felt like he had been blindsided again. This did not happen to him often, and certainly not in such rapid succession.

"You know about Joe?"

"Yes," Mike said, pouring him another round of the moonshine. "Emily told me what happened with Eve."

"Good lord," Sam said, resting his hand in his head. "How many humans are we going to bring into this?"

"Apparently, one more." Mike had a cocky smile on his face, showing a dimple on his cheek.

"So she really brought you all in?"

"Yep," Mike said, sipping his water. "I have heard about it all now. Everything that happened with Eve, Chris, the Covenant. How you have established an angel base here. I'm in."

Sam watched Mike touch a pendant around his neck that looked suspiciously like the one Emily always wore. He picked up his glass and downed it. Mike poured him another.

They sat in silence, each sipping their drinks.

"So. You are in." Sam said, staring into the other man's eyes. "Just like that? You believe all of this and you are just in?"

Mike sighed.

"Sam," he said, placing the glass down onto the bar and standing straight. "I'm an addict. Falling all-in quickly is part of my personality."

Sam scoffed, eyeing him. He raised his glass. "To being all in."

"To being all in," Mike parroted, clinking his glass.

Things just got even more interesting. Sam wondered how after eight centuries of life, this period had turned out to be the one where the surprises never stopped.

EMILY

Clair was not the same.

Ever since that mission, meeting and subsequently assassinating her father, Clair was a ghost of her former self. Emily tried to coax the old Clair back out. Tried to fill at least some of their time with normal, everyday things. Movies, popcorn, painting their nails, giving her a haircut. Anything to try to break through to the woman she once knew.

Emily blamed the Covenant for the person Clair was now – this dark, scabbed soul constantly lashing out at anyone but Chris.

As the days went on, any mention of the Covenant fired poison directly into Emily's veins, fueling her hatred into one solid, pointed edge – a knife she yearned to plunge into the heart of Augustus.

Emily liked the new angels and the new group they were building. She felt like it was not just them against the world, operating in a bubble apart from everything else. The world had stepped in to meet them and they were rolling with it. She enjoyed being a part of it all with Mike right alongside her. She was not sure what had transpired between him and Sam, but they had both shown up together one day and Mike kept showing up after that.

She also hated it. She hated that it needed to exist at all.

"Exactly," Clair said, and Emily startled so hard that the coffee she was drinking spilled out over the edge of her cup and onto the maps below. Sam and Mike both looked up at Clair.

"Clair! When did you get here?" Emily asked, grabbing a nearby towel and starting to sop up the mess.

"I didn't see her come in," Mike said, eyeing Clair like one might a wild bear that crept into the house.

"I was agreeing with you," Clair said, cocking her head at the maps in a disinterested way. "It shouldn't exist."

Mike looked at Emily, and Sam gave Clair a questioning look.

"I didn't…" Emily looked at Clair, whose eyes were still perusing the maps. "I didn't say that out loud."

"Didn't have to," Clair said, tapping her finger twice on the side of her head. "You thought it so loud I heard you loud and clear." Clair folded her arms across her chest and leaned against the table, facing Emily and ignoring Sam and Mike. "And I agree. None of this should exist. It's all just some game that we can't win."

Emily stared at her friend. "I don't think that God is playing a game."

"No?" Clair seethed. Emily realized that she had yet to see Clair blink. "What if he asked you to kill Mike?" Clair spat, her eyes growing dark. Emily felt as if she was being judged and weighed and found lacking. "Do you think any of this matters to anyone other than us? Do you truly think the Ultimate Powers give one shit about us?"

The way Clair so casually mentioned killing Mike made Emily snap.

"God's not asking us to do anything right now!" Emily yelled, getting in Clair's face, refusing to back down. If Sam taught her anything, it was never to cower in front of a predator. "In fact, I don't even think He's asking us to convert the world. I don't even know for sure the Catholic God is the only god - but Clair, I mean, you're a freaking angel, how can you not believe?"

"Am I? Am I an angel?" she scoffed, closing her eyes and stepping back. "Or am I something we don't fully understand?" Clair opened her eyes, looking off into the distance at nothing. "I feel the oppressive weight of time and responsibility pressing upon my shoulders today."

"We don't know for sure what we are," Sam interrupted, walking around the table to stand next to Emily. She felt her body relax. She could almost feel the power he was amassing in case he needed to use it. Against Clair. How had they gotten this far from what they were? "But that isn't as important as what we *do*, Clair," he said, willing her to understand.

Clair glared at them both, eyes flitting over one and then the other before she turned back around and began walking toward the door. "None of it has any meaning, Sam. You of all people should know that."

"Clair!" Emily admonished. "What the hell is wrong with you today?"

"What's wrong with me?" Clair turned back around, eyes beginning to glow with barely suppressed power. "What's wrong with me is that we are trying to rebuild something that's just going to fall apart again anyways. The Covenant is gone. It's done. Augustus is lost – hopefully dead. Why try to organize a bunch of angels that have no business being organized in the first place? Maybe the world is better off without us." She started walking away again.

"Clair, you don't mean that," Emily said. "Look at all the good things that have happened. Look at all the *magic*."

Clair sighed and turned around once more. When she looked up, Emily could see the weight of kings in her eyes. The Clair she had known before the Covenant was gone. In her place was a hollow creature full of pain and envy and hate.

"You're playing with magic. I *am* magic."

CLAIR

lair was sitting alone in the dense forest basin again.

This had become her spot to think. To wait. To ruminate on her power, grief, and guilt.

Guilt?

Clair looked up and spotted the wrinkled old man approaching her in the forest. He leaned heavily on a cane, each step requiring enormous effort. She narrowed her eyes.

"Not the type of soul you usually like to inhabit," she said, scoffing and returning her gaze to the trees. She almost missed the Gate. It would be nice if that unhinged Eve could make an appearance and rid her of this constant pest.

The old man laughed, plopping next to her on the ground with a grunt. She could hear his bones creak with the effort it took. She imagined his bony butt being pricked by the rocks, and it made her smile.

"There she is," the Ultimate Evil said, turning his yellowing teeth in her direction. "How was your trip?"

"Fuck off," she said, picking up a rock and tossing it into the trees.

"Testy today, I see," it said, cracking its neck. "Where is your little angel helper? He tends to make you less cranky."

"Working, with the rest of them."

"Ah," it said, taking a deep breath. "Seems our Samuel has taken in more strays. Typical of him."

"Actually, I think it's very atypical of him," she said, turning to face it. "Was this your goal all along?" she asked, sighing heavily. "Setting me up to dismantle the Covenant?"

It chuckled, looking out at the trees for a moment before turning back to her.

"Look at these hands," it said, gently touching her fingers with its withered ones. They were surprisingly warm. She had expected nothing less than stark cold from the Ultimate Evil. "These hands have power. They hold the opportunity to embrace or to inflict pain. What the owner chooses to do with them is entirely up to them. The hands – they are simply the tool."

Clair looked up into its golden eyes which would remain as long as it possessed the body. "So, that's it. I am merely a tool to you. To all of you." She did not need any of them. She did not need Sam, Augustus, or any of the angels. She had come so far since Eden that she felt limitless. If she had Chris in her orbit, she could do anything.

"What am I but a tool in any religion's hands?" it said, looking into her eyes. "But tell me," it continued. It loved to talk. "Which is scarier— a mythological creature roaming the earth doing evil, or the idea that every single person out there has two voices warring in their heads, and sometimes," it touched the tip of a finger to its temple and twisted it like a knife, "the bad voice wins?"

"Oh please," she said, for once feeling on even ground with it. "I've had worse problems than you." She gestured around them where Eve had attacked her.

It continued, "The Bard once wrote, 'All the world's a stage, and all the men and women merely players. They have their exits and their entrances; And one man in his time plays many parts.' You have played many parts, Clair, but this may not be your final stage. Eve was the least of your problems," it said.

"My problems will never stop finding me. They started – this all started – that fateful night years ago. The night a sad girl climbed into a tub and invited the water to smother her. The night I first started hearing voices. That voice led me to fight, led me to glory and power beyond belief. Now, I have ascended to greatness. I am the most powerful being one can see on this earth." Clair considered what it had said. "Are you suggesting there is more than one world?"

The Ultimate Evil picked a small yellow flower from the ground, twirled it between its fingers, and popped it into its mouth. Clair cringed.

"I'm saying that if someone enjoys doing something, they rarely stop after doing it just once," it said. "I have potential everywhere. Every human on this earth can be moved to madness, to evil with a single thought." It touched a finger to its temple.

Clair observed it disdainfully, her heart unmoved.

"You were raised thinking that like yin to yang, there must always be balance. Where there are angels, there must be demons." The evil stood, much too fast for the body he inhabited, the bones screamed with the exertion. It turned, arms thrown into the air as it laughed. "Oh, Clair. I don't need demons. I am the ultimate master of the mind. I am the motivation of demonic thought." It turned to face her, "I am unending."

She watched the old man dance through the field where the Gate had once stood. She heard the bones breaking with each step, yet it did not stop. It did not slow. It did not feel.

"So much more damage can be done by a single thought than any good deed," it exalted, a haunting sound amid the snapping of twigs and bones. "Most people dismiss their intrusive thoughts as simple lapses in their brains, but simple has nothing to do with it. That thought was a spark, and if fanned and fed properly, that spark can burn into a triumphant flame." The Ultimate Evil turned to face her.

"That is why humans are so important to what I am."

"And what are you?" Clair asked.

He stared at her. "Fear."

Clair narrowed her eyes.

"You are my flame, Clair, and I intend to let you loose on the world. But," it continued, hobbling beside her her and placing a hand on top of hear head. "I can't allow you to remember this conversation."

Clair looked out at the empty field. It was wonderfully quiet. She took a deep breath, enjoying the solitude.

When she stood to leave, she noticed blood on some of the twigs around where she had been sitting, and wondered what poor animal had died here.

EMILY

"You don't think that he would?" Clair demanded.

All they did was argue.

Emily was styling Clair's hair. With all the chaos of establishing a new base for the angels, this was the only opportunity they had to spend time together, just the two of them, anymore. Emily refused to call it the New Covenant because that original had caused too much suffering for people she cared deeply about. Not to mention, the remaining loyalists were out there wreaking havoc on the world as they spoke, releasing demons in droves on every continent.

If Emily had not trained so determinedly with Dotty to learn to protect herself, she would be freaking out right now.

The number of minor angels appearing and having no help except what they can figure out for themselves must be in the thousands by now. Humans were noticing a spike in homelessness, but not connecting that those people were actually stranded angels.

It was a giant mess.

A mess Sam was trying to clean up.

Emily still could not believe they were all working together. Mike being brought in was both wonderful and terrifying – her two worlds colliding. She loved watching him work with the angels and working with him to help solve problems neither of them could have conceived of mere months ago. Mike was entranced with it all. It shocked her, but why should he not be? It was magic, plain and simple, and they were the two lucky humans who got to be a part of it.

Emily tuned back into Clair.

"What do you mean?"

"Don't you think that if you and Mike have a kid," Emily immediately pulled back the scissors before she accidentally snipped something vital. A kid? What? "And one of the Ultimates wanted to use you to some end, and getting rid of that child would get you to where you *need* to be, he would do it? We're all just pawns in the games the Ultimates are playing."

Emily missed the old Clair.

Emily had hoped it might just be a phase, that Clair needed time to work through what had happened. When Clair told her the story of finding her father, of what he had said, of how he had chosen to free himself from any responsibility, Emily had rallied around Clair. She had lamented the father Clair deserved, a parent with unconditional love for their child, not just himself.

They had cried together, drank, and shared stories. They had discussed the future they wanted to have, what they could become. They had reconnected.

Even after all that, Clair just was not the same. She was not working through it. She was deteriorating.

Jaded. Withdrawn.

It was like looking at a mountain you had always seen in the sunlight suddenly always darkened by cloud-cover.

If Emily was being honest, watching her interact with Sam lately, Clair scared her. She doubted Clair would ever be the same again.

None of them would.

"You think that the Ultimate Good, or God, in my opinion, would sacrifice my hypothetical child if he needed to in order to get me where he needed me to be?"

Clair stared at Emily's reflection in the large salon mirror, her light green eyes hollow. "Yes."

Emily resumed her task. She did not know if she agreed with Clair. The God of the Bible she had been raised with was both loving and vindictive. Emily would never consider herself devout – she was currently living in sin with her fiancé, after all. She thought of herself a Catholic "CEO" – a member of the flock who made appearances at Christmas and Easter Only.

She also believed in free will, that everyone had the ability to make choices in their lives and that the course of human lives were not preordained by a higher power.

She was thrown when she considered the role of fate, though. When she thought about how she, Clair, Dotty, Mike, Sam, and Chris had ended up together… If she had not chosen step up for her family instead of just helping herself, she never would have run into Clair that day at the Brown Bear. She never would have encountered angels, magic, or hope. Was this destiny or was this her reward?

Emily was not sure.

"I don't know, Clair," she said. "Part of me thinks you might be right. That whoever is pulling the strings of fate would choose whatever they needed to get to the outcome they desired…"

Clair nodded.

Emily continued. "But a bigger piece of me believes in choice. We make choices and those choices create outcomes. Maybe everything is just a choice."

Emily thought about her choice to learn magic with Dotty. She placed the scissors down and touched the small vial around her neck. Clair eyed it in the mirror.

Emily had asked if Clair knew what it was, since Dotty refused to tell her. Dotty only said that she needed to always wear it. When Emily made a second one for Mike and told him to do the same, Dotty had only nodded in approval.

Clair knew specifically what the vial contained, but she only said the same thing Dotty did – it was protection from magic. Powerful protection.

Emily felt the vial warm beneath her touch as Clair stared at it, and wondered how much of the magic in it was her creation, and how much had been amplified just being around all the magic that circulated among their group.

Regardless, she would take it.

She would protect what was hers and do everything in her power to help.

CLAIR

lair watched the liquid pouring into the shot glass.

Clear like water. It felt wrong that something so potent could be so clear, so clean.

It should have been murky and filled with specks of debris, marred by its source.

It was pristine. Perfect.

And deadly.

Oh, so deadly.

Clair knocked back the shot and tapped the bar for another.

She was back in that bar again, the one where she had met Cole.

Cole, who had been a pawn for the Covenant the entire time. Cole, who was still out there somewhere helping Augustus attempt to take down the world. Cole, who she had kissed before Chris returned, who she had thought she was attracted to when she thought she was moving on from Chris's dusting.

From the moment Chris arrived at the Covenant, broken and believing she had died, Clair had lost all of the anonymity Dotty had spent her life curating. Before she had even returned from Eden, the Covenant had set its traps to lay claim to her privacy and her future. Augustus had planted Cole within her reach. Another set of eyes and ears to watch and woo the potential weapon, the seraph.

Never Clair. Always the seraph.

The bartender brought her another perfectly clear shot of gin.

She stared at it, and even though she felt like they were one in the same, Clair could not help but hate the liquor. Hate that she needed it. Hate that she resembled it. Hate that it existed and then would simply cease to exist, and no one would remember.

No one would remember what had happened.

"Oh, Clair, try not to be so morbid."

Clair glanced over at the Ultimate Evil, in possession of yet another poor soul. This time it greeted her as a middle aged man, with grey at his temples and lines around his eyes. He was still handsome and fit, wearing expensive jeans and a white button-down collar dress shirt.

"Just came from work myself," the Ultimate Evil said, gesturing to the bartender. "I'll have what she's having."

The bartender nodded before walking away.

"I am not accepting any drinks from you," Clair said, sipping the shot.

"As if I would ever offer. You're buying me this drink," it said, taking the shot from the bartender and gesturing to Clair. The bartender looked from the Ultimate Evil, who stared at her expectantly, to Clair.

Clair rolled her eyes. "Put it on my tab."

"So nice of you, thanks."

"What the fuck do you even want?" She finished the shot and tapped for another. Anytime she met the Ultimate Evil was a good night to get drunk.

"I'm not here for you," it said, tapping the bar when the bartender turned to him. "I just so happened to be here and here you are. I thought you would be at home, with your little minor angel, sailing off into the sunset."

Clair snorted into the shot glass. "You know that we aren't and you know why."

"Enlighten me?" it asked, tapping for another shot. Clair was glad she had access to Sam's money now.

"Oh, you know," Clair said, leaning onto the bar and turning toward him. "Augustus is out in the world trying to bring down humanity and create an even cultier Covenant in the process."

"Ah, that," the Ultimate Evil said. It cocked its head. "So what? We both know none of that is your problem."

Clair raised her eyebrows incredulously. "Not my problem? You really think it's that simple when all my friends and family are doing nothing but working themselves into the ground to stop him and save the world?"

"No," it said, drinking two more shots before turning and eyeing the crowd. "What do you care if Augustus fails or succeeds? You can protect your own family, friends, and whoever or whatever appeals to you. You have the power now to do whatever you want. You took that power. You earned it." He turned to look into her eyes. "I think you know that. In fact, I think that's part of the reason you are here tonight and not out there planning and plotting and fighting the good fight. You know, that in the end, you can protect what's yours, and you're okay with that." He tapped the bar once more. "It's enough. Leave the rest of the world to fend for themselves."

Clair looked out at the dancers, the fog throwing light all around the bar.

He was right.

She could protect her own. Deep down, she knew that when push came to shove, she could keep everything and everyone she cared about safe.

Why did the safety of the world have to fall to her?

Her freedom, her happiness, her time, her future… She had given enough to the world. It was time the world sorted itself out.

Clair looked back at the Ultimate Evil, but it was gone.

When she returned that night, Clair found Emily sitting on her couch, a cup of tea in her hand and a book open in front of her. Seine perched contentedly on the couch next to her.

Clair sat down in one of the plush armchairs across from Emily. Seine watched her from Emily's side, his eyes flashing gold in the low light.

"How was your night?" Emily asked, glancing up from her book.

Clair felt how deeply strained things were between them.

"What are you reading?" she asked, ignoring the question.

Emily huffed, closing the book. "Another deep-dive on the magical properties of various elements. Dotty continues to push me, even though I've passed most of her tests."

Clair watched Emily gently hold the pendant hanging from the gold chain around her neck. Dorthea had her own brand of magic, separate from angelic magic, which Clair thought was irrelevant to her and had never bothered giving a second look.

"If you don't want to do it, then don't," Clair said, crossing her legs, staring at the cat. Seine always made her uneasy.

"Sure, Clair," Emily said, huffing. "It's all that simple, right? Just don't do something you don't want to do. Don't worry. Don't be concerned that an angelic war is beginning, that we can't find Augustus, that we're sure we have more enemies than friends."

Clair turned her gaze on Emily, cocking her head. She saw Emily grip the pendant tighter.

"Enemies…" Clair said, looking off into the distance. "I'm not sure the ones we think are our enemies are really our enemies."

"What is that supposed to mean?"

"It means," Clair said, looking back at Emily. "That we'll never really know what anyone's motivations are for sure." Clair looked back at Seine, feeling a headache form behind her eyes. She rubbed them.

"You're burning the candle at too many ends, Clair," Emily said, picking back up the book. "You should just be focusing on the cause. Helping Sam and Chris. Does your head hurt?"

"I've been losing time," Clair whispered, and instantly regretted it. She looked up at Emily. Concern was etched into her features. "I need you to forget that," Clair said, feeling the power rise to her. Emily's eyes widened, but as Clair began reaching for her mind, she met resistance. Clair looked at the pendant around Emily's neck.

Emily gasped and leapt to her feet, knocking the book to the floor. "You were trying to take my memories!" she exclaimed, shaking and backing away from Clair. "How dare you, Clair? How dare you!"

Emily ran from the room.

Dotty had stronger magic than Clair thought.

JUDE

There was something deeply peaceful about listening to the crickets. Something calming and meditative about the vibrations of their leathery wings reverberating around him in an unrelenting, unpredictable cacophony. A sound to soothe a troubled mind. Scientists had determined there were a few specific warnings behind the cricket's different chirps, but no one knew exactly what they were saying to each other. All Jude truly knew was the serenity that came when the cricket songs were in the air.

It was a special type of music that helped him forget that he was wandering the forest alone at night, in a twelve-year-old body. Or was he thirteen now? Yes. He was now thirteen again. His most recent set of parents had tried to throw him a surprise birthday party with his school friends. It had been such a disappointment, he was sure they would never try again.

Jude did not have any friends. He preferred it that way. It was easier to forget the constant stream of faces, names, and personalities. It was always much easier than remembering. When a soul traveled through an endless series of lifetimes – be they long or short – and remembered everything, things got messy. Lines blurred, people blurred. He did not even remember the man he first was anymore— the man considered by many to be the ultimate betrayer.

Though he started over in a new body and his new lifetimes never exceeded nineteen years, his soul had aged so many lifetimes that who he once was and who he was now were further a part that this galaxy and the next.

The crickets stopped chirping.

Jude wondered when he would stop being compelled to seek out the darkness. When he would stop feeling it hum beneath his skin like a freshly plucked guitar string.

Probably never.

There she was, sitting on a fallen tree, gazing up at the stars.

The seraph. The light-bringer. The survivor of Adam and Eve. The most powerful angel on earth. A young woman, not much older than he was now, whose destiny would either be a blip in his existence or a monsoon.

"Good evening, Clair," he said, striding over to sit next to her. She turned her head toward him, her eyes glassy.

"Jude?"

"Yes," he said, feeling the stillness of the moment. The trepidation. He knew what came next, but it was terrifying every. Single. Time.

Jude watched as her eyes bled to a deep, billowing gold. The irises glowed in the darkness like a predator with too much prey. Its eyes uplifted toward the stars and it took a deep breath.

"*Jude,*" it said, turning toward him with a malicious smile on its face. "***What brings you out into the forest this night?***"

"Oh, you know," Jude said, leaning back against the log, his palms scraping against the old wood. On the outside, a relaxed position of ease, but internally his heart was thumping wildly. His mortal body knew danger even if his soul was unafraid. "I do so love a stroll through the darkened woods at a god-awful hour. How about you?"

"***God-awful, you say?***" it laughed, twisting its head left and right, moving its fingers. Testing its control. "***Yes, yes, yes. God-awful indeed, but the daylight hours are for the other things. The secret things that glow in the light. The nighttime is for us – the things that exist between the shadows.***"

Jude turned his face away to look at the stars. So serene and so useless. The moon had its uses – the light, the pull on the earth – but the stars? They were simply pinpricks in heaven. Nothing more.

Jude turned back to look at the Ultimate Evil. "You are... more in control now." He said, watching the fingers twitch and the mouth contort. Jude wondered, briefly, where Clair's consciousness went when she was being manipulated. Maybe she just dreamed. He hoped she dreamed.

"*Yes*," it said, turning its face to the stars. "*And you are trapped in an unending loop, soul crosser. You are bound by a pact older than time itself. You are no longer allowed to play games with the fate of the world. You are denied influence. Denied opinion. Denied existence, in any way that counts. Your lives will always be meaningless, your days numbered. You will never have children. You will simply continue to exist and then die, over, and over, and over...*" It began cackling, a vicious sound like thick coins scraping glass.

The darkness pulled in around them and began blotting out the stars.

It turned back to look at Jude, Clair's head cocking to an almost comical angle.

"*You are not pleased?*"

Jude started, his heart beating much too fast. "Pleased with what?"

"*This is what you want, too. We all want it. This will be good for you. For everyone. It's time to reset the clock.*"

Jude sighed, staring at the Ultimate Evil. "We can never reset the clock. Time continues on, whether we are ready or not."

It narrowed its eyes, robust power seeping from Clair's pores.

"*I will never give up. My time has finally come. You will see. You will all see...*"

There was a brief pop in his ears. Clair closed her eyes and then opened them. She glanced around, regaining her bearings, before turning to look at Jude.

Jude stared at the seraph, who he knew would remember none of this in the morning. She would wake in her bed, her memories of him, of the Ultimate Evil controlling her lost. All of it lost forever. Burned from her brain like a seeping wound being cauterized.

With another pop she disappeared from sight, returning to wherever it was that she went.

The crickets began chirping again, slowly, as if testing the air.

"Let the battle begin," Jude said, into the night. And he could not help but feel like the music from the crickets was an anthem of war.

CLAIR

I think you should go," Clair said, pulling on her shirt. Sam and Kioko were leading a small team somewhere, attempting, yet again, to intercept Augustus, only this time it was further away – in Europe. Why they were even still trying was beyond Clair. He was too slippery, too well-connected to ever be caught by the ragtag team of angels they had on their side. It was precisely this line of thinking that led Clair to the conclusion that this was the perfect mission to let Chris go on without her.

He would not be in any danger. He would be with Sam. He would get to be on his own, apart from her, independently making his own name with the team. They would miss Augustus, again, and then he would come home having put some of the energy that was pent up in him to good use.

They had spent the night at his house, watching a movie and eating popcorn. It was such a normal experience that Clair thought maybe she had dreamt it.

"You what?" he said, staring at her.

"I think you should go," Clair said, turning to look at him. "You did all that training and you're not using it, because you're so worried about me." She sat next to him on the bed, admiring his bare chest. "But I'm fine."

Clair was definitely not fine. She felt more powerful and strong than ever before, but she had been feeling off for days. She was losing time again, but she did not know why. She needed space from Chris to explore this new power without endangering him and to figure out what was wrong without troubling him. She did not want to risk him –

to potentially tap into something uncontrollable and put him in danger – but he would never leave her side willingly if he knew what she was planning.

So she poured the lie into her eyes. She made him believe that she would be fine, that everything was normal.

After all, they had just had the most normal night since they had met.

"You'll be with Sam, Kioko will stay here with me, and we both know how much joy it brings me to suck the fun out of her life." Clair smiled playfully and Chris chuckled.

"Are you sure?" he asked, pushing a strand of loose hair behind her ear.

"I am sure," she said, grabbing his hand and kissing his palm. "We were apart much longer than five days before."

Chris frowned. "Never again," he said, his eyes serious.

"Never again," she echoed, leaning in to place a chaste kiss on his lips.

"Now," she said, leaning back. "Do you want to tell Sam, or do you want me to?" She grinned.

"Let me be the one to tell Kioko I'm taking her place, Clair," Chris said, chuckling. "You can tell Sam."

Clair playfully slapped him on the shoulder. "You're taking all my fun away."

"That's my job," he said, waggling his eyebrows. "Keeping the big-bad seraph from having any fun."

"Oh," Clair said, crawling toward him. "I think you have plenty fun with your seraph…"

Later, Clair slid into the cool silk sheets, resting her head on her hand as she sat up on her side and looked down at Chris. He smiled at her.

It was always going to be his smile that held her heart.

She brought her hand to his face and gently caressed his cheek with her fingertips. His eyes closed on a sigh.

It was always like this when they touched. As if they were two magnets that had been separated finally coming together.

She let her fingers wander down over his strong jaw, feather-light over his throat where she felt him swallow.

Clair traced her fingers over his collar bones and then lower over his chest. Her fingers circled one of his nipples and he let out a puff of air for a laugh, cocking one eye open to see her wry smile.

"Tease," he said, pulling her toward him. "Again?"

He kissed her slowly, just a brush of lips on lips, before deepening the kiss. His tongue traced the seam of her lips and she allowed him entrance. His tongue danced with hers in a ritual so instinctual, she forgot she had been leading.

His hand snaked up the back of her neck into her hair where he fisted it, pulling her more forcefully into him.

Clair moaned, straddling him beneath the covers. She loved the feel of him between her legs, the heat of his need matching hers.

Clair let herself be consumed.

They did not get to Sam's house for another hour.

The mission was set. They were leaving. Kioko was pissed and Clair got everything she wanted. She spent a little while watching Chris fall into his element, planning and discussing tactics with the other angels, pouring over maps, before walking back into the main house.

Clair turned the corner and came face-to-furry-face with Seine.

She had never liked the cat but tonight its eyes were too yellow. Too similar to the Ultimate Evil.

She began walking up the stairs.

"*Hello, Clair,*" Seine said, stretching his legs. Clair stopped, turning back toward the cat. She shook her head, making sure she was not dreaming.

"You possessed a cat?" she asked it, for it was no longer Seine she was addressing.

The absurdity of the situation consumed her. She knew she should be concerned, but she could not bring herself to be. A cat? Seriously?

"*Cats are…*" the voice hissed, forced through a mouth not made to match human sound, the cat's maw nearly breaking to accommodate the foreign speech. "*Fun.*"

"Sure," Clair said, walking over and picking up Seine with one arm.

"*What are you doing?*" It sounded almost indignant, but not surprised.

"You aren't allowed in my house," Clair said, opening the back slider and tossing it out. "Seine, when you're back to normal you can come back inside. But not before."

The cat coughed a laugh.

"*Oh, Clair,*" it said. "*You walk the earth assuming everyone is playing by the same basic set of rules. That there is a game that everyone is a part of, and that your team or your opponent are stuck in certain character roles. But what are those rules? Name them. And what are those roles?*" It spit, shaking its head.

It was odd hearing the Ultimate Evil's voice coming from a cat.

"*In reality, you are all completely unaware of what goes on inside each other's minds. Completely at the mercy of random happenstance. You know this better than most — you, who wields so much power through influence. There isn't a difference between power and influence when you're an angel. You simply do.*"

Clair stood in the doorway, staring at it.

"Then I simply choose to ignore you."

She slammed the slider and walked away.

SAM

It always feels like he is one step ahead of us," Sam said, pulling the kettle from the stove and pouring the hot water into the two teacups he had retrieved. He handed the floral one to Dorthea. He knew she preferred them. "It is as though with every step we take to get closer to him, he takes three in an opposing direction. We struggle to reach the new minor angels before him and his flock of fanatics— the fallen angels who believe in his rhetoric and want to see the fall of mankind. Sometimes..." Sam sighed, handing Dotty her tea. "Sometimes it just feels hopeless."

"It's never hopeless, Sam," Dotty said, gently touching his shoulder. She looked tired. She had seemed more defeated since Clair returned. Since the fight of the angels landed fully on her doorstep. Sam was positive a piece of Dotty had fractured irreparably the night Clair returned after killing Elijah.

Sam made a mental note to keep a closer eye on Dotty, to make sure she was getting enough rest.

"You should go to bed. We've got this," he said, placing his hand lightly over her wrinkled one.

"You know what? I think I might do that," she said, patting his shoulder. "Thank you for the tea."

"Of course," Sam said. "Anytime."

Dorthea smiled at him and left the room.

Sam walked back into the antique shop, to the table where they had set up the war station. Kioko pulled his attention back to the map. They were leaving tonight– Chris, a small team, and Sam. Augustus had been sighted along the east coast of Italy. Their flight was in two hours. Kioko had refused to let up on the planning, despite, as she grumbled, the fact that she would be staying back to babysit the demon angel.

"You really need to stop calling Clair that," Sam said, continuing to review the map.

"Why?" Kioko said, sending off the necessary coordinates to the team on the east coast who had secured them weapons. "That's what she is. Harbinger of death. Seraph of multiple personalities."

Sam turned toward her. "Clair is dealing with a lot."

"Clair killed a human and her own father," Kioko said, ignoring Sam when he tried to protest. "Those are facts, Samuel, not opinion. She's the most powerful angel on earth right now and where is she? Hiding in her room, screwing her boyfriend, and drinking. She needs to get over what she did and start using her powers to help us put a stop to Augustus before he establishes a new, much worse Covenant."

Sam sighed. "I agree with you, to a certain extent," Sam said. "But you weren't there when she thought she lost Chris. It was a long time before she even seemed remotely herself again. We're lucky she's even letting him out of her sight for this trip."

"How does she do it?" Kioko asked.

"Do what?"

"How does she wield so much power? I didn't think it was possible for one being to use so much power."

Sam thought for a minute. "When she casts a spell, she uses her life force to support it, whereas you take energy from around you. She stopped using the little angels and started pulling the energy from within her own body."

"So she could exhaust herself."

Sam thought about it. "Maybe," he said, pondering. "I would need to look into it."

"We don't have time, Sam. We don't have time for anything anymore." Kioko sighed. She finished preparing the document package for him and handed him the small bag. "Here are the passports and resources you'll need to get past security, and the security encrypted location of the safehouse where our allies are currently bunked."

"Thank you," Sam said, placing his tea on the table. "We'll be back in five days."

"We'll be here," Kioko mocked, slumping into a nearby chair. "Just me and Dotty, babysitting."

Sam rolled his eyes. He walked over to the desk and pulled out a book he had been saving from the bottom drawer. He tossed it at Kioko, who caught it smoothly. Sometimes he forgot the depth of her skillfulness.

"Here," he said, watching her look at the book. "All the contacts from your old pal Sylvester in Romania. One of the local teams pulled it from the archives before they fled. I've been saving it for you for when you needed some cheering up."

Sam watched as Kioko flipped through the book, her face turning menacing. "Perfect," she said. "I'll get to do a bit of light plotting while you're gone. Much appreciated."

"I figured," Sam laughed, turning to leave. "I'm going to get Chris and we'll be off. Call if anything happens."

"Please," Kioko said, sparing him only a glance. "In this town?"

DOTTY

otty, finally, made it to bed.

As she laid down, she felt the plush comforter beneath her dip, just a bit, as it conformed to her body.

She loved the soft mattress. She knew she needed to replace it, that it was much too old, but it knew her. It had a space for her, crafted by her body from so many nights.

She chuckled; her mattress was the most consistent thing in her life.

But she was so tired. So very, very tired.

Her body was achier than it had ever been. Her joints felt like they scraped against each other as she moved. Being around all the angels magic had helped, but she was feeling her age more and more. So much more.

And since Elijah…

She was so tired.

Dotty closed her eyes, took a deep breath, and slept.

She dreamed.

It was fuzzy, but Dotty always seemed to know when she was dreaming. She did not have access to her normal senses, but she was somehow partially awake. Always. Sometimes she would be flying, or performing magic, or doing impossible feats. Other times she would be doing mundane things like cooking, cleaning, or walking.

Sometimes her dreams would manifest in real life, giving her intense déjà vu.

But this place… She would know this place anywhere.

She was walking along the river Seine. The sun was just beginning to set on the horizon. She could see blurry silhouettes of people walking by her, hear muffled voices as if she was underwater. It was like a painting in her mind, all blurred colors and soft shapes. Just vivid enough to know what they were, but not crisp enough to truly feel like she belonged within it.

Dotty walked across the cement bridge, tracing her hand along the railing. She missed the rough texture she had been accustomed to all those years ago. Was the bridge cold at night or did it retain heat from the sun? Dotty could not remember, and apparently her dream brain could not either.

She stopped in the middle of the bridge and looked out across the blurry water. She could see the water but not hear or smell the sea.

The lights from the nearby buildings were beginning to turn on, complementing the warm tones of the setting sun. Dotty always loved the river at dusk – it was her favorite place to walk with James.

They had met in France. She was in the Louvre, conducting research for a university paper in which she identified transitional features in works of art that connected French Neoclassicism to Romanticism, spending hours in rooms 75-77 in the Denon Wing on the first floor. She loved the older paintings – how the paint, though chipped, was restored to the best of the curators' abilities. How they reflected a different time in history altogether – a time when paintings were one of the only media to capture faces, and bodies, and movement.

She loved the colors, the depth of the art. That artists were able to create so much beauty with such limited resources astounded her. It fed her love of art and compelled her to hunt it like long lost treasure... She would imagine herself a pirate, sailing the sea, finding lost works of art.

Oh, how she had longed for adventure in her youth. Maybe it was this longing that captured James's attention. He would always tell her that she had drawn him in with the unbridled awe reflected on her face as she stared at the paintings. He said that she was striking. She had been unapologetically beautiful. Her parents had taught her to love herself through how they showed their love for her, and she never let that confidence die. James told her there was something glittering in her eyes when she turned toward him that first day, and he knew.

She was for him, and he was for her.

And so, Dotty and James's adventure began.

Though it had not been what either of them expected.

Dotty sighed in her dream, the muffled voices of those around her on the bridge walking by.

Then, she felt him.

She turned, and it was like that day in the Louvre all over again. He was beautiful, just as he was all those years ago. Perfectly imperfect masculinity, tousled together with a rumpled shirt, jeans, and windswept hair. He was a god amongst men – a work of marble come to life, and there he was – looking at her.

"James," she sighed, her heart pounding in her chest. "You've come back for me."

He walked toward her, and as he did, her heart beat impossibly fast, the voices around them becoming clearer and crisper. She could smell the water below her on the bridge, feel the cement of the railing on her fingers. As he approached her, Dotty felt more alive than she had in a long time.

He was inches from her face, his breath ghosting across her lips. He smelled of amber, pine, and the antique shop all rolled into one. He smelled like home. Dotty's heart tried to leap from her chest.

He kissed her.

Her heart stopped.

She opened her eyes, and her senses were flooded by sound and smells and light.

It was like coming up out of the water. The sights, the sound, and the smells all came rushing to her. She felt gravity take hold of her on the bridge and would have collapsed if James had not caught her. She gripped his shirt with her hands…

Her hands.

Her hands were now smooth, free of lines and dark spots. She stood on shaky legs and brought them to her face, marveling at the way her fingers could so easily curl without pain of arthritis.

She touched her face with the now smooth pads of her fingers, finding the skin on her cheeks soft and firm. Her hair, too, fluttered in the breeze. Long, as it had been so many years ago, and full of color, warm browns with hints of amber.

She was no longer touched with age, the wrinkles that told the tests she had endured no longer present. She felt lighter in her bones.

She was as she had been when she met him, before her life changed forever.

"James?" she whispered, touching his face and feeling the texture of his skin. "James?"

"Yes, love," he said, placing his hand over hers. His voice was so lovely it brought tears to her eyes. As deep and full as she remembered. "You're here. You're safe. I came to get you myself."

"I…" she said, staring into his eyes. Feeling the breath come in and out of her lungs.

"I'm dead."

"Yes," he said, cupping her hands in his own and bringing them up to his face. He gently kissed her fingers, tears springing into his eyes. "I am so sorry, my love. It was a heart attack. I wanted to be there… I needed to be here for you."

Dotty felt her own tears come to her eyes. She was dead… but Clair.

"Oh, Clair," Dotty breathed, leaning against him.

"Yes," James said, cupping her head, his other hand rubbing slowly across her back. "Clair has her own demons to face now. It was time for you, my love. It was time to leave. Trust me."

"I have always trusted you," she said as she looked up into his eyes. "I've missed you so much."

"I was always there," he said, rubbing her cheek with his thumb. "I need you to know, I was always there."

"I know," she said, reaching up to cup his cheek with her hand. "I love you."

"I love you, my Dorthea. You were so strong – you have been so strong. But now, it is time to rest."

Dotty chuckled, rubbing her face into his shirt. "Rest?" she said, looking out over the water, hearing his heartbeat beneath his breast.

She sighed. "I could use a little rest."

They watched the sun set, locked in each other's arms. She would never have to worry about him disappearing ever again.

CLAIR

She was dreaming again.

No longer the black dove being drowned in white falling from the sky. No longer the insecure girl running from yellow eyes trying to swallow her whole.

Now Clair dreamed of an empty, dark room – an endless, pitch-black night.

She woke, covered in sweat, her head pounding. It was still intensely dark outside. She could not have slept for more than a couple of hours.

She swung her feet off the bed, clutching her head.

It was getting worse.

She was losing time.

She was losing her mind.

Clair heard it then…a whisper…

She stood, walking over to the wall to turn on the light. She flicked the switch, but nothing happened.

A power outage? That never happened.

Clair stepped out of her room into darkness. Pitch-black darkness, like her dream. It felt like there were clouds swirling around her feet and she was walking into fog. Something was in the house.

She started to run – down the hall, down the stairs.

She ran and ran and ran.

The hallways began to twist and turn and rise again. She thought she was climbing more stairs when she heard a noise to her left.

Someone was in the house. Something was in her house.

KIOKO

ioko was tired.

She had stayed up too late tracing back over the latest maps. They needed to find him. Chris and Sam had taken the team on the plane a couple of hours ago. Kioko should have returned to his place to sleep, but she was still in this musty antique shop, looking at maps and stats she had read a thousand times before.

She sighed.

It was never going to be enough.

No matter what they did, no matter how many angels they saved, how many came over to 'their' side of the war – it would never be enough.

Sometimes Kioko wondered what the point of it all even was, but that was the thought of someone who had given up, and she was not the type to give up. She had not escaped Augustus just to be defeated by her own mind.

She stood, lifting her arms above her head and taking a moment to stretch. As she went to leave, the lights sputtered and died.

"What now?" she said, attempting to walk around the desk but stubbing her foot. She felt around for one of the many candles she had seen around the antique shop. She used her powers to light the wick, grateful for the small burst of light in the darkness.

She heard a creak on the stairs in the house, and assumed Dorthea or Clair was investigating the issue. Kioko hoped it was Dorthea and not Clair.

As she walked into the house, she heard voices coming from upstairs, but it did not sound like Dorthea or Clair…

Kioko ran up the stairs and into the hallway, where she saw Clair leaning wide-eyed against a wall. She was sweating, her t-shirt soaked through. Her hands were bloody, and in the wall, Kioko could see gouges where it looked like she attempted to claw her way through it.

"Have to get out," Clair panted, wild-eyed.

"Clair?" Kioko held her hand out in front of her, slowly approaching Clair as one would a wild animal. "What's going on?"

Clair stopped panting, stopped even breathing. She she turned her impossibly wide stare on Kioko. Her eyes were unseeing, clouded by darkness. She cocked her head, forcefully cracking her neck, and it jerked like a dead thing, a wretched thing, thrust too far to the side to be a human reaction.

Kioko dropped the candle and pulled out her knives. She watched it roll to the wall, watched its flames begin to lick up the curtains of a nearby window.

Then Kioko heard the other voice.

"Kill them."

Kioko watched a knife appear in Clair's hand. Clair stared down at it, tilting it, watching it gleam in the glow of the flames.

"Clair?" Kioko asked.

When Clair turned back to look at Kioko, the yellow-gold eyes of the Ultimate Evil looked back at her.

Through everything Kioko had faced in her life, through all the missions and training and the angels she had watched disappear, Kioko had never felt like she was facing death. Not until now. She was frozen with fear.

Kioko took her final breath and watched the knife plunge into her heart.

EMILY

mily got the call around two in the morning.

"We need you. Something's happened. The house is gone."

Sam was so matter-of-fact, it took her brain a minute to catch up.

"What do you mean?" she asked groggily. "What house?"

"Firefighters called me. They are at Clair's house," Sam said.

"Why would they call you? I don't understand."

"Emily," Sam said. "You need to wake up. They called me because I took over Chris' house in my name and paid the deed, and we are the closest house. Now you need to wake up." He was unfathomably calm.

Emily could not tell if the sirens and the people shouting she heard were in her head or outside of the Brown Bear.

"What's happening?" Mike turned toward her, rubbing his eyes.

"Bring Mike," Sam dictated. "We're on a flight back. We were at a layover in Maine when I got a distressed text from Kioko. You need to get there. Keep me updated."

Sam hung up. Emily stared at her phone.

"What is it?" Mike was sitting up in bed beside her.

"Clair's house is on fire," she said, still staring at her phone. She felt the bed shift behind her. Mike was standing, throwing on jeans, and tossing one of her sleeping t-shirts at her.

"Get dressed, Em," he said. "I know you're in shock, but we have to go."

"Yes," she said, pulling the shirt over her head. "Okay."

It was a disaster.

They could see the flames from the road, through the darkness. As they neared the house, the blaze flared into the night sky.

Two firetrucks and three police cars surrounded the property, blasting it with water. Firefighters were running around, some in masks, shouting to each other. They were desperately fighting to keep the flames from the trees, from the forest.

All Emily could do was stare, in shock, at the house.

There was barely any house left.

"Clair…" Emily breathed, Mike pulling her closer to him as they stayed near their car.

"Emily, stay here. I'm going to go talk to one of the police officers." When she did not respond, he pulled her face toward him. His eyes were lined with worry, the smoke was starting to make her eyes water. She thought it was the smoke. "Emily, please stay here. I am going to find out what is going on."

Emily nodded, and he released her, walking over to one of the many officers on site.

Emily turned back to the house. The antique shop. All of it.

It was gone.

The firefighters were doing a good job containing the fire in the house, away from the forest.

Emily never thought her intelligence was something that she would ever question about herself, but as she stared up at the burning building, she could not seem to comprehend what was happening. Kioko, Dotty, and Clair had all been inside. They were inside.

Where were they?

She felt her phone buzz in her hand. She did not remember bring it. She briefly wondered if she had even set it down after Sam called. She flicked it on and held it up to her ear. "Hello?"

"Emily!" It was Chris, he was frantic. "Emily, are you at the house? What is happening? Clair isn't answering her phone and I feel like something's really wrong."

She could hear the desperation in his voice, but all she could do was stare at the house. "I don't know."

Chris stopped breathing. She heard it down the line.

Mike came back over to her and took the phone from her. "Chris, put Sam on."

"What do you know, Mike? What is happening?" Chris practically screamed.

"Chris," Mike said, more forcefully this time. "Put Sam on the phone. Now."

Sam must have come on the line because Mike started talking.

"The police informed me that the fire started about an hour ago. They have it mostly contained but the building is a lost cause. The antique shop and house are both gone." He paused, looking at Emily, who was hanging on his every word. "And they found a body."

Emily felt the ground reach up to swallow her.

CHRIS

I t's been seven days, Chris. We can't wait any longer."

Sam was right. Chris knew Sam was right, but every time Chris drew in a breath, he felt his lungs fracture, as if he was freezing internally with no way to get warm.

Clair was out there somewhere, alone.

Sam had received a single text from Kioko before she went dark.

"Something's wrong."

That was it.

They had tried calling and texting her as soon as they landed, but eventually the line had gone dead.

Then Sam got the call from the police.

They had boarded the next flight back. It was chaos.

Emily and Mike had tried to deal with the police, but everyone involved had been left with more questions than answers.

Chris could still see the charred remnants of the house in his mind's eye. It had burned almost fully to the ground.

And Dorthea…

They had found her body in her room.

The coroner had conducted an autopsy at Sam's request. Sam must have sensed something they all missed. The coroner confirmed Dorthea had died before the fire, that she had suffered a heart attack. It was not the fire that had taken her. Clair was still missing and Kioko…

Based on the timing of her text, the devastation of the fire, and where Sam had found the scorched remains of Kioko's phone in the house, Sam was certain that Kioko was dust. Chris supposed that had Kioko survived she would have found a way to contact them, but a sliver of him held onto the hope that she was not gone forever. He preferred to think of Kioko as lost.

What had really happened?

Where was Clair?

How could she be missing this?

"I know you want to wait," Sam began, pacing in front of his sliding glass door. He was dressed in all black. Emily had made the arrangements in Clair's absence, assisted by Mike.

The funeral was set to take place in an hour. The whole town had been invited.

Amid the chaos of the angelic schism, none of them had felt comfortable having a potluck at their houses. Thankfully, Jean had stepped in, offering to host a gathering at the flower shop, surrounded by all the hybrid lilies she had created from Clair's.

Clair would be proud of the work that they had done.

"I know," Chris said, turning to Sam. His dark grey suit and emerald tie were in place. He had to borrow a pair of Sam's dress shoes. The ones from the Covenant were white, an irony that was not lost on him. "I know why we can't wait. I just…she's got to be so heartbroken, and I know she would want to be there for Dotty."

"Then where is she?" Sam asked, stopping dead in his tracks and facing Chris. "Where is she? And what the hell actually happened? Everything was fine when we left. I know she's been off since the mission, but the house bloody burned down, Chris!"

"I know that!" He turned to face Sam, his chest heaving. Warmth began seeping into the hole where his heart used to be. "I don't know where she is, but Clair wouldn't, she couldn't— she didn't do this!"

Sam stared at Chris and his shoulders slumped. All the tension in the room dissipated as quickly as it had come. "I do not want to believe that Clair is capable of something like this, but we should have looked closer. We didn't see it."

"No," Chris said, turning away from Sam and walking toward the door. "She didn't do this. She didn't. I'm going to help Jean set up for the wake."

Sam let him go.

Jean had dressed in a knee-length black velvet dress and woven white lilies into a plait in her hair.

"Thank you for hosting this, Jean," Chris said, moving a small table from one side of the room to the other.

"Of course," Jean said, sounding tired. Chris had never really noticed her age before. She had always been kind to him when he lived in the hills and kept to himself in those early years. Though he had never seen Jean and Dorthea interact, Clair had mentioned their friendship. He knew it must have been special for her to be doing all this.

Jean stroked one of the lilies in her braid. "Dorthea was different," she chuckled, walking over to a beautiful wreath of roses, carnations, lilies, and lilac. "Most people didn't get why she preferred to be alone, but I did. We – the unconventional people – have to stick together." When she looked up at Chris, it was as if she could see through him. He held his breath as she continued to talk. "We don't need to know everything about one another to know we are unique. We exist on a different wavelength than most people."

She looked away from Chris, who started breathing again, and back to the wreath, hanging a small bell in the center. When she lifted it, the bell chimed. Chris could imagine it would chime beautifully in any little gust of wind. "Dorthea was one of those unconventional people, special and skilled."

Jean walked back toward Chris with the wreath, who gingerly took it, and they walked out of the shop and toward the funeral site.

"She had already been through so much in her life when she chose to raise that little girl as if she was her own daughter," Jean said. "Later on, she began bringing in other people into her little circle." Jean glanced sideways at Chris, who nodded.

They were silent for a bit, both lost in their own thoughts. They arrived at the cemetery near the forest on the border of town.

When they got to the funeral site, Jean went to greet some townsfolk she knew and Chris placed the wreath gently on the stand near the coffin. Sam was standing next to a couple other bouquets, frowning at one in particular. A gaudy, black arrangement. The white flowers had all been dyed a deep, dark burgundy and were held together with a thick, black ribbon.

Chris walked up to Sam.

"It's from Augustus," Sam said, handing the card to Chris, who took it with shaking fingers.

For the woman who raised the bringer of the new world. Until we meet again, - A

"Even in death, that man has to get the last word in," Chris scoffed.

More people began arriving.

Emily and Mike joined Chris and Sam near the flowers.

"Still nothing?" Emily asked. Her eyes were red-rimmed, her nose rubbed raw. Emily and Dorthea had grown extremely close during their time together. Mike was holding her hand as he scanned the crowd.

"No," Sam said, gesturing to the black lilies. "But Augustus made sure to send his regards." He handed Emily the card, and Chris watched Mike's hand tighten over hers as he read the note.

"We shouldn't be here," Mike said, eyes returning to the crowd as if one of them were about to attack. "We shouldn't have invited the town. We're too exposed."

"Yes," Sam said. "You are correct that we are too exposed, but it is out of necessity. Dorthea was human. All human. If there was no funeral or record of her death, it would cause more problems down the line."

"But lying about her leaving on a burning candle?" Emily said. "It just feels wrong."

"Technically, it was a candle, or multiple candles, that started the fire. As for Kioko…" Sam paused, clearing his throat. "She did not officially exist. With Clair missing, we cannot place her at the house, or her story could become muddy too. We stick to the plan."

"Clair is too filled with grief to be here after losing her last remaining relative," Mike parroted. "We've got it. So really, we just need to make it through the funeral uneventfully, be seen at the wake, and return back to Chris's house or ours."

"Speaking of houses, we need to re-ward everything. Dotty used to do that," Emily said, tears collecting in her eyes again. "I never—well, she taught us, but it wasn't our job. The house…" Emily pulled her hand from Mike's so she could cover her face with her palms. "It's all gone. All her research, all that history. Their whole lives… gone."

Chris inhaled sharply.

"Clair isn't gone," he said, ignoring the way Sam's eyes slid to the side. "She isn't. I don't know where she is, but something must have happened. She's the legacy Dotty left behind. Clair and us."

The funeral director began calling everyone over.

They all looked at each other. They were all that was left. They had to keep going.

And Clair…

She would come back to him. Always.

CLAIR

She was in the forest.

Even with her eyes closed, she could hear the sounds of the birds in the trees, feel the slight rumble of the earth as the squirrels and small rodents ran to and from their homes. She could smell the mold of the fallen leaves and taste the fog in the air.

Clair opened her eyes.

She was in the bowl, lying where the Gate had once stood.

Even now, she could feel the slight thrum of the earth where it had absorbed all that power.

That was nothing compared to the power she could feel pulsating in her veins yearning for release.

You are awake.

Clair sat up and looked around. She was not afraid.

"Yes," she said to no one. "Why am I here?"

You are here because you needed to rest.

"I needed to rest in the forest? Why didn't I go home? Where are you?"

No answer.

Clair stood on shaky legs and her stomach rumbled. Her lips were dry and cracked, and when she was fully standing, she needed to pump power into her blood to remain upright.

"What happened?"

They're having a funeral.

The memories started flooding back to her, like the clean nick of a razor pulled too quickly against the skin, a trickle and then a downpour.

She remembered the darkness and the light. She remembered wandering her house, the fear. She remembered the enemy…

But she was not an enemy.

"Kioko," Clair cried, bringing her hands to her face. There was no blood. She felt like there should have been blood, like the memory required it. She needed to see it. Needed to experience the full weight of what she had done. Kioko had faded away as if she was never there, as if she never existed. Did she exist? Clair looked down and the knife appeared in her hand. It was clean, no blood. No gore. Just the reflection of the light in her eyes.

"I killed her," she said, watching her shaking hands.

She never truly existed.

"She existed and I killed her!" Clair yelled into the ether.

She took a shaky breath.

"They're having a funeral?" she asked. "I need to go."

Yes.

She blinked and suddenly found herself standing on the hilltop, looking down at the procession. She did not bother to question how. She was beyond questioning her abilities.

The whole town had shown up.

At the very front, surrounded by Chris, Sam, Emily, Mike, and Jean, was a coffin carved from a dark walnut wood, its rounded top covered in flowers.

Beside the coffin was a picture.

Clair felt her soul fracture.

"Dotty."

Clair stared at the coffin, at the scene below her. She stared at it, willing it to be fake, willing it to be another hallucination.

"I killed her."

Yes.

"I killed them all. My family—I can't breathe. I can't—"

I can fix it all.

I can help you.
Turn to me.

Clair felt herself let go.

CHRIS

A t that moment, Chris felt Clair's pain like a fissure in his heart.

He felt the pull of her presence and looked up at the hill. He saw Clair standing there, partially obscured by the trees, and in that instant he understood.

"She didn't know," he whispered, and everyone near him turned to stare. They all watched as Clair's eyes became molten, two golden pools blocking out her sight.

Clair turned from them all and disappeared.

It's time to return to the dark place, Clair.

CLAIR

She was *alive*.

More alive than she had ever felt before. Alive to her fullest potential. Throbbing with power. It was burning through her blood, seeking an outlet.

She was fully alive now without feelings getting in her way.

Nothing reached deep within her to hold her back. Nothing could suppress her any longer. She was nothing more than magic. A vessel for magic.

It sounded right.

It sounded smart.

It sounded detached, but in a reasonable way. A reasonable sense of detachment.

She did not need anything or anyone else.

She was infinite.

How had she not seen it before?

She was alone again, but it did not hit her heart like it used to. She knew, realistically, that she had the power to ensure that Chris was somewhere out in the world alive. No matter where she was, her power would protect him. He was hers. He belonged to her. And now she – she belonged to herself. She belonged to the magic and power flowing in her veins.

She belonged to the world.

She had grown accustomed to the darkness in her eyes and she could see clearly now. She observed her surroundings with her grim detachment. She was near a lake or a large pond, perhaps? Surrounded by trees. She did not know this place. It looked abandoned, untouched – beautiful. Nature as nature should be, without all of the technology, cars, and humans…

She cocked her head in consideration, as she walked into the lake.

Humans.

Why had she not realized sooner that she was not one of them? Why had it taken her so long to accept the inevitable future of her life?

In a way, Dorthea being gone was a good thing.

Yes.

Yes. A good thing.

She was no longer beholden to anyone. Chris was around, yes, but he was hers like the earth belonged to the sun.

Yes.

"Yes? So you agree with me then?"

Clair walked forward until the water stood up to her breasts.

Yes, I agree with you Clair. I've always agreed with you.

Clair stripped the clothes from her body, indifferently watching them sink into the murky depths. She felt free. Truly free. She was reborn.

It's like a river.

"What is like a river?"

Power, Clair. Power. If nothing gets in its way, it will turn and wind, carving away the earth, around and around until it has covered as much space as possible.

You were meant to explore this world, to encompass it, to be a part of it. You were never meant to be a pretty little prop for the Covenant, a chess piece in their little games. You are infinite.

The angels are supposed to be more than that.

"Yes. We were all meant to be more, then we wasted our potential. We wasted all that time trying to build something that should never have existed in the first place."

The fish began to die around her as she descended further into the lake, into the night.

You are mine.

SIX MONTHS LATER

I wish we were the birds,
Who dwell among the stars.
I wish that we could fly away,
And forget all our scars.
I wish there was a song to play,
To ease your broken mind.
I wish that we could fly away,
And end the race of time.

CHRIS

Chris sat at the metal table in the command center.

They kept the new base away from Healdsburg, even though Sam, rightfully, assumed that Clair would never return there again.

They went underground, both literally and figuratively. The primary base was subterranean, but they had established numerous safehouses around the world. Sam's network of angels living on the fringes of society was vaster than Chris had realized. There was an entire faction of angels living independently and acting apart from the Covenant within the world he thought he knew.

He had been pouring over the most recent map of events for over an hour. The coffee on the table next to him had gone cold.

He heard the door open and shut but ignored it.

"I don't think you're going to get anywhere with that tonight, Chris." Emily sat down next to him, shuffling some of his discarded maps, and reviewing the broken mess of a path Clair had created.

"We just need to catch her, Em. I just need to be face-to-face with her."

Emily dropped the map she was holding and looked at him. "Do you really think that will work, Chris? It's been months. *Months*. She's destroying the world. You really think you can save her?"

He was silent, looking back at the map in front of him.

Could he save her?

He was not sure, but he had to try.

He looked up at Emily. She had aged noticeably in the six months they had spent underground.

"How is Mike holding up?"

"Oh, you know," she sighed. "About as well as I am. I miss the sunlight, Chris. I miss my family. Hell, I even miss working. I want things to go back to normal. As normal as we can be after all this."

He nodded. Normal would never be the same for him.

"He says his team has developed a new way to neutralize the natural disasters," Emily said. She was talking about Sam or Erik.

In the last six months, Clair had been systematically destroying the planet by causing natural disasters. She had started slowly at first, but her output was rapidly increasing. The worst part was she was simply accelerating the natural direction of humanity's war on nature – oil spills, global warming, toxic air.

Sam was spending nearly half of his resources on hunting her, and the other half on feeding lies to the media confirming that the disasters were, in fact, natural. There were some things he could not hide.

"You don't think humans are going to notice all of these disasters are happening at once? They're too coordinated to be random. It was lucky we released that 'disease' to help keep them out of the line of fire," Erik had railed in a meeting three months ago. It was the only time Chris saw Emily break down. She had been against it, but the sickness had stopped the world from functioning as normal. The disease kept most people out of planes and off the streets, but it had killed hundreds of them in the process. It was reckless and heartless.

Chris did not know if what they were doing was right anymore, but he did know that what Clair was doing was wrong.

"I know she's still in there, Emily," he said. "She lost so much, she broke. We didn't see it. I didn't see it. I knew she was struggling when she came back from the mission, but she hid it from me. She didn't tell me about the dreams or the meetings with the Ultimate Evil. He got to her right under my nose, Emily!" Chris shouted, slamming his hand on the table. "He got to her while I was with her."

Emily sighed, shooting him a miserable look before rubbing her hand over her face. They all pitied him now. Pitied his faith in her. His love for her.

"There was nothing you could do," Mike said as he walked in, dropping a stack of papers on the table before placing a swift kiss on Emily's cheek. He rounded the table and sat down on Chris' other side. "This was the plan from the beginning. Someone else's plan, Chris. You couldn't have stopped it. Now, we just have to figure out a way to limit the damage."

Chris dropped his head into his hands. He felt Emily begin to rub his back. He remained hunched until the rest of the angels came in for the daily report and briefing.

They were wrong.

This was all his fault.

THE WHITE ROOM

Clair opened her eyes.

She was clutching her knees to her chest, lying flat on her side. It was calm and quiet where she had awoken. She raised herself up to sit and took in her surroundings.

She was lying on a hazy line. Behind her, darkness extended so far that she could not see its end. There were no stars like she would see at night, only a dense and black form. Before her was the brightest light she had ever seen. She could not look straight at it for too long because it hurt her eyes, like the sun.

Clair looked down to where she was sitting.

The colors almost blurred into a beautiful grey beneath her bottom.

She was not wearing her own clothes anymore. The clothes she had been wearing when she fled from the…

Dotty.

Dotty was dead.

She had killed her own grandmother.

Clair felt the tears pool in her eyes and drip slowly down her face and onto her chest. The white shirt and pants she was now wearing became soaked in her misery.

Her grandmother, who she loved more than anyone. Who had raised her. Who was the only one strong enough to hold them all together.

Dotty was gone.

Clair was an orphan.

There was no one left.

Clair closed her eyes and laid back down.

Clair woke again the in the white room.

It was almost circular. The line she was on seemed to wrap around the light in the center, as if everything stretched from it.

Clair sat up.

She needed to figure out where she was, how she got here, and whether or not she wanted to leave.

Her emotions were all over the place. She was distraught, depressed, and confused but her feelings were all heightened. She had never considered herself an overly emotional person, but here, her emotions were all consuming.

She deserved it.

She deserved to feel the worst despair, the worst pain. She was the cause of all their problems. She was the reason Dotty was dead. She was the reason her father was dead and her mother.

She had no one left.

Clair looked as closely as she could at the white light.

She stood, the loose white pants billowing around her ankles, and stepped toward the light.

It burned.

She flinched back, moving further into the space with the darkness.

It was freezing.

Clair pitched herself back in the middle between the light and dark, where it was neither hot nor cold.

Slowly, she moved her foot toward the light.

It burned. The light was fire. She felt the heat seep into her toes and sensed that it would burn her alive if she got too close to it. If she stepped into it.

Clair turned and looked toward the dark.

Slowly, she slid her foot along the tile-like floor.

She felt her toes freezing, blood vessel by blood vessel.

She pulled her foot back.

She sat, turning between the light and the dark, in the safe middle space.

She sat and she waited.

"Clair," the voice said, no longer in her head.

Clair stopped breathing.

CLAIR

I t was quiet.

She could not recall it ever being this quiet in her head.

Not since she killed her father. Not since she killed the man guarding him.

Everything before that felt so distant.

Removed.

She scanned the sea of people walking around her.

When did they get here? She did not remember leaving the lake. She did not remember finding clothes.

She looked down at her black leather pants, stiletto heels, and the tight black top that accentuated her breasts.

You know how much I love to dress up my toys, Clair.

"Your fetishes are your own problem. This getup is impractical, to say the least. Who can commit chaos in heels? The movies have always been lies."

Always so pragmatic in this state.

"I am what I was made to be. Where are we?"

Fort Lauderdale.

Interesting.

Clair looked around at the buildings. There were so many buildings clustered together that they blocked the view of the landscape. Car horns blared on the busy streets lined with discarded trash. The smells of decaying food mixed with the stink of too many bodies pressed together on the packed sidewalks in the humid summer air.

Humanity was destroying the earth faster than any living creature. It had subverted the laws of nature with science, and the earth could not develop fast enough to sustain it. The earth was not full of infinite resources.

Clair walked around the city. Just another city. There were too many cities, too much noise. Too much motion from too many people.

"There are too many people."

Yes.

"Why are there so many people?"

Evolution.

Overrun. Loud.

A man approached her on the street and outstretched his hand toward her, shoving a flyer in his face. He was yelling at her about something, trying to get her to take the paper in his hand.

He kept coming closer, too close, into her space.

"Shhh," she whispered, and the man froze in place. His eyes were open and unseeing.

Finally, there was quiet.

Clair looked past the man to see a frozen crowd, the people all stopped mid-step. In the distance, she could hear sirens, screaming, and crying. But right here, in her frozen bubble, there was quiet and stillness.

It was time to bring more stillness to the world.

Wonderful. Let's begin.

She sat in front of a burning candle.

Where are you now Clair?

"Shouldn't you know?"

It laughed.

I am of you, yes. I should. Yet I do not.

"I have no time for riddles tonight, devil."

No, no... No time. Riddles are not important now. Now, we destroy. We claim. We right wrongs.

"No. Tonight I watch. Tomorrow, I see. And you? You leave me to it."

Yes, Clair.

There was silence in her mind. Blissful silence.

Who is he to you?

She circled the man. Thin and balding, his ribs protruding from his almost transparent skin. He wore a beard that fell to the ground in intricate braids.

"Just another religious leader," she said, circling him. The man could not see her, but he could feel her.

She had gone after Augustus first.

His death had been quick.

Too quick, if she had been in her right mind.

But she had not.

It was easy to find him huddled in the corner of his impenetrable safehouse. Easy to ignore his pleas for sanctuary, his pleas for her to understand his side, to join his mission to establish angelic rule on earth. It was too easy to walk over to him, this man she had feared for so long, and choke the very air from his lungs.

As she watched the life fade from his eyes, her only thought was that it was too easy, that he should have somehow been harder to kill.

From there, she had tracked down all of the other religious leaders who had been in the room while she was attacked.

One. By. One.

She destroyed them all.

"You prey on the weak and the lost. You are vultures who feast on the carcasses of living beings. You promise salvation, for money, as long as they live under your rules. You tear families apart and rip babies from mothers' arms."

The people are the pieces that you see – the ones moving them are the authority.

"Yes," Clair said, looking out at humanity. "Time to bring the whole thing down."

THE WHITE ROOM

The voice was making her relive it.

She did not want to see it. She did not want to face it, to think about it. She could not bear it. It was too much. She had nothing but her thoughts in this room. Nothing but the light and the dark, and the voice.

The casket, the mistakes, the burned house.

Murderer.

She was a murderer. Family killer. Seraph with all the power and yet no power at all, stuck in a prison of her own making. Stuck in this white room, between the fire and the frost.

She never should have lived.

"No."

She should have died in that tub.

"No, there's more."

"Stop lying to me! You're always lying!" she screamed into the light.

"No, I do not lie, Clair."

"There is *nothing* more!" She pulled at her hair. She felt the strands dampen, like the invisible water from that night. The tub, the pills, the hopelessness, even then. The fear. The rejection. The voice was wrong. It was wrong.

Always the rejection. Everyone.

She should have just died that night in the tub.

SAM

"Florida is still reeling after the recent tsunami that crashed into the coast killing hundreds last week. The state, which had only recently been hit by —"

Sam turned off the truck radio.

It was a rare for them to be above ground. They were always hiding now, trying to stay under the radar.

But even angelic armies needed supplies.

Sam was currently driving a truck very similar to the one he had purchased for Chris what felt like long ago but could not have been more than two years. Chris was sitting shotgun, his elbow perched on the window, his head resting on his hand.

He was distraught lately, and rightfully so.

What Clair was doing was unforgivable, but Sam knew Chris would find a way. He would always forgive her. He truly believed in Clair, believed she was his purpose and his light.

As the months of destruction had continued, Sam had questioned it all. Questioned whether or not Chris was more like him than either of them had ever imagined, whether Chris was destined for a life separated from everything he thought he knew. A long, lonely life.

There was only one thing Sam was absolutely certain about: Clair was too far gone to be saved.

He had seen the videos of her destruction. Walked among the broken bodies left behind in her wake. She might be disguising the death with natural disasters, but she was causing it. She was choosing to do these things. Her mind was no longer her own and if she ever managed to get it back, he knew she would never recover from the damage she had inflicted upon the world.

Even if Chris got to her, he would not be able to bring her back. The girl they had both known was gone. Her body was now a vessel for magic—magic that had been contaminated by sorrow and an evil bent on destroying the world.

No, Clair would never return.

It was over.

They had failed.

As Sam slowed to a stop at a red light, he wondered what would stop Clair.

He glanced over at Chris, who was lost in his own thoughts. He had grown to love him over the years and respected his accomplishments, his fervor. Sam loved this boy.

Sam was sure Chris was Clair's only remaining tether connecting her to the world she had once loved. He was her anchor. Anchors were always connected to their vessels by a rope.

Sam felt for the knife he always carried in his pocket.

The ship notices immediately if you sever it from its anchor.

It would be so simple to draw the knife and drag it quickly over the other angel's throat. So simple, and then they would be done.

It would all be over. It would lure her out. The area they were in was remote. There would be fewer casualties this way. He could end this war right here, right now.

Sam clutched the knife with his left hand and looked over at Chris.

Chris, who looked like he would prefer to be dead. Chris, who had sat with him in the forest for hours on end. Chris, whom Dorthea had adored and knew was the best of them. Chris who was always hopeful. Sam held the knife and looked at Chris and knew he could not be the one to end him.

He would not.

As the light turned green and they moved on, Sam let go of the knife and let go of the idea of ever killing Chris.

CLAIR

This was set in motion a long time ago.

She was flying through the clouds.

It was calm here. Cold, but her body no longer mattered. The angelic part of her would protect her. Her skin was becoming sallow. She was no longer eating. She was not sleeping. She was pulling in so much power that it could sustain her.

Because she was no longer Clair.

Yes, it said. *You are infinite.*

Clair could do anything. When she strode on the ground, she could feel the earth beneath her feet. She could feel the molten pressure deep between the plates and pull it up and up then push it down.

She could even take chunks of it with her. She was more than an earth affinity; she was the nature's sword, come to fight the disease infecting the land.

Clair pulled a cliff from the earth, bringing it up with her into the sky. It floated, ethereal in its levitation.

She dropped it.

She could no longer discern whether these were her choices or if someone else was in control.

She no longer cared.

This has been determined from the beginning. Everything is as it should be.

She was sitting on a park bench, staring at a sign that read, "You're going to hell! Repent!"

Was this not hell? Clair could think of no place else where could she find more pain and suffering. The answer was simple.

There was no heaven or hell.

There was only life and the absence of life.

"Why would anyone assume that the Ultimate Good would say that?"

Why wouldn't he?

It's unfair to place either of us in a box.

It's unfair to attribute all the joy in the world to him and not the suffering.

People blame a nameless evil for all the wrongs that happen in their lives.

But ultimately, it all boils down to the same thing.

The idea of two opposing deities, spirits, or divinities affecting our lives is wrong.

Good and evil are two faces of the same coin.

Two parts of the same piece.

Destined for duality.

Glued together throughout time.

Acting as one.

Being as one.

The bad with the good.

No one to blame.

The hardest thing for humanity to accept: fate determines which side the coin landed on for them.

SAM

Sam was seated on the bunk in his room.

He really missed windows. He missed the sunshine. He missed life before the Covenant, before Dorthea, before Clair had lost it.

He heard his door open and looked up from the book he was reading. Chris stood in the doorframe.

"May I come in?" Chris asked.

"Of course," Sam sitting up taller, watching Chris as he closed the door and strode into the room. He looked, well, he looked terrible. He was not sleeping and was barely eating. His skin was shallow and his eyes were dull. They had all tried to pull him from his thoughts, his pain, but it was starting to consume him.

Chris walked over to the bunk set across from Sam's and sat to face him. "I felt her today," he said, and Sam had to force himself not to barrage him with questions. Chris looked up at Sam. "I felt her. She's...unravelling."

Sam took a deep breath, watching Chris slowly drag his hand through his shaggy, disheveled hair.

Suddenly, Chris stood and began pacing the small room.

"I felt her but something's not right. She didn't feel right. Which, I know sounds like it makes sense because of what she's been doing, but it was like part of her was *missing*. Maybe lost? I can't quite put it into words. It was like there were two of her." He looked over to Sam with a question in his eyes for which Sam had no answer. Chris started pacing again. "I know she's in there, but it's like she's dissociated

~ 230 ~

herself from the human portion of her consciousness," Chris said, and stopped to face him. "I could sense that she's unstable. The chaos has been ramping up lately. Her attacks are happening much more frequently. All the destruction we have seen is nothing compared to what I feel is coming. That brief glimpse into her—the feeling I got..."

"We need to stop her," Sam said.

Chris took a shuddering breath and fell to his knees, sobbing.

Sam knelt down next to him, pulling him into his chest and letting him grieve. The boy was too cold.

"It's going to be okay, Chris," he said.

It was not.

THE WHITE ROOM

here's more, Clair. There has always been more."

She was retreating further and further into her own mind. Days, weeks, hours, minutes, seconds, months. She did not know how long she had been sitting there, her thoughts a jumbled mess, her emotions rising and crashing like the ocean waves she knew she would never see again.

She imagined her wrists torn, bleeding out onto a silent bed in a dark room.

Alone.

Always alone but never alone.

"Just let me think!" she shouted within her own mind.

Just let me be.

Just let me die.

"No."

She took to crawling around the line of the circle.

Never going too far into the darkness and never going too far into the light.

She took to circling and circling and circling, until she could not move any longer.

She did this over and over and over again.

Whenever she gained consciousness, she would circle the room, round and round as the madness seeped in.

CLAIR

he was sitting in an airport.

She had never been in this airport before. It was loud.

Yes, it said. ***Very loud. Overcrowded.***

"You just described the entire world," she said to it.

"Excuse me?" The woman next to her was reading a magazine and had turned to her. Clair cocked an eyebrow.

"I wasn't talking to you," Clair said, turning back toward the window. The woman huffed, stood, and moved away, muttering about weirdos and new-age outfits before returning to her magazine.

Clair looked down at what she was wearing.

It was a three-piece black suit with a black collared shirt and black snakeskin boots. Her hair was pulled back into a severe low ponytail. Gold adorned each of her fingers and a fancy gold watch sat on her wrist.

"You dressed me like a rich businessman," she said to it.

You don't like it? I think you look perfectly menacing.

"Men make women out to be the devil because they fear us. I look fine," was all she said. Clair really did not care how she looked. She really did not care about anything anymore. "Why are we here?"

So you can pick a plane.

Clair looked at all the different gates.

All the different places.

Before she chose, she reached out her senses and tugged on the thread that connected her to Chris.

She felt him, alive and well, miles and miles from her.

I told you, it said. *I will not harm the boy.*

"No," she said, turning and walking toward a gate with the heading Montreal in it. "I will not harm him. You are nothing without me."

We are nothing without each other.

Clair approached the woman scanning tickets.

"Ticket?" the tired woman asked. She looked frustrated that she even had to ask Clair for a ticket.

"This is my first flight," Clair said, reaching into her pocket for nothing. She pulled out nothing, but to the woman and anyone watching, a first-class ticket appeared to be in her hand.

Upon seeing the status of the non-existent ticket, the woman perked up. "Right this way, you should have been boarded first! Our apologies. Have a great flight!"

"Thank you," Clair said, depositing the air into her pocked before stepping down the ramp.

First class was my idea.

"I'm sure it was," Clair said. The plank leading into the plane was like a rat's tube – one of those tunnels given to a small pet for enrichment time. The air was musty and stale. Gross.

It isn't much better on the plane.

"I'm aware," she said. "This isn't my first flight. Maybe try commenting on something useful."

Bit chatty today, are we?

Clair scoffed.

She passed through the small entryway at the end of the tube onto the plane.

She took her seat in first class, and waited. When the plane reached cruising altitude and the passengers had all been served their drinks, when some had even begun to doze, that was when she started the storm.

Clair made herself invisible and plodded down the aisles of the shaking plane.

People were screamed and cried out in fear.

She stole the air from their very lungs, felt it leave their bodies in a soft puff. Watched as they sat frozen in their chairs, staring helplessly at each other, pleading silently to whatever force they hoped would save them.

To whatever force would not come.

When she was in the middle of the plane, Clair looked down at the seat nearest her.

In it, sat a little girl clutching an even littler brown teddy bear wearing a silky red bow tie.

The girl must have been traveling alone because the adults near her were screaming and completely ignoring her, while she stared straight ahead as the plane bobbed and dipped around her. Clair wondered if she had already killed the girl's parents.

She was small – a tiny thing not yet talking who stared up into the space where Clair was standing and swirled her hand in the air. Clair, too, used to see the little angels floating around when she was younger. Angel kissed – this girl must be a descendant of one of her kind.

The little girl kept the plane in the air that day.

Clair sat, feeling the sharp wind prick at her face, watching the man on the ledge.

He could not see her, she did not allow it. She observed as he debated the next step in his life.

She had followed him for days, watching him, hearing his thoughts, his desperation. She knew this was inevitable. He walked invisibly through life, surrounded by people but alone, just another fish in a school waiting to be devoured by a sly predator.

Unfortunately for him, the main predator in his life was his own mind. He just needed a little urging.

"Jump," she breathed into the wind. "Jump. It's easy. It's so easy." One less life to fuel the fire of retribution. One less human to destroy the earth. "Jump." She watched as her words drifted on the wind like a spider's web to his ears, finding dainty footing in his mind.

"Jump."

Clair looked up at the stars as the man took a step forward and plunged into the air.

SAM

As everyone clear on their objectives?"

They finally had a plan.

They believed Clair was stationed somewhere in Southeast Asia. The team had assembled on Phú Quốc Island, Vietnam. With its strategic location and relatively small population of 180,000 inhabitants, Phú Quốc was the perfect place to lure Clair in an attempt subdue her. They had decided the meeting would occur on a remote beach in an uninhabited corner of the island.

Sam looked around at everyone assembled. Emily and Mike would clear the hilltop area facing the beach just before dark, leaving Chris alone on this section of the island. Then he would call for Clair and Sam would threaten to hurt him if she did not come.

Then it would be all up to Chris.

If he could not stop her, Erik had the laser trap ready.

Erik had developed an easy way to activate electric fencing over a designated area of land. It required multiple boxes positioned at different intervals. Once activated, the netting would form a dome-shaped trap. It would have the power to take down a T-Rex, Erik assured them, if they still roamed the earth. It would give them a chance to at least talk with Clair. Chris was positive it would not come to that.

Sam assumed they would need to use the laser trap but admired Chris and his undying optimism.

"Yes, we are all good to go," Chris said, his shoulders dropping as he watched Erik set up the laser points. "I need to go meditate for a bit."

"Good idea," Sam said, watching him walk away.

"We know what to do," Emily said, looking at him. "But Sam," Emily said, reaching over to grab Mike's hand. She looked up at Mike, and he nodded, before looking back toward Sam. "There's something we need you to do for us first," Emily said. Sam felt his anxiety rise. They were being very serious.

"What do you need?" he asked, wondering what could possibly be wrong. They had been spending a lot of time together over the past six months. He quite liked the both of them, even considered them friends. Mike had been extra affectionate with Sam since the devastating losses in Healdsburg and Emily had seemed more than fine with it. Sam worried he had overstepped a boundary somewhere.

"We want you to marry us," Emily said. "We want you to marry us before we set the trap, in case something goes wrong. It's time. We don't care about a fancy wedding or our parents being here—any of it. We want to be married and we want you to officiate."

Sam was awestruck. Marry them?

"I can honestly say, in my extremely long existence," he said, looking between them. "I have never married anyone before."

"Well, perfect," Mike said, coming over and patting Sam on the back. "There's a first time for everything."

Sam laughed, looking between them.

"Alright," he said. "How does one get ordained?"

It had been surprisingly easy to get ordained online.

By the time they reached the cliff, the sun was high enough in the sky that they still had a couple hours left before they needed to set their plan in motion.

Sam, the freshly ordained minister, stood at the top of the cliff flanked by Mike. Sam had dressed formally in all black, from his button-up shirt to his slacks and dress shoes. The groom had opted for tan pants and white button-down rolled at the sleeves with no shoes.

They were waiting for Emily.

She emerged at the bottom of the hill in a long, white, silk dress. The backline was low, the straps small and dainty. White flowers cascaded along the line of her waterfall braid. The only jewelry she wore were the pendant around her neck and her engagement ring. She was barefoot, walking across the grass toward them like a goddess of spring. The trees creating the perfect aisle for her to walk down, their flowering branches swaying peacefully in the breeze.

Sam felt his heart stutter. He looked over to Mike and noticed a tear fall from the man's eye.

When Emily reached them, she smiled at Mike and took his hands.

They stared deeply into each other's eyes.

"We are gathered here today," Sam began, then stopped. "No."

They both looked slightly concerned before he continued.

"No," Sam went on. "You two are extraordinary. Your wedding should be, too."

Sam made sure no one was near them then inhaled deeply. He focused on the earth around them. Slowly, he pulled all the fallen leaves and flowers up to float around the couple.

Emily gasped, tears forming in the corners of her eyes.

"Now we can begin," Sam said, admiring how her eyes shone in the magic of the moment. "Marriage is so often seen as the ending – a culmination of a love so great that you want to tie yourself to that person forever. Or it's seen as a beginning – a new step in a relationship that clearly separates the past from the present and the future. But it's both – marriage is both a culmination of love and new beginning. It is a statement to yourselves and to the world that you are choosing this person, forsaking all others. You are committing to choose this person over and over again. Mike, please tell Emily why you are choosing her."

"Emily," Mike said, gazing into her eyes. "I have watched you face demons. I have watched you look into the eyes of terrifying magic and not be afraid. I have watched you persevere through circumstances that seemed utterly hopeless and come out even stronger in the end. I have seen you do all of this and more. You took a broken man and made him whole. You showed me a new world, a better world. You inspired me to grow beyond my wildest dreams. You will always make me a better person than I was yesterday and for that I will give you my life. I will do anything to see you safe and happy. I love you, Emily."

Happy, emotional tears slid silently down Emily's cheeks. She squeezed Mike's hands.

"Emily, why are you choosing this man?"

"Mike," Emily said. "I knew you before you were living up to your potential. I watched you become a man who always strives to do the right thing. Who loves me, supports me, and cares about our futures together. You stepped into magic with me," Emily paused, looking over at Sam before returning her gaze to Mike. "You stepped into magic and never once questioned it. You've done nothing but support me, and this team, and you have learned alongside me. Because that's what we are, Mike. We are a team – and I cannot wait to spend the rest of our lives together."

Sam pulled the rings from his pocket, giving one to Emily and one to Mike.

"Mike, place this ring on Emily's finger and repeat after me. Emily, with this ring, I thee wed. I thee cherish. I thee love."

Mike repeated the worlds, tears flowing slowly down his cheeks, and placed the ring fully on Emily's finger.

"Emily, place the ring on Mike's finger and repeat after me. Mike, with this ring, I thee wed. I thee cherish. I thee love."

Emily slid the ring onto Mike's finger, repeating the words.

"I now pronounce you husband and wife. You may kiss the bride."

Sam watched them embrace and felt something shutter in his heart. He did not fight the tears streaming from his eyes.

The bride and groom turned to him and pulled him into a fierce hug. They stood there together, the three of them laughing and crying until it was time for the couple to retreat for a moment alone before the mission.

Emily and Mike disappeared to walk along the beach and change before the plan was to be executed.

Sam had headed to their hotel gift shop in search of a bottle of soda, when he felt someone slide up next to him.

"Hello, Sam."

Sam twisted around to see an older woman, shorter than him by almost half his length. She was wearing a bright pink t-shirt dress and black sunglasses pressed through her permed, greying blonde hair. Her flip-flops showcased her bright pink toes. When she smiled, Sam could see crooked teeth and cigarette stains on her mouth.

It was her eyes, that forbidden molten yellow, that stole the breath from his lungs.

"Oh, Sam," the Ultimate Evil said. "Not happy to see me?" The old woman tutted, grabbing a beer from the fridge before turning back to him. "We have a long history, you and I."

"We have no history," Sam heard his own voice whisper out, like a breath on the wind. He could not seem to move.

"Oh, but we do, loads. But that's not why I am here today. Do you know why I'm here today?"

Sam held his breath, attempting to blank his mind lest their plans show on his face.

"Oh no, Sam," the old woman said, cocking her head. "Those tricks don't work with me. I know everything there is to know. It's part of my burden. But now I am going to burden you."

She a feral smile erupted on her face.

"We all know, given the ultimatum, who we would choose to save over another." Sam thought about Emily, Mike, and Chris. He thought about how he would choose to save them over other people. The thoughts were yanked from his mind like slime from a too-tight container. He thought about Chris, and how he was a threat to all of them because he belonged to Clair. The memory of Sam and Chris in the truck, and the knife, sprang into his mind. "Oh, Sam, we have been naughty. The problem is, I know who *she* would choose to save and that is dangerous knowledge."

They knew. Clair knew about the plan, the trap. The Ultimate Evil told her or was going to tell her. It knew Sam had briefly considered killing Chris. It knew that if it came down to it, Sam would kill Chris to save humanity. It would not be an act or a ploy to get to Clair's attention.

The old woman pulled out a knife from somewhere deep within her shirt. Its edges were chipped and dull, like she had been running it over a rock. She pointed it toward her chest.

Sam looked at the Ultimate Evil, his own knife poised, as it talked.

"The sword of destiny has two sides," it said, before thrusting the knife into his victim's heart.

Someone screamed. Sam ran, calling for help, before sprinting from the store.

Clair knew. She knew and she was coming for them.

The sword of destiny has two sides.

CLAIR

You were never there. You are not here now.

She was standing in the waves as they swelled and crested, somewhere in the middle of the ocean, immovable as the tide ripped around her. She watched a pod of whales drifting lazily in the current below the surface. Below her feet, the water appeared dark and still like a sea trapped frozen in time.

It almost stirred her heart. Almost.

Then she heard Chris.

SAM

Sam made it back to their hotel suite in time to catch Emily and Mike packing their supplies.

"What's going on?" Mike asked with concern when he saw Sam's panicked expression. He rushed to Sam's side. "What happened?"

"Where's Chris?" Sam asked, looking wildly around the room.

"He already left," Emily said, coming over to stand with them. "Why?"

"She knows," Sam said, grabbing a pack and texting Erik that the mission was off and if Chris was with him, please send him back to the hotel. He needed to go underground. "She knows. She knows that we are setting a trap. She knows that we're using Chris as bait. She knows—she knows I would kill him if I needed to."

He watched the shock and disbelief hit Emily's face, while Mike just nodded. He had never said it out loud before. He could not believe he said it out loud.

"I cannot allow her to hurt more people!" He threw his arms out. "If it came down to it, Chris is one angel compared to all of humanity. Until the Ultimate Evil brought it up, I had not realized I had even been entertaining it as an option in the back of mind. A final, desperate option if Clair had refused to talk. But she and the Ultimate Evil know what I would have done, and now she's coming. We have to warn Chris. We have to get him safe, underground, anything!"

"Let's go," Mike said, shoving past Sam and stuffing the last few items in his pack.

Sam looked at Emily, who shook her head.

"It's all gotten so out of control, Sam," Emily said, rubbing her hand down her face.

He sighed and pulled her in for a hug. He needed to hold her, if only for a minute. "I know."

He felt her take a deep breath before they pulled away from each other and followed Mike out into the dusk.

CHRIS

can get to her. I can make her stop."

It was the mantra in his head and heart. If she would only talk to him, he could help her. He could stop her.

Chris got to the cliff early.

He was standing on the edge of the circle, staring at one of the hidden net units. This was not right. This was not the right way to handle Clair. She would never be fooled by this.

Chris was reaching down to disable the marker when he heard her.

He stood and turned.

She was perched on the edge of the cliff. She was wearing tattered black pants and a holey dark shirt. Her once rich brown hair had fallen out in patches across her scalp. Chris felt his heart squeeze when he noticed she was missing some of her fingers, the ends broken and bloody.

"Clair…" he breathed, walking toward her. She cocked her head at him. "Clair, what happened?"

"Everything," she whispered. He was almost to her when he heard the shouting.

"Chris!" Sam was running up the hill, with Emily, Mike, and Erik close behind him. Erik was attempting to activate the trap.

"No!" Chris shouted, extending his hand toward them.

He heard the electrical units in the ground whir and activate, but nothing happened.

They all stopped running, and Chris turned to look at Clair who was staring at Sam with molten eyes.

"I see your heart," she said. "And it is as black as mine."

Sam fell to his knees, clutching his head.

"Clair!" Chris shouted, falling to his knees beside her. "Stop, please! Please, Clair, I am begging you to stop."

She turned to Chris and Sam stopped screaming. Chris heard Emily talking to Sam, saw her holding him. He had to stop this, he had to get Clair to see reason.

"Reason?" Clair asked, looking into his eyes. He missed her eyes. "Reason is all I have become. I am going to set the world right."

"Clair, this isn't the way! Reason without heart, heart without reason – it's destined to fail."

Clair walked toward him and the air charged with her magic.

"But you are my heart, Chris. And now…"

She was close enough he felt the crackle of magic against his face.

"Now, I have you."

SAM

Sam was in agony.

His head felt like it was splitting open.

From the moment Clair looked at him, he felt her there, in his mind. It was not the controlled power she had used when she helped him recover his memories. No, this was a shredding, ripping assault. She pulled the memory of him in the truck with Chris, of the knife in his hand, of his wavering choice. She forced it to the front of his mind and then she raked her claws across his brain.

Magic flared to life around him, consuming him. It was all he could do to remain conscious. He felt his body fall to the ground as he clutched his head. He heard Chris shout and the pain lessened. Then Emily was there, holding him, comforting him, trying to get him to resurface.

Sam opened his eyes. Clair was walking toward Chris, speaking softly. She was too close.

"Chris," he groaned, watching her approach him. "No."

Sam watched helplessly.

He watched as Clair reached for Chris and they disappeared.

She took him. Chris was gone.

Sam screamed.

Thrusting his hands into the grass he screamed his frustration into the ground. The cliff shook and large pieces broke off into the water, but Sam continued, releasing the energy into the earth, shaking, crying.

Through it all, Emily continued to hold him, her firm grip almost painful across his shoulders. Mike shouted something and Erik tried to dismantle the trap that had sparked around them.

She had come for him.

Chris was gone.

Sam felt the darkness take him.

"What do we do now?"

Sam was slowly regaining consciousness. He felt a plush bed beneath him and a light blanket over him.

"I don't know," it was Emily, and she was near him on the bed. Mike must have been on his other side. "We need to get him back somehow, right?"

"I don't know," Mike said, and Sam heard him sigh. He opened his eyes. They were in the hotel room. It smelled like them. It must be their room.

Mike looked down from where he was lying on the bed. "Hey," he said, and Emily moved closer to Sam on the other side and brought her hand up to his forehead to check his temperature.

"No fever anymore," Emily said and Sam groaned, turning onto his back, his hand coming up to cover hers on his head.

"What happened?" Sam asked, rubbing his face.

"How far back do you remember?" Mike asked, turning to lean on his elbow.

Sam thought. The cliff. Chris. Clair – his head. The pain and then—

Sam felt the tears spring into his eyes. "I lost him."

"No," Emily laid down next to him, awkwardly hugging his side. "No, she took him. We didn't lose him. You didn't do anything wrong."

"I did," Sam said, the tears tracking down his cheeks. He felt Mike move closer. "I did." He took a deep breath. "Back in Healdsburg, after Clair first lost control and started to destroy the world, I thought about killing Chris to stop her, to destroy her enough to that she could not recover."

He heard Emily's quick intake of breath, and opened his eyes. She held her hand to her mouth and Mike was staring at him. "It might have," was all he said.

Sam nodded. "But it wasn't the right choice. It wasn't the *good* choice."

They sat in silence for a bit, each lost in their own thoughts.

"We've lost so many," Emily said, taking a deep breath. She was still cuddled into his side, with Mike on his other. He wished they could just stay like this forever. "How do we stop the inevitable?"

Sam did not know. He did not know what to do now, but he could feel in his bones that everything had changed.

Clair was going to come for him.

"Emily, Mike," he said. "You need to leave. You need to get on a flight, get off this island." He took a deep breath. "Clair is going to come for me. She is not done with me. We thought that by being on an island we could limit casualties in a worst case scenario but I cannot help but feel like I pulled a pin and a bomb is about to go off."

He felt Emily's fingers flex on his shirt and saw her share a meaningful glance with Mike. He nodded. "We aren't leaving you," Mike said, laying on his back next to Sam. "We're in this. We've been in this. We will think of something."

Sam admired his optimism, even if he did not share in it.

They slept that way, together in the bed, and waited for the sun to rise.

CHRIS

The last thing he remembered was a cliff.

When he opened his eyes, he was chained to a stone wall and the shackles were digging into his wrists. He looked up. Clair stood before him. Her eyes were sunken, open and dry. She was not blinking.

"Clair," he breathed, standing, and getting as close to her as he could, as close as the chains would allow. "Clair!"

"Hello, Chris," she said, but her voice was wrong. It was not her—the woman he loved was nowhere in that haunting voice.

With only two words, he finally knew. He finally understood what Sam had tried to tell him, what he had tried to get Chris to understand.

Clair was gone.

"Oh, Clair. What have you done?"

"I did what I had to do," she said, staring hollowly at him. He realized she was not breathing.

"No," Chris cried, tears beginning to stream down his face as he struggled to come to terms with the wretched truth standing before him. "You did what you *chose* to do, Clair. You did what you chose to do and now people are dying. So many people, Clair. So many people are dying. So many people have died." He hung his head, his hands cradling his face, as his tears spilled onto the cold concrete. "You can't come back from this, Clair."

She continued to stare at him, emotionless. Stone.

"I don't need to come back from this."

CLAIR

lair was having a vision.

She could see him standing there.

She could see them all.

Emily on the cliffside watching the waves over the island, hugging a pregnant woman next to her. She could see Mike assisting an unknown angel in a chapel somewhere on the far side of the island. She could see the angel warriors fighting to protect humanity across the world. She could see the humans fleeing from the disasters befalling them. But most prominently, she could see Chris right in front of her. He was staring at her, his eyes clouded with emotion and his mouth slightly parted as he begged for her to stop.

She had brought him to her bunker. It was filthy. And underground, but he would be safe. He was shackled to the wall. He was too close to her power now, he could use it to escape.

"Clair," Chris said. She was not sure how long he had been asleep. Time meant nothing to her now. "Please. You can stop this. Please come back to me."

"I am with you, Chris," Clair said flatly, looking at the world, at Chris, at everything all at once. "Now that you are with me, you will be safe."

"Oh, Clair, please," Chris groaned, bringing his shackled wrists to his head.

"But they must do it themselves. Humans. It is not something that can be done for them. Opportunities might be missed, but they are not my opportunities to give or take. My opportunities will remain answered by myself, and I will watch the world go by as it does."

She was not sure Chris understood her, but he would.

She was back in the clouds, staring at the island.

It began gradually.

A trickle, like the rain beginning on a bright day.

Unexpected, yet inevitable with the dark grey clouds circling.

Clair pulled the ocean to her, up and up and up.

She pushed it forward, crafting a tidal wave higher than the tallest building on Phú Quốc.

EMILY

I need you to take this," Sam said as he thrust a thumb drive into her hands. They were packing up as much as they could. They were evacuating to shelter with the rest of the island's inhabitants. There had been a tsunami warning. It started at sea and grew faster than it should have. It was heading toward the island.

Clair was going to drown them all.

"Emily," Sam grabbed her chin, tilting her face up so she would look into his eyes. "It has all of my records in it. My lifetimes of research, my passwords and access codes, and the locations of all properties with information on how to take them over."

"Sam, no!" Emily screamed, trying to give it back to him. "You have to come with us. You said we would figure this out together - the three of us. Please!"

"Emily," he said as he pulled her close, tilting her tear-soaked face up to him, brushing a wayward curl back from her face. "You were always a part of my purpose - both of you. Because of that, I need to save you. I will save you. Now go!"

He pushed her toward Mike, who began backing her away as she cried and thrashed against him. She could not let this happen.

"Thank you, Sam," Mike said. "Thank you."

Sam nodded.

Mike pulled her into the elevator, and it closing felt like a slamming door in her heart. "We can't let him do this!" She turned to Mike. "We have to help him!"

Mike turned to her. "We are."

She stopped trying to halt the elevator and turned to him. "What?"

"Of course we are," Mike said, looking at the numbers as the floors continued to go up. "We're not going to let him do this alone. We're not leaving him. We're going to help as many people as we can get to safety, and then we're going to face this with him."

Emily launched herself at Mike, sealing her lips to his. "I don't know what I did to deserve you."

"Emily," Mike said, as the door dinged open. "I will live the rest of my life earning a place at your side. Now, hurry up. We have work to do."

The hospital was in chaos.

As the tallest building on the island with the most options for first aid, everyone on the island in need of assistance had been directed there.

She feared it would not be high enough.

It looked like pictures and tables had been overturned in the earthquake. The lights kept flickering overhead. People were shouting and pushing against each other demanding help. Mothers clung tightly to their young, crying children and she noticed that some of the frailest among the elderly had had no choice but to sit on the floor. The overwhelmed doctors, nurses, and administrators were attempting to triage the massive influx of people while sending the more able-bodied up the stairs to safety.

Emily saw a flash of dark hair. "Erik!" she yelled, pulling Mike's arm in his direction before running over to him. "How can we help?"

"What's left of our team volunteered to help the hospital staff and they put us in charge of getting those who can't walk up the stairs up to the higher floors. The elevator's no use, so we have been carrying individuals up on gurneys. If we make it through this, it'll be a shit show explaining who we are and what we were doing here."

"I think our highest priority is making it out of this mess, Erik, not fixing it after," Mike said, continuing to scan the lobby for possible threats.

"True," Erik scoffed, rubbing a hand through his hair. Emily noticed with a cold shiver that there was blood smeared in his hair.

"Mike, come with me to help lift some of the bedridden patients up the steps. Emily, head to the highest floor – that's where all the babies and expectant mothers are. We need to make sure someone is guarding them from the crowds." Erik turned away, heading toward the back of the building.

"Emily," Mike said, placing his hands on her shoulders and turning her to face him. "I love you. I know you. Do not put yourself in harm's way."

She reached up and grabbed his head, pulling him in for a quick, fierce kiss. "I'll do what I have to, and I know you will, too. Be safe. I love you."

Mike pressed his forehead to hers, sighing, and ran in the direction where Erik had disappeared.

Emily pushed her way through throngs of able-bodied people going up the stairs, jogging up the many landings until she reached the top floor. When things were secure, she needed to figure out a way to help Sam. She wondered if any of the spells she had learned could protect him.

Emily clutched the pendant at her neck. If only she thought to create one more, or if she had given hers to him, maybe…

"Help!" cried a woman with light brown hair. She was clutching her stomach and as Emily approached, the woman leaned onto her for support. "Help, please," she said again. "I need to get to the roof."

"Ma'am," Emily said, supporting the weight of her as much as possible. There was a wet stain on the woman's dress. "We need to find you a doctor. Let's get you to a bed, you're in labor!"

"No!" she shouted, pulling away from Emily and heading toward the door with a little placard that read, FOR ROOF ACCESS. "I need to be on the roof. I need to be outside. It needs to be me. It needs to be me!"

Emily walked after her as she stumbled and grabbed the woman's arm to keep her from falling. "Okay, okay," Emily said, pulling her arm over the woman's shoulders to help support her as they slowly made their way toward the door. The woman was breathing heavily. Emily could tell by the way she intermittently paused and clutched her stomach that she was having contractions, but she knew this woman was determined enough to go on with or without her. Emily could not just leave her alone. "We can go outside."

Emily felt the woman instantly relax. "Thank you, thank you," she breathed.

When they reached the roof, the woman gestured toward a corner of the building with a view of the sea. They slowly made their way to the edge and looked out at the coming wave.

"There," the woman breathed.

She did not need to point. Emily could see him, the lone figure on the shore.

Emily clutched her heart.

Sam was facing the sea.

SAM

e was standing back on the cliff, watching the sea withdraw from the land.

The wave was coming.

He knew what he had to do and hoped he had the strength to do it.

Sam turned from the sea to face the island. Most of the people were heading inland or to the tops of the highest buildings.

Sam began to draw his power to him; he beseeched the invisible angels to lend him their help. He begged, cried, and pulled.

He felt the earth's crust inflate under him and the molten earth expanding to fill the gaps he was creating. He pushed the magma to form unnaturally fast, to cool and grow over and over. Sam felt the blood begin to pool behind his eyes, but still he pulled. He pulled and the island began to rise.

Sam ignored the monstrous roar of the wave growing louder behind him as it approached. He dug his feet into the earth and pulled the island higher, up from the sea, away from the water. He focused on the higher ground, on lifting the people from the certain death the wave was bringing.

"Sam!" he heard her voice call to him. Turning, he saw Emily on the top of the nearest building, miles away. How he heard her scream his name, he would never know, but he could see her, hear her, and noticed she was not alone. Emily was supporting a heavily pregnant woman in the throes of what must be a contraction. There was something familiar about her.

As he stared at the pregnant woman, the waves began crashing around and over him. Suddenly, Sam knew that it was *all* his purpose. Every year he had spent on this earth, everything he learned and accomplished, every person he had met, helped, and cared for, had lead him to this. In that brief moment, Sam knew that every moment of his uniquely long life had been part of his purpose. Every second of his existence. Sam was not just saving the entire island, he was saving himself.

That pregnant woman was his mother.

As the wave blocked the sun from his sight, Sam sighed, letting the water sweep him away. The water filled his lungs and the darkness took him. Finally, he could rest.

CHRIS

hris sat on the cold stone floor.

He did not eat. He did not sleep.

He thought he would die of hunger or exhaustion, simply waste away, but Clair was pushing power into him constantly. Being this close to her was like being a flower too close to the sun. There was so much energy, so much burning.

He missed the Clair he loved.

He missed the person, not this conduit for suffering.

The woman he loved was broken, gone. She was being destroyed from the inside out. There was too much power, too little humanity. He watched her bones protrude from her chest. He watched her hair fall out, her face grow increasingly sallow and pale. He watched as she lost another two fingers from the cold. Her eyes were sinking into her skull and blisters streaked across her face from reaching too close to the sun.

The Ultimate Evil entered the room.

Today it was dressed in a new human skin. A man in his late forties, starting to grey, clad in an immaculate suit. It picked fancier humans every day. Every day it got closer to getting what it wanted.

Destruction.

"Good evening, my angels," it crooned, barely glancing at Chris before walking over to Clair at the command center. "I have a present." It pushed a lock of Clair's patchy hair behind her ear, and it took everything within Chris not to wretch onto the floor.

Clair tiled her yellow eyes toward it.

"I finally did it. I got the codes," he said as he produced a metal box, flipping it open to reveal a nuclear switch.

"No..." Chris breathed, heaving himself up to standing and straining against his chains. "Clair, no! No! Please!"

The Ultimate Evil turned back to look at him with placating eyes. "She can do whatever she wants, angel."

THE WHITE ROOM

lair."

Clair opened her eyes. She took a deep breath and turned toward the light.

"Clair, it's time to decide."

Clair! She heard his voice like an echo in the room.

Chris.

"Chris?" she said, looking from the blinding white and into the darkness. "Chris?!" She stood, walking the circle of grey light, keeping well away from the cold and the heat.

Clair, no! You can't do this! Please don't do this!

His voice was coming from the light.

"Chris," she said, the tears beginning to fall down her cheeks.

Clair, yes! It's me. Please, please don't do this. I love you. Please don't do this.

Clair fought to see through the blinding white. The more she focused, the clearer the vision became. It was like watching a television through her own eyes. She was in a stone room with a metal box on the console in front of her. Her hand was raised over a button. Next to her, a man in a suit was talking, but she could not hear him. She willed the vision to shift, she forced it, feeling the blood drip down her nose as she turned to face Chris.

He was chained to the wall. His skin was pale, he looked bruised and battered. He was straining against his shackles, his wrists chafing and bleeding.

Clair! Oh my god, Clair! Please! Do not do this!

Clair looked back at the box, where her hand still hovered over the button.

Clair, please. I know, know it's the end for us. But, I love you. Please don't do this.

Clair looked back at Chris. He was crying now. He knew, just like she did, what she needed to do. How she could stop herself.

"It's time, Clair," the voice said. "It's time to choose."

Clair looked at the desperation in Chris' eyes and felt the tears stream down her cheeks.

"I'll lose you," she cried. The man next to her was screaming, trying to get her attention, but she only had eyes for Chris.

You could never lose me, he said. *You're my purpose, Clair. You were always my purpose. I will always love you. But please, you need to end this. Please...*

The vision faded, replaced by the blindingly white light of the voice. There was silence.

Clair took a deep breath, and started walking.

Fire licked up her feet, burning her, killing her, but Clair kept walking. She kept walking even as her brain felt like it was boiling inside of her head. Even as her skin began to melt, as her heart caught fire. She could feel the tension within her grow tired as she became flame. She could feel herself dissolving away and she welcomed it.

It was an exultation. A sigh of breath carried away on the wind. A culmination of energy dissipating.

Clair embraced the light.

CHRIS

Chris screamed.

He had reached her somehow, but now the golden hue had clouded over her eyes again. She was just standing there, hand over the launch button. The Ultimate Evil was screaming in her face, pulling out its hair, and shaking with rage but he was not touching her and Clair was not moving.

Chris watched as her hand dropped away from the button.

"Clair?" Chris pleaded.

A voice in his head interjected, *It's time to stop what has been started.*

"I love you," Clair said, staring into his eyes.

Chris sucked in a breath.

He watched as the golden light in her eyes was replaced with blinding white. The Ultimate Evil stopped thrashing and turned to look her in the eyes.

They stared at each other, evil and good, both waiting to see what happened next.

Finally, the Ultimate Evil smiled maniacally and turned to Chris, waved, and vanished.

Chris let out the breath he did not know he was holding and watched as everything around him was flooded with a light so bright all he could do was close his eyes and hope that death did not hurt.

EMILY

mily stood clutching Mike.

The news outlets were going wild claiming nuclear war was imminent. People were screaming. There was so much death already. There was so much fear.

"I love you, Emily," Mike said, crushing her close. "I love you."

"I love you, too," she said, tears flowing down her face. She kept thinking that this was not supposed to be the end. They were supposed to grow old together. They were supposed to change the world.

Emily clutched Mike, feeling the pendant dig into her cheek where it rested against his chest.

A blindingly bright light tore through the hospital, and Emily screamed, clutching Mike, waiting for the pain, but none came.

The light passed.

Emily opened her eyes. Mike was breathing hard. She lifted her head from his chest and looked around.

The hospital was restored. The walls that had shaken and crumbled were pristine. All around them, people were going about their business, as if nothing had happened.

"Mike," Emily said and she looked up at him. His eyes were still pressed closed. "Mike, open your eyes. We're not dead."

He opened his eyes, peered down at her, and then looked around at the room. His confusion confirmed that she was not seeing things.

"Or maybe we are," he said, relaxing only slightly so she could fully look around. "How is this possible?"

"I don't know," she said, at a loss for words. Emily heard footsteps heading in their direction and spotted Erik walking toward them, slowly.

"Erik!" Emily said, turning fully toward him. His eyes widened at her recognition, and he walked faster toward the pair. When he reached them, he touched Mike's shoulder.

"Mike? Emily?" he said, looking at each of their faces. "You remember me?"

"Remember you? Of course we remember you. We were just fighting a war together. What is happening?"

"Fascinating," Erik said, examining the pendants on their necks. "None of the other humans around here remember anything. None of the natural disasters, not the plague, the angels. It's like none of it ever happened. It's a little early to say with full certainty, but it appears that everything has been restored to how it was before Clair, well, you know..."

"What do you mean they don't remember?"

"All the humans forgot about the angels. They forgot about us – they don't remember any of it. The war, the bombings, the unprecedented series of natural disasters – poof! That white light and suddenly it never happened." He was clutching his laptop, open to hundreds of different news tabs. "The world is all back to normal. The rest of the fallen angels have disbanded. It's over. It's done." Erik sighed, first pulling Emily into a hug and then Mike. "But you two remember." Erik looked pointedly at their pendants.

"She knew," Emily said, clutching at the pendant around her neck. "Dotty knew. She knew our memories might be taken." Emily started crying again in earnest. "She said she would take my memories unless I could learn this spell. *This* spell!" Emily pulled at the necklace around her neck, and gestured at the one Mike wore. "She was protecting us from magic being taken. She knew so long ago."

Mike hauled her into his arms, hugging her tightly.

"She knew."

EPILOGUE

The world is small and it gets smaller every day.

     We are nothing but our choices, our actions, and the greatest desires of our hearts.

"Are you interested in the house?"

"What?" Chris turned toward the voice which appeared to belong to a woman in her mid-forties, carrying a sign under her arm.

"The house," she said, gesturing behind him. He was sitting on the steps of the porch. When Clair had wiped everyone's memory of her existence, the house had reappeared, as if it never burned down. "It's for sale. The owner died recently. No living relatives."

"Yes," Chris said breathlessly, taking the card she extended to him.

"Great." The woman smiled, continuing to place her signs. "It'll be on the market later this week."

He nodded and stood.

Chris walked over to the porch on the old antique shop and sat down. Everything was like it had been before Clair came into his life. The house and shop were back to their original state, but it all felt empty without the women who used to live there.

Chris looked up at the sound of someone approaching.

"So," Jude strode up and sat next to him, "Where do you go from here?"

"I'm not sure," Chris said. He could go with Emily and Mike. They had extended the offer, multiple times, to join them in England. They were establishing new bases all over the world, picking up where the

Covenant left off, finding new minor angels and introducing them to their new lives. But where the Covenant had built an army, Emily and Mike were building a community. They had integrated a new group of humans and angels working together to rebuild the broken systems left behind by the Covenant. Sam had left them everything, from his amassed wealth to his centuries of research. Much of what they had spent on the war was replenished in the reset, but Sam, ever the planner, also had multiple off-shore accounts and international properties he had refused to sell during the war. They would be more than comfortable funding their operations for decades to come.

Chris had found Emily and Mike on Phú Quốc Island where he had suddenly appeared after the great flash. He saw the magic Sam had done. He grieved for his friends, for the people they had lost, for the woman he loved. He yearned for how things used to be.

All the humans who had died, the ones uninvolved with the magic, were restored. The angels they had lost, however, remained gone, like Terri who had suddenly dusted after offering him simple wisdom. Just another cost of the price of magic.

Clair was gone.

No one in town remembered her. It was as if she had stopped existing long before their shared history even began.

"I guess I always thought my story would end with hers, but it didn't," Chris said.

Jude grunted in reply and the pair sat in a moment of reflective silence.

Chris could not understand why things had ended the way that they did or how they had ever reached that point. Looking back, he could see the signs, but he could not pinpoint what he could have done differently to prevent Clair from giving into those desires, from losing her mind. How had his Clair grown so consumed by darkness that she had become foreign to him? Like the father she so despised, she had been consumed by power, unable to control it, unable to see past the logic of her heart, unable to face her emotions. In the very end, she had returned to him briefly but powerfully and then was gone. Somehow he was supposed to continue to exist without her.

It had been one month without her. Chris had replayed the months before he lost her over and over in his mind, but he still could not figure out a new path that would have solved everything. There was nothing he would have done differently but now he wished that he could go back and try again. He wished that he had seen what Clair was becoming. He wished that he could have saved Kioko. He wished that he had been with Sam in the end, but he had been with Clair, and then he was alone.

"It's so weird to be here without them," Jude said looking back at the house. "Everything's so weird."

In moments like this, Chris was reminded that Jude was technically a teenager. It almost made him laugh.

"It just doesn't make sense," Jude continued. "This has been my most eventful life in a while, and normally when big events happen, I can see why. You know, why things ended the way they did. But for this one," Jude looked up at Chris. "I just don't see why your stories wouldn't have converged and ended together."

Chris thought maybe he should have been offended by the fact that Jude was suggesting that he should be dead, that his purpose should have been fulfilled alongside Clair.

But he was not because he agreed. "What was the point of it all?"

"We'll never know," Jude said. "It's not our fate to know. Honestly, it doesn't matter. It happened. We can't change it. The only thing we can do is keep moving forward."

They sat in silence for a while longer, listening to the birds in the trees.

"I think I'm going to go back home now," Jude said. "These parents aren't so bad. Anyway, I only have a couple of more years left in this body before I go back to the beginning all over again."

Chris nodded then froze.

"What did you just say?"

"That everything feels pointless and like a spinning top of–"

"No, before that." Chris was already standing.

"I said I'm going to go back home."

"You said you go back to the beginning. You go back to the beginning! That's it!"

Chris ran.

Up the hill and through the trees, he ran. As fast as his legs could carry him through the forest.

Clair killed herself. She killed herself to stop the Ultimate Evil. She walked into the light. She chose. She made a choice. This was what the choice was for – it had to be.

The breath heaved in and out of his lungs and his muscles strained, but he still ran. He had to know if what Adam had told Clair all those years ago was for him. He remembered it now. It had to be for him. Adam had told Clair to tell him to go back to the beginning.

Chris ran down the slope toward the field, toward the spot where the Gate had stopped. He finally stopped in the clearing, where their story had begun. The spot that had been the backdrop of some of their most important memories. The beginning of their adventure.

It was devoid of the Gate's presence, but Chris could still feel the magic of the place. Lilies were sprouting from the ground, covering the field in big white blossoms. They should not have been there; they were never there before – only the magic kept them alive.

Chris inhaled sharply, drawing air to his lungs, and looked around frantically. This had to be it – this had to be what all of it was for – this could not be the end for them. It could not be.

He turned.

She appeared in a shaft of light. She had been waiting for him.

Chris ran to Clair.

Later, Chris would wonder about the Ultimate Evil and Good standing together in the field. He would wonder why they had brought Clair back to him, together. So close together that Clair was standing between them.

Later he would realize what Clair had, that they are one in the same. That there is no good without evil and there is no evil without good. What matters in the end is only choice.

As Chris and Clair walked away hand in hand, there was a whisper on the wind.

Until next time, my friend.
Until next time.

ACKNOWLEDGEMENTS:

This book has been in my head since 2011. Maybe even before then. It started for me in 2009, when I tried to take my own life the same way Clair did in the prologue of *The Gate*. I had gone through the toughest time in my young-adult life, and I did not see the point anymore. It was a half-assed effort, as evidenced by the fact that when I actually put my mind to something I can create something amazing, but it affected me. I still remember hearing that voice say, "No, there's more." And there has been more. So, so much more. I would like to start by thanking my family. My amazing husband, who does not like to read so he may never actually see this – but who has supported and been my best friend since the moment we met. My amazing son Kayden, who, by the time he is old enough to read this, will cringe that his mother wrote it. I would like to thank all my friends and colleagues who never doubted I could complete this series while I worked multiple jobs over the last ten years. I would also like to thank everyone who ever asked me how the writing was going – everyone who cared about these characters that I have loved for so long. Thank you for reading.

Made in the USA
Monee, IL
20 March 2023

30259325R00164